Antônio De Salles, M.D., Ph.D., lives in Brazil. Fascinated by brain function during his medical school years, he learned how to improve it at the Medical College of Virginia, Harvard University, and Umeå University in Sweden. He became a world-renowned neurosurgeon and neuroscientist, eventually becoming an Emeritus Professor at UCLA. He writes to raise awareness of state-of-the-art brain surgery. His novel, *Why Fly over the Cuckoo's Nest? Psychosurgery in My Brain, Please!,* is already a success in four languages, with the second edition entitled *The Brain of the Player, Love and Soccer.* Now the story continues with *The Musician's Brain: Science and Sensibility,* bringing more information about brain function and the intricacies of deep brain electrical stimulation with pacemakers to improve human life. The reader leisurely learns about the brain's underpinnings and the ethical dilemmas of its modification. Resilience through love for music, science, and loyalty to patients needing medical care immerses the reader in the acumen achieved by health professionals and dedicated musicians with their art.

I dedicate this story to my family for giving me support and space for my selfish hobby of storytelling in writing, and specifically for my wife for being my unconditional music appreciation companion and partner in the operating room and life.

Antônio De Salles

THE MUSICIAN'S BRAIN

Science and Sensibility

AUSTIN MACAULEY PUBLISHERS
LONDON * CAMBRIDGE * NEW YORK * SHARJAH

Copyright © Antônio De Salles 2025

All rights reserved. No part of this publication may be reproduced, distributed, or transmitted in any form or by any means, including photocopying, recording, or other electronic or mechanical methods, without the prior written permission of the publisher, except in the case of brief quotations embodied in critical reviews and certain other non-commercial uses permitted by copyright law. For permission requests, write to the publisher.

Any person who commits any unauthorized act in relation to this publication may be liable to criminal prosecution and civil claims for damages.

Ordering Information
Quantity sales: Special discounts are available on quantity purchases by corporations, associations, and others. For details, contact the publisher at the address below.

Publisher's Cataloging-in-Publication data
Salles, Antônio De
The Musician's Brain

Illustrated By: Marianna De Salles

ISBN 9798895431269 (Paperback)
ISBN 9798895431276 (Hardback)
ISBN 9798895431290 (ePub e-book)
ISBN 9798895431283 (Audiobook)

Library of Congress Control Number: 2025902924

www.austinmacauley.com/us

First Published 2025
Austin Macauley Publishers LLC
40 Wall Street, 33rd Floor, Suite 3302
New York, NY 10005
USA

mail-usa@austinmacauley.com
+1 (646) 5125767

I am grateful to my beta readers, Dr. Ricardo de Oliveira, Maestro João Carlos Martins and his wife Carmen Valio for their constant encouragement since the very birth of our story. The highly musical intellectual dinners hosted by Carmen, and the Maestro's performances at those homely encounters brought the inspiration for the characters and details of the music scenes that punctuates the thrilling moments of our dystonic musician boy's journey, including the flow of the concerts he in which stars. Additionally, it is impossible only to acknowledge the invaluable importance of Bruno's and Marianna's artwork, Emma's Spanish translation, and Jucilana's and Giulia's Portuguese translation. I have their photos and short CV highlighted in the book, as they are young rising stars needing recognition, each in their field of work, respectively, a neurologist, an artist, a marketing specialist, a neurosurgeon and a neuroscientist. I also acknowledge Thais Lopes, my secretary who did the first diagramming of the manuscript, making it ready for the eyes of the early readers.

*Talent hits a target others miss,
genius hits targets no one else sees.*
Arthur Schopenhauer

My heartfelt thanks go to Dr. Alessandra A. Gorgulho, my wife, partner at work, an inspirational female neurosurgeon, and my doctor. She is an outstanding mother to our son Lucas Gorgulho De Salles, who is also inspiring as a sportsman and student. I took time from interaction with my family to research and create this story. Marianna De Salles, who drew the cover, is an artist who, during her youth, spent time in an anatomy laboratory at UCLA to learn medical art. From Marianna, I learned that an artist needs freedom to create without barriers; she exemplifies this as an artist. Dr. Bruno Galo deserves all the credit for the anatomical drawings; out of his generosity, he showed me his computer art and created the brain illustrations, which were so necessary to give this text clarity for lay readers. Carmen Valio provided the readers access to the music by preparing links to accustom readers to enjoy her husband's art while learning from this text. Her dedication to Maestro João Carlos Martins managing his social media and receptivity to their friends in her home attests that love does exist.

Dr. Roberto Martinez Alvez has been my best friend in neurosurgery, my mentor in Spain, and my first novel's translator (to Spanish). Although I met Roberto late in my career, he became a partner in behavioral surgery, the modern and highly scientific form of psychosurgery, after I retired from UCLA. Additionally, I am grateful to Thaís Alves Soares for her dedication as a secretary during the development of this story. Finally, I cannot forget all my mentors in the past, in Brazil, the United States, and Sweden, and last but not least, my patients, who trusted me with their lives, believing that my thirst for learning would be a source to help them.

Table of Contents

Prologue	**23**
Part 1: Brain, Music, and Plasticity	**27**
Chapter 1: Troubled Brain	*29*
Chapter 2: Plasticity	*31*
Chapter 3: Music and the Nodal Network	*35*
Chapter 4: Gelastic	*37*
Chapter 5: A Sardonic Smile	*40*
Chapter 6: Out of Commission	*43*
Chapter 7: Home, Music, and Love	*46*
Chapter 8: Focus on the Network	*51*
Chapter 9: Music and Synapses	*53*
Part 2: Virtuosity	**59**
Chapter 10: Sensibility	*61*
Chapter 11: Motor Skills, Aggressivity, Sensibility	*64*
Chapter 12: Overreaction	*66*
Chapter 13: Child Depression	*69*
Chapter 14: Gamma Rays	*72*
Chapter 15: The Virtuoso	*75*
Chapter 16: Ready for Recitals	*76*
Chapter 17: The Competition	*78*

Part 3: Consequences of Success — 83

Chapter 18: The Emergency Room — 85

Chapter 19: Shock and Tragedy — 89

Chapter 20: Mom Action — 92

Chapter 21: The Protocol — 97

Chapter 22: The Protocol Music and Touch — 102

Chapter 23: The Touch and Music Experts — 109

Chapter 24: The Colburn Community's Heart — 112

Chapter 25: The Walk for Dystonia and Music — 116

Chapter 26: The Fundraiser — 122

Part 4: Doctors, Musicians, and Dystonia — 125

Chapter 27: Scientific Plan — 127

Chapter 28: Surgery and Recovery — 130

Chapter 29: Music Power and Pleasure — 143

Chapter 30: Music Healing — 147

Chapter 31: Motor and Sensory — 150

Chapter 32: Boys Success — 155

Chapter 33: Boys and Maestro — 161

Chapter 34: The Maestro's Story — 163

Chapter 35: Plasticity Revolution — 167

Part 5: Tours and Concerts — 169

Chapter 36: Boys Bach's and Chopin's Preludes — 171

Chapter 37: True Science and Music — 182

Chapter 38: Concerts — 188

Chapter 39: Beyond Music — 191

Chapter 40: Meeting the Queen — 199

Chapter 41: PTSD — 204

Chapter 42: Over Ethernet	*208*
Chapter 43: All Together to Help	*213*
Chapter 44: Technology for Music and Brain	*218*
Chapter 45: Vienna	*222*
Chapter 46: One More Device	*226*
Chapter 47: More Concerts in Europe	*229*
Chapter 48: Perfect Teamwork	*233*
Chapter 49: Another Surgery	*235*
Chapter 50: Maestro's Gratitude	*242*
Epilogue	**246**

The more I study nature,
the more I stand amazed at the work of the Creator!
Louis Pasteur

The Nature of This Work

Observation, reason, human understanding, and courage.
These make the physician.
Martin H. Fischer (1879 -1962)

This is a work of fiction. Based on my observations as a neurosurgeon in a major academic center, the story is built on imaginary patients and doctors. It was also inspired by professional musicians, some of whom are real characters, while others are imaginary. All compositions and scientific publications are real. The science and art represented by the cover, anatomical illustrations, comments on architecture, and musical scores are used to raise ideas about novel therapies for nervous system diseases. Because of the fictional nature of the great majority of the characters and therapies, as well as the conjectures about the future, the story is a literary creation. However, it uses verified scientific findings to support suggested therapies based on music and hard scientific facts. The most inspirational character is an outstanding musician, Maestro João Carlos Martins, an icon of the Brazilian classical music scene, along with his wife are central to the story, as is the story of his fight against the brain/muscle disorder, dystonia. This work was created to raise dystonia awareness, teach lay readers science and music, and provide ideas for young physicians. I hope it is an entertaining story with credibility and value to music, medicine, and science.

Cover by Marianna De Salles

Artist and Teacher at Redondo Beach, CA, USA, University of Hawaii—Department of Arts and Art History.

Spanish Translation by Emma Ferro

Palmer Trinity School, Miami, FL, English College, Uruguay,
Pablo Giménez School, Uruguay—Visual Communication & Fashion Production
Australian Pacific College, Australia—Social Network Marketing.

Portuguese Translation by Jucilana dos Santos Vianna

Neurosurgeon by Rio de Janeiro State University and Functional Neurosurgeon and Radiosurgeon by I D'Or and NeuroSapiens®, and Vascular, Skull Base Neurosurgeon by University of Sao Paulo, Brazil.

Anatomic Illustrations by Dr. Bruno Gallo

Physician at Pontifícia Paraná Catholic University (PUC-PR), Brazil. Fellow in Neurology and Postgraduate at the Department of Neurology, John Hopkins School of Medicine, Baltimore, MD, USA.

Portuguese Editorial by Giulia Martins Cavalcante

Universidade de São Paulo, Brasil
Student of Psychology and Neurosciences at Merrimack College (MA, EUA), Resercher on children behavior and human brain development.

Music Organization

Carmen Valio de Araujo Martins. Maestro João Carlos Martins' Wife and organizer of the musical demonstration in the book.

Neurology Preface

By Ricardo de Oliveira-Souza

In *The Musician's Brain-Science and Sensibility,* Dr. Antonio De Salles comes out with an enthralling novel that takes us to the core of the brain of a young musician who is badly injured by a cruel father who cannot accept the fact that his son loses a contest at a famous American school. After this tragic beginning, the story takes a turn that reveals how noble and generous human beings can be, even when they risk losing their reputation and work. Antonio embellishes this journey with insights into the brain underpinnings of music perception and enjoyment that can be provided only by someone who has devoted a lifetime to caring for patients with the most severe types of neurologic ailments. As in his earlier novel, *Why Fly Over the Cuckoo's Nest? Psychosurgery in My Brain, Please!* Antonio exercises his natural gift of translating hermetic neuroscientific concepts into colloquial language without belittling them for the sake of simplicity. Readers will be taken to the edge where fiction meets reality, pointing to the infinite possibilities now within our reach to give life back to legions of people who have lost all hope and, worse, their dignity. *The Musician's Brain* is an ode to music, faith, and creativity.

Music Preface

Keeping the Music Alive
By Maestro João Carlos Martins

My story as a dystonic pianist

Having to abandon the dream of making music is the most terrifying prospect a musician can face, and it is also the most tragic.

It nearly happened to me several times over the course of my 70-year career. I've endured 30 surgeries, dozens of treatments, contradictory diagnoses, and two life-altering injuries. But none of the obstacles that crossed my path could force me to let go of that vital dream.

When I was only 18—in 1958, just six years after making my professional debut as a pianist in my native Brazil—I began experiencing involuntary tremors in my right hand.

It took until 1982 for the chronic condition that affected me to be diagnosed as focal dystonia. This complex movement disorder wreaks havoc on the lives of at least 1% of professional musicians, according to the neurologist Dr. Alexandre Kaup[1].

For years, no one could explain what was going on. When my symptoms first started, some doctors even suggested that perhaps I wasn't comfortable playing in public—that it was a psychological problem.

The reality was exactly the opposite. I loved playing live recitals and concerts as much as I loved recording in the studio, and my respect for the audience was uncompromising.

Even if it meant playing with metal braces on my fingers, which I also tried. The problem was agonizingly physical. Close to the end of one concert, I noticed drops of blood speckling the piano keys. But I fought through the pain until the last chord.

---

[1] Dressler D, Altenmüller E, Giess R, Krauss JK, Adib Saberi F. The epidemiology of dystonia: the Hannover epidemiology study. J Neurol. 2022 Dec;269(12):6483-6493. doi: 10.1007/s00415-022-11310-9. Epub 2022 Aug 11. PMID: 35948800; PMCID: PMC9618521

Looking back, I don't know how I managed to play more than 1,000 recitals and concerts with major orchestras across the United States, Europe, Asia, and Latin America.

At times, the pain in my hands became nearly unbearable. But my determination to communicate with my audience inspired me to keep on playing.

What also helped was learning how to trick my brain. After all, that's where the neurological misfiring that causes dystonia originates. For many years, I wasn't bothered by involuntary movements until after the first two or three hours following a good night of sleep.

So, no matter where I traveled, I discovered how to use this to my advantage and arranged my schedule to allow me to sleep until 15 minutes before each concert.

This trick gave me the feeling that I was playing at 7 in the morning, just after waking up. My right hand would become spastic after the concert.

But these coping mechanisms didn't always work. I stubbornly insisted on matching emotional expression with perfectionism of technique. That left me satisfied with only 70% of my performances. I didn't like 15% of them; the rest I canceled.

At times, I descended into depression. I even tried to escape music altogether. This happened over two extended periods, each lasting seven years. The goal was to be able to focus on my mental health.

'Living with musician's dystonia,' as Dr. Kaup observes, involves 'a mix of frustration, pain, shame, and struggle' that all too often results in a foreshortened career.

But this disease could not destroy a passion that is as essential to me as air or food. Much as I found ways to trick my brain, I adapted to the changing circumstances that confronted me.

One of my many surgeries rendered my right hand entirely useless in performance. So, I concentrated on repertoire for the left hand alone—until I lost usage of that hand about 20 years ago.

But I couldn't give up. So, how do you win a battle after it seems you've lost the war? I found a way: by turning my attention to conducting, building up my own orchestra, and encouraging the young generation.

It is in that spirit that I made my return to Carnegie Hall, in the city that was my home for many years. I first played there 60 years ago. At Carnegie, I gave one of my most memorable performances, the First Book of Bach's *Well-Tempered Clavier*, in a comeback concert in 1978, following the first of the long interruptions in my career.

I'm sharing my story with the hope that it can inspire others struggling with dystonia and similar challenges. I myself found inspiration in my friendship with the late Leon Fleisher—in my opinion, the greatest American pianist there has been. His bravery in coping with focal dystonia has become legendary.

We met in 1958. Over the years, we have tried to help each other by exchanging ideas on practice techniques and fingering strategies to combat the problem.

Along with its physical toll, dystonia can affect mental health. Artists, in particular, are susceptible because of their perfectionism and the anxiety that comes with a life devoted to professional performance.

The work being done internationally by experts like Dr. Dévora Kestel, director of Mental Health and Substance Abuse at the World Health Organization, offers a beacon of hope in improving our understanding of this aspect of focal dystonia.

In the long term, I am convinced that doctors and scientists will find more lasting solutions to focal dystonia. Even at 82, I remain young in spirit: my own career and struggles have taught me to expect the unexpected.

For example, I could never have predicted that Ubiratan Bizarro Costa, a brilliant industrial designer, would invent a pair of bionic gloves for me. Thanks to this palliative—for me, miraculous—solution, I can play some pieces again after so many years.

Music has always remained in my heart, even when my hands were completely gone. And I will continue to keep it alive as long as I can.

Because of focal dystonia for musicians, we lost dozens of the best ones in the world.

Some of them thought about committing suicide themselves.

This is why *The Musician's Brain-Science and Sensibility,* a marvelous book by Antonio De Salles, a fantastic neurosurgeon, is so important. It explains this rare disease and why I wrote those few lines to show how I kept music alive despite all the adversities I had during my life.

Radiation Preface

By Luiz Larrea

Antonio De Salles, in this entertaining fiction novel, around the complex brain of a musician, perfectly describes the actions of brain radiosurgery in tumoral and functional pathology such as epilepsy. He highlights crises of laughing, a complex gelastic behavior related to a benign brain congenital defect. A small hamartoma that in the brain of a child generates a significant dysfunction for his life.

In this story, he shows how to treat a hamartoma with radiosurgery to eliminate it with the judgment and precision of an expert neurosurgeon.

Radiosurgery causes a series of reaction events in brain cells ranging from permanent damage such as apoptosis. It induces damage with independent cellular repair of neurons and their axons, glia, blood vessels with their nets and permeability, and to exposed blood cells. Importantly Antonio stresses the functional changes of part of the irradiated cells leading to disease cure.

It must be considered that radiosurgery applies a very high dose of radiation to the hamartoma, usually a non-necrotizing dose, knowing that inside the malformation there is an area that will receive very high dose. Around the hamartoma, cells receive radiation in decreasing doses of 50%, 20% and even negligible amount. Importantly is that neurons, glia, blood vessels, lymphocytes, macrophages, and other elements in the hamartoma are affected to halt the harmful effects of the hamartoma, preserving the surrounding cells' function. The technique provides diverse responses to different doses, from necrosis to complete repair. The response to different doses varies according cell type, leading to a curative reaction. Through the process of radiation injury and cellular response, the brain adapts and restores its normal functionality in the musician's brain environment. This is what is known as radiomodulation of the nervous tissue after radiosurgery.

Thanks to the neuronal plasticity, Antonio De Salles illustrates the beneficial effects of radiomodulation in the life of an exceptional musician, showing the beautiful integral harmonization of his brain and senses.

I have shared with Antonio our experiences since the beginnings of radiosurgery on the phenomenon of functional plasticity. The effects of neuromodulation in many of my patients convinced me of the beneficial effects of radiosurgery, which today are in universal use. The mechanism of action and modulation led by radiation we do not understand with the details we would like; however, this intriguing scientific story at the fringes of real and fictional telling explains the importance of the continued quest for finest and creative uses of radiation.

Antonio's great experience in the radiation field is shown graphically in this wonderful, detailed work.

Prologue

*Music expresses that which cannot be put into words,
and that which cannot remain silent.*
Victor Hugo

Dystonia is a spasmodic abnormality of movement or posture that imposes an involuntary twisted position on the affected body segment. It can affect restricted segments of the body, such as the hands and the head, or be generalized, in which case it leads to grotesque distortions of the body figure due to the sustained torsional attitudes it imposes on the face, head, trunk, and limbs. Dystonia may be triggered or worsened by attempts to move the affected parts largely as a result of the involuntary co-contraction of muscle agonists and antagonists. Dystonia disturbs the lives of thousands of musicians and millions of people throughout the world. Frequently, it affects musicians at the pinnacle of their careers. It mainly affects those playing technically highly demanding instruments **(Figure 1).** Classical piano and string instrument players are the most affected, although those playing wind instruments can also suffer from dystonia in their laryngeal muscles.

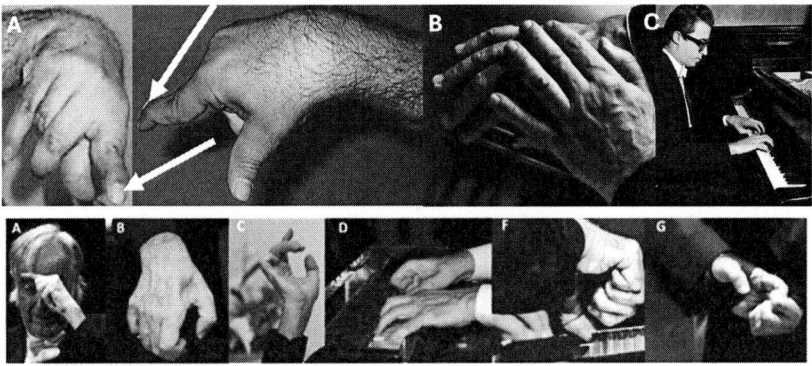

***Figure 1**: Dystonia Hand and Maestro's Hands*

Dystonia Hand and Maestro's Hands : Above, right arm dystonia adopts bizarre attitudes in the three space planes. *Courtesy of the neurologist Ricardo de Oliveira-Souza*. Below (A), (B) Maestro João Carlos Martins' hands before his severe musician's dystonia, and (C) Maestro João Carlos Martins' playing at the beginning of his difficulties with the right hand. (A), (B) e (C) Evolution of the Maestro João Carlos Martins' dystonic hands. Notice not only the dystonic attitude in (A) but also the muscle atrophy (B) secondary to several surgeries leading to nerve damage and botulin toxin (Botox) injections during the Maestro's highly successful career. (D) and (F) disclose the difficulty playing the piano and conducting the orchestra in (A) and (G), *Courtesy of Carmen Silvia Valio de Araujo Martins, Maestro João Carlos Martins' wife*.

This fictional story shows the anxiety and dedication of high-level concert pianists, as well as the drama brought about by motor diseases affecting these professionals. It is based around life in a major research medical center where health professionals, bioengineers, and scientists strive to help the victims of this professionally devastating disease.

The inspiration for this story came from over 40 years of dedication to alleviating the suffering of patients with functional diseases of the brain and from becoming acquainted with Maestro João Carlos Martins and seeing his resilience and success. Despite having severe musician's dystonia, he enjoyed a long and successful career. He made his struggles with dystonia, nerve damage, and head trauma an inspiration for other musicians and patients battling diseases of the nervous system.

The most common movement disorders, namely, essential tremor, Parkinson's disease, and dystonia, have baffled medical doctors throughout the twentieth century. These diseases remain unsolved at the dawn of the twenty-first century; however, humanity is poised with technology to conquer their cure. Molecular and anatomical imaging, such as Positron Emission Tomography (PET) and Magnetic Resonance Imaging (MRI), as well as genetics, immunology, bioengineering, robotic medicine, computerized analysis of brain waves, artificial intelligence, and the mastery of the diverse energies applied in medicine and with recent acquired capability of changing the genetic code as CRISPR, medicine promises to finally put an end to the suffering of those affected by genetic, traumatic, and degenerative diseases of the brain.

The text is light science fiction. It is based on factual knowledge about music, diseases, and the history of medicine. The information is offered as a romantic mystery, which allows the reader to learn the nuances of medical care, including tough decision-making, present and fictional therapies, and ideas for future developments. Pharmacotherapy is not the focus of this story; instead, it is directed to possible surgical approaches to a definitive resolution of central nervous system diseases, or at least decreasing the need for palliative pharmaceutical products and human suffering.

Part 1
Brain, Music, and Plasticity

Chapter 1
Troubled Brain

People pay the doctor for his trouble.
For his kindness, they still remain in his debt.
Seneca (4 B.C.-65 A.D.)

Four-year-old Randy sat with his toys on the floor next to the piano, listening to his mother Jill playing. She was a young Asian neurosurgeon at the University of California Hospital in Los Angeles (UCLA). He was an agitated boy with a fleeting and restless attention span who could not concentrate on any task for more than a few minutes, even when playing with his favorite toys. This dark-eyed, black-haired little boy had striking features, a mix of Asian looks acquired from his mother, and a strong Mexican-Latin-American genetic background from his father Charles. Once a national soccer star, Charles was now a bioengineer professor at UCLA, running a neuro-device development laboratory.

Randy reacted aggressively when his toys were moved from the careful location he had defined. He was meticulous about the way he organized them and remembered the arrangement of his cars for a long time, just as they had been aligned in his imaginary parking lot and gas station set. Paradoxically, given his fleeting attention, he accurately remembered everything he did and learned. With his fast, restless brain, he created imaginary situations that often agitated him, making him panic. Jill could not understand the stimuli or reasons that provoked this, so during his panic attacks, she didn't know what to do to calm him down.

A loving, dedicated mother who was overburdened with professional demands, Jill felt powerless about dealing with these episodes. She didn't want to give Randy medication at such a young age, as she knew the importance of letting his brain develop freely without the suppression of sedatives. She fostered Randy's creativity, quick thinking, and curiosity, which are important qualities in the development of any intelligent child. Amazingly, music had the power to calm him. She played for him for one to two hours after her hard day of work at the university. Her piano-playing soothed him to the point of him falling asleep listening to the familiar pieces he had heard since his fetal life in Jill's womb. An avid pianist as a child, she had always used music to rest, a habit she maintained during her career and pregnancy. Randy responded wonderfully to the music. We know from experiments that the fetus enjoys music while in the womb. Early on, babies show a preference for tunes they experienced during their gestation.

Jill's difficult moments were eased by her daily piano sessions. However, her passion for knowledge of the brain was greater than her love for music. When she entered medical school, science had progressively reduced the space for her music; the profession occupied 12 to 15 hours daily. There was very little left for the family and herself. However, her own need for music was reinforced by the positive effect on Randy. Early in his life, she knew that her music and science would greatly benefit his education. He had taken music lessons since he was a two-year-old at a dedicated school for toddlers' musical initiation. Children became familiar with all the string instruments, percussion, wind, and especially the piano. Knowing the effect of music on Randy, Jill had taken a particular interest in understanding the power of music over the brain. Would music from the womb to adulthood make him a musician?

Chapter 2
Plasticity

Every man, if so determined, can be the sculpturer of his own brain.
Santiago Ramón y Cajal

As a neurosurgeon and a neuroscientist, Jill knew that her task of raising Randy would be full of challenges and that her knowledge and studies would be essential to turning him into a useful being who could improve humanity. The brain responds to our demands, molding itself based on its amazing plastic capability, as the Nobel Prize neuroscientist Ramón y Cajal suggested around the start of the twentieth century **(Figure 2)**. This means that the brain is not strictly pre-programmed for pure survival, as with most animals, but it is a multipurpose organ that is highly adaptable to human needs. The proper stimulation for developing or adapting the brain's architecture molds it, building a unique, beautiful human being **(Figure 3)**. A lack of proper nurturing can lead to a mediocre or even a harmful person. It is an amazing reality.

She had been able to organize her husband's life and brain due to her dedication, love, and scientific knowledge. Now, her task was to work on Randy, who apparently had a similar but more challenging disease than that of his father, Charles. She was able to operate on her husband and cure his impetuous aggressivity by implanting a brain pacemaker. She knew her love and intelligence would be pushed to extremes if she wanted to create a good and productive human from her baby. She had been able to accomplish a remarkable task with Charles when they were young, full of dreams, and intensely in love. After an apparently insurmountable challenging period of suffering, her efforts led to Charles being a major support in her life. He was a dedicated father, an excellent teacher, and a bioengineer already known nationally for his professional soccer fame, scientific skills, and being the first human to benefit from a closed-loop implant to control aggressive behavior. [2]

Figure 2: Santiago Ramón y Cajal Monument to the 'Father of Brain Plasticity' Santiago Ramón y Cajal Monument to the 'Father of Brain Plasticity.' The Spanish neuroscientist was the pioneer of the visualization of nervous system cells and the concept of neural networks. He received the 1906 the Nobel Prize for Physiology and Medicine, jointly with the Italian Camillo Golgi. Santiago Ramón y Cajal was a medical doctor, a neuroscientist, and a bodybuilder. He is well depicted in the statue. Note the inscriptions on the monument and the bullet scars acquired during one of the World Wars. By his side is the author (right) and Dr. Roberto Martinez Alvez (left), pioneer of the Gamma Knife® in Spain, a neurosurgeon dedicated to the modern development of behavioral surgery (Madrid, April 2023).

Knowing Randy's needs, Jill focused her studies on various diseases that would give her a clue as to how to educate her son. When a baby is born, they have a brain to be written on, a white sheet of paper that parents, schools, and society work on in order to bring the best out of that person as they grow up. The worst aspects a human may develop when the environment is completely

---

[2] De Salles A (July 2011) *Why Fly Over the Cuckoo's Nest? Psychosurgery in My Brain, Please.* Writers Guild of America. CreateSpace, Amazon.com.

hostile. Genetic make-up is important; however, the early environment that the parents, the raising foster parents, or the orphanage give children leads them to be bad, good, or outstanding adults. There is now a lot of research on epigenetics, genetics tailored by the environment to define one's personality. Epigenetics plays a huge role in the formation of the brain. The reality is that we can indeed develop certain areas of the brain and atrophy others through education, training, proper foods[3], and the demands of the environment. The controversial 'Mozart Effect' studied by Francis Rauscher, a famous psychologist from Southern California, is an example of the important way that music, at an early age and beyond, can mold the brain's nodal networks[4]. Music stimulates almost all our senses: sensory, motor, vision, hearing, sensibility, mathematics (through rhythm), and the feeling of making music to please oneself and others. It can be a true tour de force in the way it stimulates the brain.

It had been discovered that Randy had a hamartoma with a high capacity for electrical outflow. This outflow had caused a febrile seizure when he was a baby, showing the limited ability of his nodal network to suppress unwanted neuronal electrical discharges. A magnetic resonance image (MRI) disclosed this cluster of abnormal neurons located intrinsically in his hypothalamus, which had already caused some disturbing effects on Randy's behavior. Jill's experiences with her husband Charles' disease during her medical school days had given her a detailed understanding of Randy's brain.

The hypothalamus is the crossroads of human behavior [5]. Randy already had some personality traits that made Jill worry about his education in a very particular way. One of the traits was an extreme sense of justice and the tendency to become violent when he felt someone was being unfair, either

---

[3] Ekstrand B, Scheers N, Rasmussen MK, Young JF, Ross AB, Landberg R. (12 May 2021) 'Brain foods-the role of diet in brain performance and health,' *Nutr Rev.*, **79**(6):693-708. doi: 10.1093/nutrit/nuaa091. PMID: 32989449.

[4] Pauwels, E. K. J., Volterrani, D., Mariani, G., & Kostkiewics, M. (2014) 'Mozart, Music and Medicine,' *Medical Principles and Practice*, **23**(5), 403-412. doi:10.1159/000364873

[5] Barbosa D, de Oliveira-Souza R, Monte Santo F, de Oliveira Faria AC, Gorgulho AA, De Salles AAF (September 2017) 'The hypothalamus at the crossroads of psychopathology and neurosurgery,' *Neurosurg Focus*, **43**(3):E15. doi: 10.3171/2017.6.FOCUS17256. PMID: 28859567.

toward him or his loved ones. He frequently bordered on serious violence, like his father once had. Additionally, when he was playing, he sometimes stared at his toys and smiled for no reason. Jill assumed that he was imagining funny stories, although she knew it could be a sign of seizures, specifically the type known as gelastic.

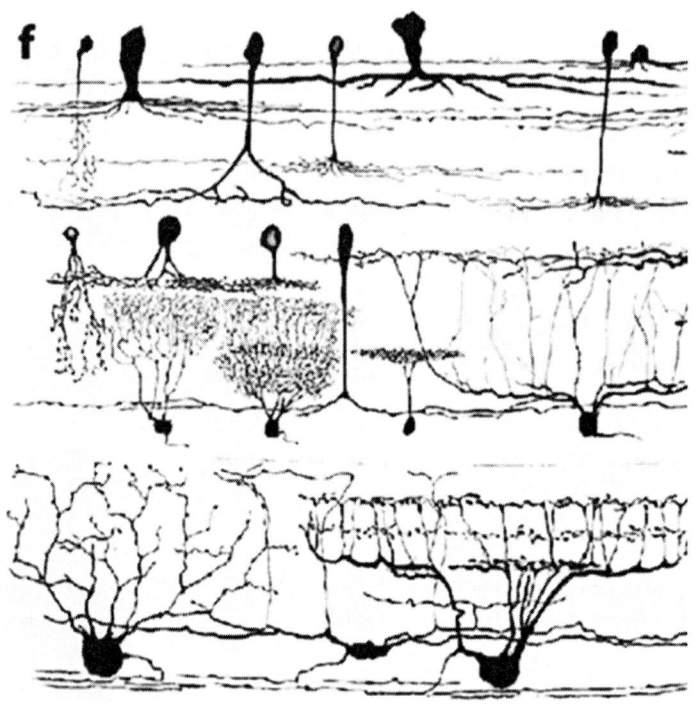

Figure 3: Excerpt of Santiago Ramón y Cajal's 1893 drawing
Excerpt of Santiago Ramón y Cajal's 1893 drawing of his visualization of a lizard's retina cells. Notice the neurons and the multitude of dendrite types. They multiply to enhance brain function based on epigenetic environmental demands causing plasticity. This classic scientific art piece was captured through a primitive microscope available at the end of the nineteenth century. It resembles a musician's music score. Cajal's work is largely available in the public domain, demonstrating his generosity as a scientist and teacher[6,7].

---

[6] Erlish, B (2022) *The Brain in Serch of Itself. Santiago Ramon Cajal and the Story of the Neuron*, Farrar, Straus and Giroux, ISBN-13 978-0374110376.

[7] Lefebvre, J. L., Sanes, J. R., & Kay, J. N. (2015). 'Development of Dendritic Form and Function,' *Annual Review of Cell and Developmental Biology*, **31**(1), 741–777. doi:10.1146/annurev-cellbio-100913-013020

Chapter 3
Music and the Nodal Network

*Rhythm and harmony find their way
into the inward places of the soul, which they mightily fasten.*
Plato

Music has the power to penetrate not only the brain network of a person but also that of a whole crowd at the same time. Concerts that attract thousands of people listening and dancing to the tempo of the same band attest to the power of music over a crowd's brains. Music can bring an entire religious congregation to a trance state in unison, affecting similar networks in the brains of thousands of people at once. Then, music can influence millions of neurons, inducing them to progress through the brain's developmental pathways. We know that at seven months intra-uterus, the hearing apparatus is ready to present music to the fetus's brain, affecting its nodal neuronal network and connections[8]. As Jill had provided music to Randy's brain since his fetal life, it must already have affected his brain in a unique way.

However, it did not prevent the development of the hypothalamic deranged cluster of neurons that formed his hamartoma. Would music influence this cluster of neurons, making them less epileptogenic? This was a question that gave Jill immense anxiety, even though Randy had only had a single seizure in his baby days. Also, that seizure had been triggered by a fever, a not uncommon benign occurrence in children. The great majority will go on to develop normally without further seizures.

---

[8] Massimello F, Billeci L, Canu A, Montt-Guevara MM, Impastato G, Varanini M, Giannini A, Simoncini T, Mannella P. (Apr. 2022) 'Music Modulates Autonomic Nervous System Activity in Human Fetuses,' *Front Med (Lausanne)*, **14**;9:857591. doi: 10.3389/fmed.2022.857591. PMID: 35492323; PMCID: PMC9046697.

Too much knowledge is always a source of anxiety, especially knowing the details of a disease that threatens the well-being of a loved one. Jill knew that if Randy experienced too many seizures, it would affect his cognition. She knew that the hamartoma could lead to more varied types of seizures. She also knew that hamartomas could lead to precocious puberty, depending on the location in which it settles in the hypothalamus. The latter is only 4mm in size but is responsible for all our hormones, sleep cycle, sexual drive, rage control, temperature control, and many other functions affected by hormones throughout the body. When affected by a disease, this delicate structure, linked to the hormonal person's make-up and deeply linked to memory and metabolism, can be the source of a multitude of deficits for a child in development. Jill continued to watch Randy's behavior and development milestones like a hawk.

Chapter 4
Gelastic

In nothing do men more nearly approach
the gods than in giving health to men.
Cicero (106 B.C.-43 B.C.)

Jill became a young faculty member at the Department of Neurosurgery at UCLA, working with Dr. Hillary, her mentor through medical school and her residency. Her qualifications and accomplishments from her research on addiction and aggression earned her a Doctorate in Philosophy (PhD), making her the best candidate for the position in Dr. Hillary's department. They were dedicated to treating Parkinson's disease, dystonia, epilepsy, and essential tremor using cerebral implants. One day, they were operating together, implanting a device to control the symptoms of a patient with Parkinson's disease, when her cell phone rang insistently. The nurse circulating their operating room finally picked the phone up, pulled a worried face, and said, "Jill, it is Randy's teacher. Randy punched a little girl at school."

"What?" Jill asked.

"Yes, and now he is sleeping," the teacher said that he is not waking up!

Dr. Hillary, who had diagnosed Randy's hamartoma said, "Go to his school now, Jill. I will close the patient. He has probably had a seizure."

Jill rushed desperately from the operating room. She arrived at Randy's school half an hour later. It was an agonizing drive north on the traffic-jammed 405 freeway. It was horrible to know that her son was unconscious, and she was not at his side. Was he suffering from a mal epilepticus? This is a state when the person enters a nonstop seizure, with their neurons on continuous electrical discharge, and when one seizure finishes another starts. This state is dangerous. Seizures can lead to poor respiration, causing insufficient oxygenation and consequent loss of brain cells, possible effects on cognition, and even sudden death. All these anxious thoughts ran through her mind as she arrived at Randy's school.

She found him awake in the classroom as if nothing had happened. The teacher said that soon after the seizure episode, he woke up confused and sleepy but had soon started playing alone in a corner, apparently not remembering what had happened. She asked him if he could remember the altercation with the little girl, but apparently, he really didn't remember anything. He had a complete retrograde amnesia of the event. Patients who have seizures often have no memory of what happened during the crisis. She decided he probably only had one seizure, leading to loss of consciousness.

The teacher explained that Randy had been playing with cubes and building a tower when the little girl destroyed his work. He hadn't done anything; just started building the tower again. When the tower reached the same height, the girl proceeded to destroy it again. Randy just suddenly punched her in the face, started smiling, rolled his eyes up, opened and closed his mouth for no reason, stared forward, and started shaking. He had fallen on the floor, wet himself, and then relaxed into a deep slumber. The little girl cried, and there had been turmoil in the classroom. As Randy continued sleeping, the teacher was able to calm the classroom down. That was when she had called Jill. Twenty minutes later, he had opened his eyes and looked around, still very sleepy. Soon, he sat down and directed his attention to the cubes, starting to build the tower again as if nothing had happened.

The little girl certainly did not come close to him again. She was fine; a four-year-old's punch was not that strong, but it was enough to teach her that Randy was not someone to mess up with. However, it did mean that Jill had to accept the hard truth that Randy had epilepsy. This needed serious attention otherwise he would not develop normally. She had to find a way to curb Randy's abnormal neuronal electric discharges, which were probably coming from his hypothalamic hamartoma. This was not an easy task, as the cluster of neurons was in the center of his brain, adjacent to important functional cells in the hypothalamus. Conventional surgery was not an option, as it would render Randy completely disturbed in his hormones and probably without memory. Antiseizure medication was an immediate option. However, all of them sedate the brain, which worried Jill very much, as only a small group of cells needed to be curbed. The medication would certainly have side effects, turning him into a zombie and possibly harming his learning abilities. She was overwhelmed with all these thoughts. She decided she needed to discuss this with Charles and ask Dr. Hillary for help.

She hugged Randy and saw that he was completely calm, unaware that he had done something wrong. She felt deeply sorry for him because she knew that the fight against his disease would not be easy. She had worked for years to help his father with his uncontrolled aggressive behavior; it had been a strenuous effort, coupled with intense suffering and irreparable consequences for many people. Now, once again, she would have to get back to the basics of her studies to help a loved one. Fortunately, her efforts would not only help Randy; thousands or millions of people would benefit from her research and technical developments. She had already been recognized in the scientific world for her work with Charles, her husband. It had repercussions in the scientific and medical fields worldwide.

She drove home with Randy, thinking about the challenges she had to face ahead.

Chapter 5
A Sardonic Smile

A smile is not always a friendly gesture.
Antonio De Salles

Jill was completely absorbed by her thoughts as she automatically drove down the 405 freeway toward home. Charles was still working in his laboratory in the Bioengineering Department. It was National Institute of Health scientific project application season (NIH grant season); he was working on a new project about a feedback loop device for Alzheimer's disease. This device would be capable of storing memories, returning them to the patient when requested by their brain. It was an idea Jill had while working with patients suffering from short-term memory loss, seeing how much patients and their families suffer as Alzheimer's disease progresses.

She had given the idea to Charles; no one had benefited more from brain-computer prostheses than her husband. The simple device Jill and Dr. Hillary implanted in his brain brought him freedom and a rewarding and productive life as a top scientist. He was in jail after an aggressive burst, causing a promising neurosurgery resident to enter into a permanent comatose state. After a staggering fight against outdated rules and regulations for psychiatric surgery, Jill was able to bring her husband back to the main curse of society, performing modern psychosurgery on him. He had become an outstanding match for Jill and often developed Jill's neuroscientific ideas. His exemplary behavior, ensured by the brain prosthesis, had earned him conditional freedom at his home and workplace, despite the serious murder charges he had faced when he was without the neuromodulation aid, having episodes of rage when he was not conscious of his actions.

She glanced back in the rearview mirror; Randy was calmly asleep, well protected in his child car seat. She fell deeper into her thoughts, planning the end of her afternoon. Arriving home, she would ask Charles to come home to stay with Randy, while she would return to help Dr. Hillary with the afternoon rounds. Mainly, she wanted to see the Parkinson's disease woman they had been operating on when she had been called to Randy's school. She was Jill's patient, a lovely 54-year-old who she had treated for more than five years until the family decided to accept that she needed a brain pacemaker implant to control her debilitating symptoms. The patient, Mrs. Biden, was already losing her ability to care for herself, as she was unable to dress and feed herself. Although Dr. Hillary must have finished the surgery without difficulties, and Jill had complete confidence that everything should be fine, she was the patient's doctor. She had a tight bond with the patient and her family. They would be expecting to talk with her after the surgery, as the patient's main surgeon must always do.

The traffic was getting heavy at the end of the afternoon when, in the rearview mirror, she noticed Randy's grimace. It was a very strange smile, which promptly alerted her that he could be having another epileptic attack. The smile was followed by a behavior identical to the one described by his teacher: he rolled his eyes up, made some strange movements in his mouth, and started shaking all over, a characteristic of a generalized seizure. Even worse, foamy blood came out of his mouth. This made Jill panic. She directed the car to the shoulder of the highway, parked it, and desperately threw her door open.

Instantly, a passing car hit her door and leg, throwing her back inside. She felt a sharp pain in her hip; she looked back to Randy and saw that the crisis had stopped. He was in a bad state but breathing. She reached for her cell phone on the dashboard and called Dr. Hillary. He promptly told her not to move or get out of the car. The driver who had hit her hadn't stopped; he sped off down the freeway as if nothing had happened. The traffic continued its sluggish flow as if nothing had happened. Then, a large truck stopped behind her car, and the truck driver came to her help.

He said, "Ma'am, are you OK?"

"I have a lot of pain in my hip, sir," Jill answered. "An ambulance from UCLA Hospital is already coming to pick us up; I called them."

"Us?" The driver asked. "Is there somebody else in the car?"

"Yes," answered Jill. "My son Randy is in his car seat in the back; he had a seizure. I see that he is already asleep again, so he will be fine; I am a doctor. Now I am worried about my leg, it is not moving, too much pain."

"Ma'am, don't you worry, I will keep my truck behind your car, so the same accident does not happen again. Your car is small, some other car could hit it again; people drive like crazy here."

"Thank you so much; please stay here while we wait for the ambulance. I am afraid that my son will have another attack, and I will not be able to help him."

"Don't worry, I am here to help you."

Chapter 6
Out of Commission

When adversity gives us time,
it is an opportunity for great creations.
Antonio De Salles

The ambulance arrived within 15 minutes. The police came first and blocked a car lane to facilitate the rescue. Jill was placed on a stretcher; she saw that her left leg was turned in a grotesque way. The paramedic secured an intravenous drip and relieved her pain with a dose of morphine. She fell asleep immediately. Randy was also placed on a stretcher, his mouth was cleaned, his vitals checked, and the ambulance took off to the UCLA emergency room. Upon arrival, Jill was immediately taken for a whole-body CAT scan; she was admitted as a polytrauma victim, meaning the doctors had to check her whole body.

Randy was promptly seen by Dr. Hillary and his team. They knew of his disease; they medicated him to prevent further seizures and switched their attention toward Jill. She was still asleep. The scan showed a fracture in the lower third of her left femur. Fortunately, it was not an exposed fracture, i.e., the broken bone had not ruptured her skin, risking osteomyelitis. Otherwise, it would keep her for several days admitted to the hospital, taking intravenous antibiotics. Nevertheless, she was taken to the operating room, and under general anesthesia, her fracture was aligned. A cast was placed, completely immobilizing her leg. She was taken to the recovery room, where she woke up without pain. Her first words were, "Where is Randy? Is he OK?"

Dr. Hillary was at her bedside, soothing her worries about Randy. He was already awake in the pediatric ward, being tended to by the nurses, playing with some toys, and asking for Mommy.

"Did you call Charlie, Dr. Hillary?"

"Not yet; it is 5 pm now. I let him work. He must have been very busy writing, so he didn't call here. I plan to send you and Randy home at 6 pm. Calling him during the aftermath of your accident would not have helped him, nor you. So, I took care of everything. All is fine now. You have a broken femur. I will keep you out of the operating room for at least eight weeks."

"And Mrs. Biden…?"

"Don't worry, I will take care of her. She is fine, she woke up from the anesthesia. She still has the tremor, but I am sure she will be doing better after we turn on her pacemaker. Do you remember the surgery?"

"Of course, I do. I didn't lose consciousness at the time of the accident," said Jill. "It was just senseless of me to get out of the car through the left-hand side. I should have cared for Randy inside of the car or left through the right front door to reach him. When I saw blood coming out of his mouth, I lost my mind. He could have aspirated in the position he was in. You know, he could have died if he stopped breathing. I went for the shortest route toward him. Well, fortunately, all is under control. But how will I stop working for eight weeks? Impossible!"

"Sure, it is possible. We will be here for you," said Dr. Hillary. "The team can take your load for a while. The residents will love having more opportunities to operate while you are away. You can keep up your intellectual work; you don't need legs for that. The project you are working on with Charles is very important for the department. Let's help him to get his project funded. You can help him immensely with his writing during these eight weeks. He is the principal investigator in this basic part, but you will be the principal investigator when we move into the clinical phase. Helping patients with Alzheimer's disease is a daunting task. Girl, we are counting on your sharp brain!"

"OK! Let's turn this disaster into an opportunity, as you always say. I will use this spare time at home well. However, we need to do something about Randy's hamartoma," said Jill anxiously.

"Jill, I have been thinking about how to handle it. Let's talk about this another time. Now you need some rest, so you can still go home today. Do you want to call Charles now, or do you want me to call him?"

"I prefer to call myself," said Jill. "Hearing my voice first will immediately assure him that we are fine. I will ask him to pick us up here in one hour, OK?"

"Yes, when he arrives, please give me a call so I can tell him the details of your leg fracture and how to care for Randy today. Talking to both of you at once will save me time. Now, excuse me, but I must finish the afternoon rounds."

Chapter 7
Home, Music, and Love

Imagination creates reality.
Richard Wagner

Since her maternity leave, Jill hadn't had a chance to dedicate herself completely to her family. Her accident created the opportunity for her to dedicate more time to Randy, just at this moment when he needed her so much. She always felt guilty for not giving him enough attention. He was attending one of the best schools in Los Angeles; however, she wanted to be at his side more often, to care for him and develop his brain the best she possibly could. She believed that overwhelming his neuronal nodal network with love and music might overcome or block the detrimental electrical bursts generated by his hamartoma, curbing its bad influence on his brain.

She theorized that nurturing his brain connections and strengthening the neural network dedicated to productive endeavors would totally suppress the discharges from the hamartoma. Finally, she would have some time she could dedicate to infusing stimulation into Randy's developing brain. Since his toddler years, she had placed Persian rugs with a lot of intricate embroidery in his playing room to stimulate his visual cortex and pathways during his crawling period. She had always found ways of reaching his neural network. Additionally, he had been watching the 'Little Einstein' video series since he was an infant. The period from four to 12 years old was the time to intensify his exposure to music.

Jill assiduously organized her schedule at home to make the most out of her two months off, focusing on Randy's care. This time with Randy was so precious that she devised a strict calendar in which she would spend most of the time teaching him music. She would help Charles with the Alzheimer's project when she could, but he could write it independently.

Every day, the family woke up at 6 am; Charles made breakfast for the family while Jill was already at the piano with Randy by her side. She started playing the pieces she enjoyed, the ones she had played during her pregnancy, Mozart and Chopin. Then, when he was completely calm, she showed him the music notes and helped him play some simple tunes. She also started teaching him to read music so she could have him playing some children's songs by the end of the two months. Her hope was that he would acquire a love for the instrument at the end of this intensive two-month period, enhance his music-related neural network, and start to suppress the firing from his hamartoma. After her piano lesson, they had breakfast, and Randy was prepared to go to school.

Their time was short though. Randy continued attending kindergarten. School started at 9 am; as Jill could not drive due to the fracture, Charles drove Randy to school. Jill always went with them, as freeway time was also precious. They would talk about family issues and sing children's songs with Randy. He was always very engaged and happy to be with his parents. He liked school; the teacher understood that she had to prevent any confrontations with other children. Learning to socialize was important at this stage of his life. He played well with other children; he was learning to share and gradually accepted the ways the other children wanted to play with him. He even befriended the little girl he had punched; she became his constant companion at school, building towers, drawing, and singing with him. The teacher encouraged their friendship.

Randy had no memory of what had happened. To him, she was just a friend. He would arrive at school in an excellent mood, usually singing the songs he had just learned in the car with his parents. His memory was amazing; he would remember all the words, sing complete songs, and even teach the teacher what he had learned, particularly if she didn't know the songs. He started to be admired by the other children, becoming a leader in his classroom. It was the opposite of his attitude back at the beginning of the year when he had been a solitary child, always trying to play alone with his own toys rarely interacting with his classmates.

The drives to and from school were also important for Jill and Charles. It was when they discussed their ideas and their project. They talked about how to inject memories into the brains of patients with Alzheimer's disease. This involved transmitting the memories from the miniature computer Charles was conceptualizing, creating a prototype, building it in his laboratory, and injecting it into the hippocampus of a patient. He was already able to inject lessons into a rat's brain from a chip he had prepared; rats were able to work out mazes much faster when he implanted an electrode into the animals' hippocampus. Now, the challenge was to construct an algorithm to transfer electrical impulses with information into the hippocampus of a human being.

On one drive, she said, "I like the concept. Very challenging, though," uttered Jill.

"Well, the technology is already partially developed here in our institution," said Charles. "Electrodes to record seizures to define their focus have been done here at the university since the 1970s.

"I have been discussing it with Dr. Wilson, the electrophysiologist who worked with Dr. Crandall. They developed an umbrella-like electrode that was implanted bilaterally in the hippocampus. This technology led to breakthroughs in facial recognition in the temporal lobes, lateralization of the functioning of the right and left hippocampus, and localized seizure-triggering sites on hundreds of patients in preparation for epilepsy surgery. It helped neurosurgeons to use resections to control seizures when medications were not effective[9]."

"Go ahead," said Jill. "It is a great start. Ultimately, we will have to find a way to wirelessly infuse memories into the hippocampus. Remember, Charlie, we are in the age of wireless technology. Soon, we will be transmitting information from the Ethernet into people's brains using Bluetooth technology."

"Great, smart girl," Charles said enthusiastically. "I already know how to do that if you can implant a receiver in the hippocampus. **(Figure 4).** Then, my device will send memories into the hippocampus and spread them throughout the cells. The device I am designing is like a miniature porcupine fish; it will be 4 mm in diameter with myriad spikes; some will be receiving antennas, and the others will be like dendrites passing memories on. Do you think it is possible to implant something like that?"

---

[9] Suthana N, Haneef Z, Stern J, Mukamel R, Behnke E, Knowlton B, Fried I. (Feb. 2012) 'Memory enhancement and deep-brain stimulation of the entorhinal area,' *N Engl J Med.*, **9**;366(6):502-10. doi: 10.1056/NEJMoa1107212. PMID: 22316444; PMCID: PMC3447081.

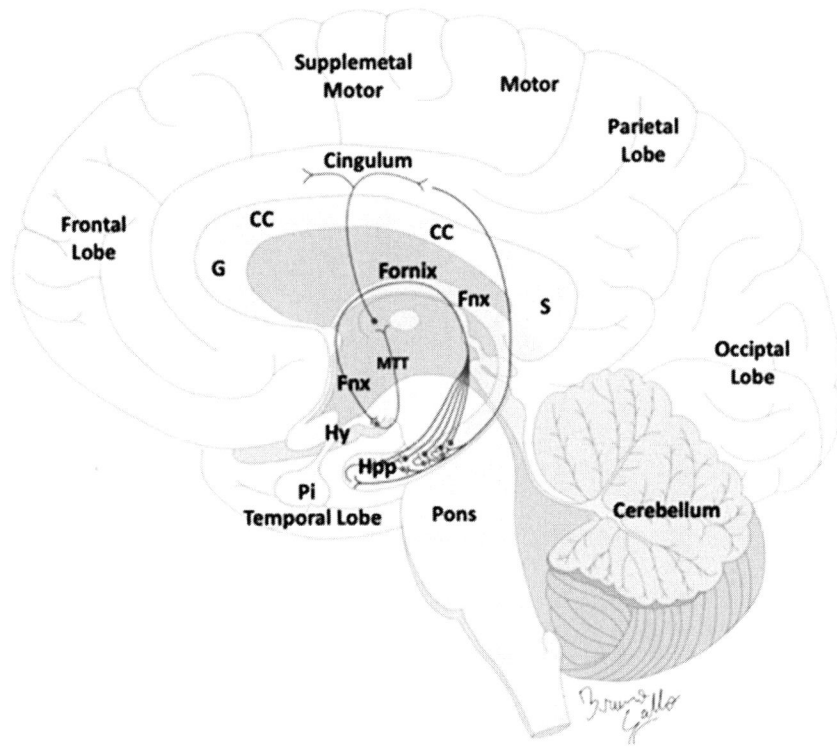

Figure 4: *The circuit of memory leaves the hippocampus*
The circuit of memory leaves the hippocampus (Hpp), where several neurons are represented in green, blue, and red. They send axons throughout the brain to connect memories with intellectual interpretation, feelings, and storage areas. The structures represented are all targets for spreading memories, such as the Fornix (Fnx). The red neurons curve toward the mammillary body, in close relationship with the hypothalamus (Hy). Green neurons are interconnecting with red and blue neurons in the cingulum and hippocampus. Notice the single long green neuron interconnecting the mammillary bodies and the thalamus; it forms the mammillothalamic tract (MTT), which is closely related to the spreading of memory throughout the brain. Additionally, there is the spread of memory through the blue axons directly to the cingulate gyrus (Cingulum), part of the Papez circuit, forming the limbic system, the house of deep feelings and thoughts reverberation. The Corpus Callosum (CC) interconnects the hemispheres. The Genus of the CC (G) interconnects the intellectual might occurring in the frontal lobes. The Splenium of the CC (S) interconnects visual and auditive information between the hemispheres. The mother gland, the pituitary (PI) influences diverse body organs with hormones. It is controlled by the hypothalamus (Hy).

"Yes, it is. I don't see any difficulty installing such a small device," said Jill. "We must find out if it does not migrate throughout the brain. The problem is that Alzheimer's disease patients don't initially suffer from losing old memories. Instead, what most handicaps them is the inability to retain recent, immediate memories. Your device has to record recent memories and inject them into the hippocampus. That is the way I believe your device will work. We have to devise an experiment on higher order animals, pigs, or monkeys to find out if the hippocampus is indeed the place to infuse the memories with your 'porcupine fish device'."

"I will explain the need for these experiments in our budget proposal to the National Institute of Health (NIH)," said Charles.

Chapter 8
Focus on the Network

Your brain does not manufacture thoughts.
Your thoughts shape neural networks.
Deepak Chopra

"Well, Charlie, my focus now is Randy," said Jill. "I want to enhance his neuronal nodal network using music."

This network is composed of neurons, dendrites, and synapses, which respond to stimulation; the more we study, the more we remember what we learn. Memory is completely dependent on synapses, the chemical connections we create in our brain in response to demands, as described by Dr. Kandel, who got the Nobel Prize for his life-long work teaching rats and checking their memories, with years of help from his collaborators in New York.

"I will use music to stimulate all Randy's senses. I will do this with maximal intensity, as I am hypothesizing that it will inhibit his hamartoma's abnormal neurons and increase his number of dendrites and good synapses, enhancing his memory. I hope this strategy will work."

Immediately, Charles brought his head down. She knew he felt guilty for what was happening to Randy, partly because of Charles' genetic heritage. He knew that 23 of his chromosomes had met the 23 Jill's chromosomes to conceive his son. Apparently, Randy had got all the good ones from Jill, but also the aggressive trait from him. He felt sorry for him and Jill, as he had seen how much she had suffered when she found out that Randy had a brain disease. Nothing in the brain is simple, especially when abnormal cells are embedded so deeply in the brain. He had put a lot of thought into how to help his son, but he had not yet worked out how to curb those misfiring neurons. He just hated seeing Randy getting in trouble like he did during his soccer life and graduate studies[10].

He raised his head and asked Jill, "Could we implant a porcupine fish device into Randy's hamartoma?"

"Maybe, but why would you do that?"

"To overwhelm the firing hamartoma's neurons with electrical impulses. Isn't that what we do when treating tremor, rigidity, and dystonic movements?"

"It is a valid thought, but I would rather try my music approach first. It is less invasive and will develop his brain comprehensively. I see Randy improving day by day. Assuring him of our love and music is my choice for now. The three of us driving to and from school have already modified Randy in a remarkable way. The teacher is amazed by his progress at school, academically and socially. She told me he is her main helper in class. He is becoming a good, influential leader… a good person. He is singing and playing musical instruments, teaching his colleagues the children's songs we sing in the car, and really behaving as a loving human being. Let's trust our nurturing a bit, Charlie. If needed, we can think of complicated solutions for Randy's hamartoma, such as a neuromodulation device, or a way to focus energy to disable it, such as focus ultrasound or photons [11],[12]."

---

[10] De Salles A (July 2011) *Why Fly Over the Cuckoo's Nest? Psychosurgery in My Brain, Please.* Writers Guild of America. CreateSpace, Amazon.com.

[11] Bystritsky, A., Korb, A. S., Douglas, P. K., Cohen, M. S., Melega, W. P., Mulgaonkar, A. P. … Yoo, S.-S. (2011) 'A review of low-intensity focused ultrasound pulsation,' *Brain Stimulation*, **4**(3), 125–136. doi:10.1016/j.brs.2011.03.007

[12] Selch MT, Gorgulho A, Mattozo C, Solberg TD, Cabatan-Awang C, De Salles AA (Oct. 2005) 'Linear accelerator stereotactic radiosurgery for the treatment of gelastic seizures due to hypothalamic hamartoma,' *Minim Invasive Neurosurg*, **48**(5):310-4.

Chapter 9
Music and Synapses

*The chief function of the body
is to carry the brain around.*
Thomas A. Edson

Jill stuck with her plan. After three weeks of intense work with Randy, she noticed the fruits of her labor. Randy woke up on time, as the routine required. He was up at 6:00 am. Charlie was already up; he helped him brush his teeth, dressed him up, and brought him down for his piano session. She played the piano for half an hour. She started with Randy's favorite pieces, always introducing a new fragment of Bach. She believed that the strict mathematical structure of Bach's compositions would progressively organize Randy's brain. She counted on the sensibility, spatial organization, and rhythm to influence his brain. In fact, she was working with his auditory cortex, temporoparietal cortex, and their connections with the limbic system. After this introduction, she would bring him to the keyboard, showing him some notes and letting him play a bit. She had completed one of the most effective ways to stimulate all his senses in less than an hour.

During her early morning time, sharpening Randy's neurons, dendrites, and synapses, Charles prepared breakfast. They had their morning family time together and thanked God for the meal. After the quick music lesson and breakfast, they left for school to continue singing and nurturing Randy in the car. One morning, after dropping Randy off at school, Charles asked Jill while driving to work what she had imagined was happening in Randy's brain after all her musical efforts.

"Charlie, we are promoting fiber sprouts in his brain tree," **(Figure 3)** she answered with a professorial intonation.

"As you probably know, children need routine, yet they need the stimulation of all their senses, the more stimulation, the better. They are born with a brain to be developed. The *homo sapiens* need nurturing and teaching more than any other species. We became the dominant species on earth because we were the only ones that transferred knowledge to our offspring for more than 20 years. The knowledge accumulated throughout the millennia is transferred from parents and grandparents to their grandchildren, but also directly from teachers, television, films, libraries, toys, music, and social interactions.

"A child depends on their parents or other caregivers for at least ten years to survive. During this period, the brain is accumulating memories and developing its network for survival. Indeed, we are born with a brain tree of neurons with an overwhelming ability to differentiate and sprout new nervous fibers. If stimulated at the proper moment and appropriately, the brain becomes an astonishingly powerful computer; indeed, it is the most harmonic and dynamic machine ever imagined. As adults, parents, grandparents, professors, relatives, and friends naturally offer this indispensable stimulation for children's brain development. The human brain is a creation of millennia of evolution; each generation gradually improves our minds."

Jill continued, "As we offer music to Randy's brain, his neurons are migrating with directional cones, chemically and electrically guided, traveling through the glial 'highway' in the direction of cortical and subcortical locations in the brain morphologic universe."

This glial highway is composed of glial cells (from the Greek for glue). These cells protect and intrinsically structure the brain through the sprouting of fibers. These fibers are called axons and dendrites, and their interfaces are the synapses. Synapses house the neurochemicals which transfer information between the axons and dendrites. These structures jointly make a constantly dynamic machine, which is always learning and evolving with new dendrites, axons, and synapses throughout the existence of a human. Of course, this process is incredibly fast during the youth, but it persists through life until our death.

When Randy was born, the 46 chromosomes he had received determined a genetic pattern that made him develop inside of the womb into a full human fetus. At seven months, his fetus was already programmed with the basic functions for survival, so he had the basic functions in crucial regions, such as speech, motor, and sensory regions needed for survival. Indispensable senses such as hearing, vision, smell, pain, taste, breathing, and heartbeat are spontaneously localized in the brain. Every function a human needs for basic survival is ready at birth, including the autonomic nervous system, both sympathetic and parasympathetic, responsible for our automatic internal functions, such as heartbeat, breathing, digestion, and excretions, all controlled by the incessant working brain. However, these functions are not enough for a baby born to survive alone in our dangerous and wild world.

Homo sapiens would already have become extinct if a baby was left alone to fend for himself against snakes, large felines, and all the aggressive wild animals, vertebrates, invertebrates, and diseases caused by microbial beings. Our ancestors had to deal with all the experiences accumulated by humanity and transfer knowledge to their descendants, in our case, Randy, so he could compete appropriately in the animal kingdom."

"Jill, don't you think that you are overanxious about Randy's education?" Charles remarked.

"Sure not," reacted Jill, and continued, "he will compete with other human beings for a 'place under the sun.' Remember, Randy was born already with an impediment. He has seizures, he overreacts when teased, and worse as you know, he can become violent. You know well the consequences of this feebleness. Therefore, we have to offer him the best environment, so we correct as much as possible his weaknesses."

"Sorry, Jill. I understand that these defects in his personality were caused by my genetic contribution. It is peculiar that he has the same weaknesses as I do. Worse yet, he has this hypothalamic seizure, this gelastic behavior that I never had, so strange. Although I feel sorry, I feel completely incapable of helping him," said Charles with an apologetic and guilty face.

"Please don't feel that way," Jill said. "This is nonsense, you are not guilty of anything. Genetic baggage is only 50% or less of a person's make-up. Studies in identical twins have shown that one of them frequently has a disease that the other doesn't. I have a patient with obsessive-compulsive disorder (OCD) who is incapable of working and has barely finished his studies, while his brother is an outstanding plastic surgeon. You can do a lot to help, and you are doing it, as your father and your mother did for you during your infancy, childhood, teenage years, and even after you went to the university. During all our difficulties, they were there for us. Since we met, I have heard your mother describing what she had to do for you to become a balanced person during your youth. We worked through incredible difficulties, fortunately winning in the end. Now you are a recognized scientist, a soccer player that your country will never forget, a loving, dedicated father, and an outstanding husband who I love." Jill placed her hand on the back of his head while he was driving. "You are my companion, my support, half of my professional success, and a superb example for your son, Charlie."

She was on the roll now. "We must stimulate Randy's brain to the hilt for the next 15 years. We know that the brain is a dynamic organ and can modify itself over demand, even in the adult and later years. Creativity, expertise, and excellence in any field of knowledge depend on a highly connected and balanced brain. That is why, during this development period, we need to transfer all the knowledge we have and more to him, making his brain a creative machine capable of surpassing ours. We can do this by harmonically developing his neuronal nodal network, spreading his dendrites, and enhancing the number of his synapses, which are the true depositories of memory. There's nothing like music for accomplishing this goal.

"Plenty of studies show that children growing up in families who provide early music education and listen to music during their studies and problem-solving achieve better grades at school. The unused neuronal network pruning occurs during the teenage years; this helps form the mature brain when a person reaches 20 to 21 years. So, we also have to stimulate the non-pruning of the neuronal network, making every fiber we can give a specific function to be useful. It is also crucial during these formative years to avoid toxic substances, such as recreational drugs and alcohol, which are impediments to brain development."

"Sure," she continued, "we can learn new things after the formative years because the brain is so dynamic. We can learn easily if we have a fully developed neuronal network with more cells, more connections, and more synapses to store novel information. Music provides these connections. That is why I am making so much effort with Randy during these two months, I want him to love music. I want him to take an instrument, hopefully, the piano, and dedicate hours and hours to it. I am training him in an appreciation of Bach, which is technically the best way to develop his eye-hand coordination and capability with mathematics and spatial visualization, not to mention sensibility and motor control. Bach's music trains the right hand to be independent of the left hand, providing unique dexterity for life, music, surgery, any fine manual work, and even sports."

When they arrived home, Charles left her there and rushed to the laboratory. He was full of ideas but convinced that Jill was right. In fact, he had been working with Randy on sports, teaching him to kick with both feet. He had a lot to teach him. Music would help him with spatial visualization, which would help in sports. What about strategies for controlling aggressive instincts at the right moment?

He asked himself, "Were those in his court? Or were they with Jill through her piano lessons?"

Feeling confused, he concluded that Jill was an outstanding neuroscientist, working on their son as if he were a project in development.

He sighed and exclaimed to himself, "Well, he is a project of an adult."

Part 2
Virtuosity

Chapter 10
Sensibility

*Emotions are enmeshed in the
neural networks of reason.*
Antonio Damasio

*Tears fall for a reason; they
are your strength, not weakness.*
Charlie Mackesy

The two months Jill took to discipline Randy and herself playing piano and teaching him to love music had major effects on her son's behavior. He was so taken by the music that she could observe changes in his mood depending on the pieces she played in the morning. Certain pieces would bring tears to his eyes, while others would lift his mood to the point of inciting him to dance, always in the correct rhythm. As Plato put it, rhythm and sensibility to music became part of his make-up, enchanting his soul.

Musical memory is intense in humans, so much so that the tunes someone learns in kindergarten will stick with that person for life. Moreover, certain tunes will be connected to your life's best others to the worst moments. The film industry uses music to stimulate our memories and feelings, enhancing key scenes. The power of music in these moments is so intense that it creates suspense, sadness, and happiness, leading us to be fully immersed in the scene.

Rhythm can have an even stronger power than melody. Since primordial times, humans have used the beat of a drum for religious purposes, for example. A tribe would then reach a trance state, and this still happens today in many religions. This kind of trance is related to communication with God and spirits in many religions. The effect of the rhythm is also extremely powerful when it comes to enlivening parties or organizing war battalions, as it has been throughout history. Recently, trance has been associated with synthetic and dance music, even taking us to imaginary planets, as in the show *Return of the Jedi,* a concert composed by John Williams and premiered in London in 2009.

Randy's schoolteacher noticed that he loved dancing during music classes, stimulating it. He indeed acquired a musician's brain. He enjoyed playing the piano; at age five, he could already identify intervals and play basic tunes independently. Jill was so proud and excited about her success that she hired a private teacher to give Randy lessons at home, knowing that neurosurgery would take her away from Randy again. Mrs. Alice was a young, energetic, and nurturing music teacher. Randy loved the lessons; he soon started playing entire children's songs and many Mozart pieces.

Jill kept playing, mostly Bach, every day at home before his bedtime. He was receiving such an input to his motor and sensory cortex that his dexterity was improving rapidly. Most importantly, the pathway from his hearing to his limbic system and the memory required to play music, involving the fibers crossing the hypothalamus, were being highly stimulated **(Figure 5)**. By overwhelming this pathway, Jill believed that the gelastic seizures would be suppressed; in other words, the fibers coming from the hamartoma would not be used and would hopefully be pruned as Randy's brain developed. Therefore, gelastic electrical impulses from these abnormal neurons would not have enough synapses or dendrites to evolve as triggers for seizures. The electrical discharges from the hamartoma would not have pathways to reach the whole brain to cause seizures with loss of consciousness, or to reach the brain centers responsible for the sardonic smile[13] and aggression.

Importantly, his brain would develop normally, hopefully, better than normally, due to the intense global music influence, leading to robust connections throughout humans' three most important centers of information capture: vision, audition, and touch.

Jill's theory seemed to be holding. As Randy's dedication to music increased, his mood stabilized, and the seizures no longer happened. He rarely

---

[13] Camargos S, Scholz S, Simón-Sánchez J, Paisán-Ruiz C, Lewis P, Hernandez D, Ding J, Gibbs JR, Cookson MR, Bras J, Guerreiro R, Oliveira CR, Lees A, Hardy J, Cardoso F, Singleton AB. DYT16 (Mar. 2008) 'A novel young-onset dystonia-parkinsonism disorder: identification of a segregating mutation in the stress-response protein PRKRA,' *Lancet Neurol.*, **7**(3):207-15. doi: 10.1016/S1474-4422(08)70022-X. Epub 2008 Feb 1. PMID: 18243799.

displayed aggressive behavior. During childhood, he was completely protected from annoyances at school and home. Two years had passed since his last gelastic seizures; Jill had discontinued the anticonvulsants, as they had been making him sleepy at school. He progressed with excellent grades.

The family progressed healthily during this period of harmony and hard work. Charles obtained the funding he needed from the National Institute of Health to develop his memory implant. His prototype was almost ready for demonstration at the national bioengineering meeting. Jill was enthusiastic about the project. It was one of her dreams to implant the device in patients severely affected by Alzheimer's disease. She also expected that, as Charles' device became more advanced, she would have options to help not only patients with Alzheimer's disease but also those with many other neurodegenerative diseases and even autistic and feebleminded children. The increasing number of these diseases in the population was astonishing because of the longevity achieved by modern medicine and the increased opportunity for diagnosis.

Chapter 11
Motor Skills, Aggressivity, Sensibility

*To control aggression without
inflicting injury is the art of peace.*
Morihei Ueshiba (1883-1969)

Charles was dedicating his spare time to Randy's education. He spent his available hours with him playing sports. Like his father, he was becoming an excellent forward. He had all his father's characteristics as a player, with the advantage of kicking with both feet. At the age of eight, he was already on the elementary school soccer team and one of the most valuable players. Soccer rapidly became his favorite occupation. It even started to interfere with his piano studies. His dedication to music thus started to dwindle. While Charles was proud of his son's achievements in sports, Jill was worried that sport was not the best pathway for Randy's life. Sure, he had complete intelligence, sports, arts, and academics. While this is commendable, representing a broad intelligence, no one can become a 'Leonardo Da Vinci' nowadays. The accumulation of knowledge in each area of intellectual pursuit is overwhelming; no one keeps up with the knowledge accumulated through the millennia by the homo sapiens, and focusing on one area to excel is important.

One day, she said, "Charlie, I am worried about Randy's disregard for his music lessons. I strongly believe that music must be the center of his education, mostly because I dread the idea that he will end up following your footsteps, suffering all you suffered, and bringing similar turmoil to our family life that your youth brought to your parents and me. Moreover, we know the consequences that uncontrolled aggressive behavior on his part could bring to others. We cannot allow our son to become a dangerous person and end up getting in trouble because one day, he harmed someone to the point of destroying one's life. What do you think?"

"Jill, I will never leave Randy alone on the soccer field. I did terrible things during my rage attacks, which we all understand were seizures now. Fortunately, those are now completely suppressed by the device that you and Dr. Hillary implanted in my brain. However, I do believe that for wholesome development and to learn how to work in a team, he needs sports. Soccer is a perfect sport for this period of his life. Don't worry about his music; I agree with you that soccer should not be his primary focus. I will never encourage Randy to become a professional sportsman, but I do want his mind and body to develop appropriately. You can argue that swimming does the same and that he is a great swimmer, but solo sports do not provide the camaraderie of team sports. Soccer is a gregarious sport played all over the world. Anywhere he goes in the world, he will easily develop friendships and integration in any community at any social or financial level. Soccer is a democratic sport; nothing matters in terms of race, height, and even strength. Despite my disease and consequential rage attacks, I never had difficulty socially integrating and being respected on a soccer field."

"OK, Charlie, you have a point," answered Jill. "But I am counting on you to instruct Randy that music must be his primary focus. Soccer must only be a hobby, a pleasure for him to rest his mind and push his body. He will play only if he excels at school and at his piano lessons. Is this OK with you?"

"Crystal clear," said Charlie. "Nothing gives me more pleasure than ending my working days and spending time listening to you and Randy creating music. Together, you are marvelous; it is true that his repetitive Bach studies sometimes get to me. However, it is amazing to observe his dexterity progressing. However, his obsession with increasing his playing speed detracts a bit from the quality of the music he produces at times."

"Everything comes at its proper time," said Jill. "He will introduce sensibility into his play when motor skills become second nature to him. Our brain can turn motor function into automatic mode, and the integration of the cerebral cortex with deep gray matter structures and the cerebellum allows for such automation **(Figures 4 and 5)**. As he recruits cortical and subcortical areas to his motor skills, he will be able to feel more at ease inserting feelings, bringing the nuances of gesture and fingering strength necessary to transmit the sensibility expected from the virtuous. This happens through the integration of the limbic system with the motor, sensory, and automatic pathways. It is the musician mastering his skills and musical interpretation."

Chapter 12
Overreaction

Put your sword back into its place.
For all who take the sword will perish by the sword.
Mathew 26:52

Randy was a sharp student. He had grown to be handsome, tall, with dark hair, and a big, dark-eyed, a strong boy. He was the tallest student in his class. He was a gentleman at school who earned outstanding grades, was helpful to his colleagues, and was a dedicated son. The family was well adapted to the routines at home, at the hospital, and at his school. Jill took on a lot of responsibility in the Neurosurgery Department after she returned from her sick leave. She was on call in the neurosurgical team every other day. One afternoon, she was called to the emergency room to see a child arriving comatose after a head trauma. It was a blond 10-year-old boy with very clear blue dilated pupils, not responding to any stimulation. The ambulance nurse who brought him in said that he had gotten into a fight at the school basketball court. He was pushed violently by a bully taller than him. The child had hit his head on the concrete less than 30 minutes before his arrival at the hospital. He was awake immediately after the fall; however, he had drifted out of consciousness while in the ambulance.

Jill immediately took the boy to the operating room and performed a portable computed tomography of his head. She diagnosed a large hematoma between the bone and the cover of the brain, an epidural bleeding outside of the dura mater, the protective cover of the brain below the skull bone layer. It was outside of the brain but very extensive, causing large deformation of the child's left cerebral hemisphere. She promptly opened the child's skull, removing the large blood clot that was compressing his brain and possibly already affecting his brainstem. As the anesthesia wore off at the end of the surgery, the patient promptly woke up crying. His pupils became reactive, showing that his visual pathways were functioning well, carrying the electrical impulses created by his retina when light was shined in his eyes.

"What a relief," Jill said to the anesthesiologist. "He was lucky to arrive here just as he was losing consciousness. He could have died in a few more minutes. He was already showing a 'Cushing response,' his heartbeat was already dropping, and his blood pressure was rising, a sign of compression of his brainstem. He would soon have stopped breathing."

"Great job, Jill," said the anesthesiologist.

"Yes, we saved his life. Thanks for your perfect anesthesia. He will recover without any neurological damage," said Jill.

She talked with the boy's family and went to the doctor's comfort area to rest. There, she learned from a nurse that Randy, her son, had pushed the boy during the basketball game. She became alarmed and desperate at her son being called a bully. The patient committed a foul on him when he went for a basket. She immediately sent a text to Dr. Hillary.

"It is time to treat Randy's hamartoma, no delays, please!"

***

While music had blocked the seizures, it hadn't blocked Randy's sense of justice and self-defense. The reaction of 'fight or flight' is intrinsic to one's survival. It is automatic and stronger than any of our feelings or reasoning. This area of the brain is controlled by the integration of the amygdala with the hypothalamus. Hormones and electrical discharges are released to trigger several other areas of the limbic and motor systems into survival mode. Jill knew that Randy's reaction at the basketball court was due to the activation of the brain region responsible for this survival instinct.

Electrical discharges from the hamartoma, which had been curbed by her efforts to infuse music in his brain to the point of controlling them, probably escaped, spreading electrical discharges throughout the brain, including triggering hormonal release. Hormones such as adrenaline, noradrenaline, and cortisol prompted a 'fight or flight' reaction. Randy clearly had a very low threshold for response.

Would the 'porcupine fish' device that Charlie had conceptualized be capable of controlling Randy's low threshold for fights? Or was it time to completely deactivate the hamartoma with focused gamma rays? She needed Dr. Hillary's opinion. He arrived in the hospital cafeteria a few minutes after her text calling him, always in excellent spirits.

"Hey, Dr. Jill Morales, why did you suddenly decide that it is time to treat Randy's hamartoma? He is doing well at school and playing the piano so beautifully. I enjoyed his playing so much when I had dinner at your house last week. Are you sure that now is the time for us to intervene?"

"I thought you knew," said Jill. "It was Randy who pushed the boy who I just operated on. I don't think he would have survived if he had arrived 30 minutes later in the operating room. I am desperate; Randy is reliving Charlie's story. We must control these rampages before one of them causes irreparable damage to someone like his father did. Charlie is still restricted, in spite of his impeccable behavior, since we implanted the pacemaker in his hypothalamus. I don't want to let Randy harm anybody, destroying his or other people's lives. Please, let's come up with a solution."

"Jill, we have talked about this before," said Dr. Hillary. "The solution is at hand with Gamma Knife® Radiosurgery. There is plenty of data in the literature supporting this non-invasive procedure. We can modify the genetic make-up of the cells composing Randy's hamartoma without a single cut in his skin, all through calculations and this amazing robotic device. We can do this without touching the cells of his hypothalamus, which are so close to the pathological neurons causing his aggressive behavior."

"Please, let's move fast with the procedure. The consequences of events like today are worse than any treatment we can offer Randy, even if it is risky."

"Let's ponder this," advised Dr. Hillary. "Discuss it with Charlie and the radiation experts in the Department of Radiation Oncology. We can organize the team to perform the procedure in a few weeks. It is important that Charlie is on board with this; if Randy's development is affected by the procedure, he may never forgive us. He has ideas of an implant to help Randy. He is working hard to build a prototype. The Gamma Knife® effect is irreversible; it is curative but has a minimal risk of permanent damage to Randy's hypothalamus, while an implant does not."

"I am sure that Charlie will not oppose Randy's treatment if you are suggesting radiosurgery. I will talk with him and plan the procedure for the next few weeks."

Chapter 13
Child Depression

No act of kindness, no matter how small is ever wasted.
Aesop

From a gregarious guy, Randy suddenly changed to a taciturn, introverted, non-communicative boy. The incident at the basketball court deeply affected his behavior at school and at home. Charles noticed and tried to talk with him about it, but Randy did not know what to say. It was not like Randy arriving home and going to his room, sitting on the floor, and neatly aligning his collection of cars anymore. There, he stayed for hours, playing and being uncommunicative.

"Is he depressed?" Jill asked. "Do you think we should take him to his pediatrician?"

"Sure, he doesn't even want to play soccer. He says he is tired. I never heard that from him; a ten-year-old boy, especially Randy, a soccer fanatic, does not get tired of soccer. I haven't seen him playing the piano either," said Charles.

"Major depression in children is a reality," said Jill, "especially when there is a causal event, such as what happened with his buddy Jim at school. He feels awful; he told me Jim did not deserve what he did."

"They always played together after class; Randy likes him," said Charles.

"What worries me the most now is that Randy is always moody, feeling sad, without any interest in piano, and unhappy to go to school. His teacher worries that his performance at school is going down, and his academic grades suffer. He does not take pleasure in any activity these days. He told me he felt guilty because he hurt his friend. It also worries me because juvenile diabetes, thyroid disease, and adrenal gland disease can act like children's depression.

Randy has reasons for us to worry about his hormones; his hypothalamus is obviously affected. I will take him to his pediatrician."

The pediatrician confirmed that Randy's symptoms indicated major depression, as his grades and his piano lessons were dwindling, but all his blood tests were normal for Jill's relief.

The pediatrician suggested they take Randy to a child psychiatrist. Jill and Charlie were appalled by this suggestion, but they knew they had to do something.

After the visit to the psychiatrist, at which he prescribed antidepressants, Jill said to Charles.

"We must treat Randy's hamartoma; I do not want Randy taking medication for a long time. It will affect his school performance and his development in general. You must intensify his participation in sports, and I will intensify my persistence with music. We have to clear his mind from the rage attack he had at school; his friend is already back in classes without any resentment toward him. Jim is a nice boy. If we foster their friendship, it may help Randy realize that he did not harm his friend at all. It will take away his guilty feelings."

During Jim's hospital stay, Jill met with his parents, they were a tight-knit family, and understanding people. They didn't have any resentment about what happened on the basketball court.

Charlie followed Jill's request. He would not let Randy isolate himself. He would insist on taking him to the soccer field and spending hours teaching him dribbles and special kicks. He taught Randy to make the ball curve in the air from free kicks. Charles also started to invite Jim to play with them. Jim's father, Mr. Arnold Humboldt, was a musician, and their school music teacher. He had seen Randy playing the piano and taken an interest in his talent. He asked Charles if he would like Randy to participate in the school choir.

"Sure," said Charles. "I will teach soccer to your son, and you teach voice modulation to mine; it is a deal. His mother will be thrilled. She is so busy in the medical center, but she is making a major effort to maintain Randy's interest in music. She arrives home exhausted but always plays the piano for at least half an hour until Randy falls asleep. Her piano really soothes him and takes the worries from work out of her, as she usually brings her patients' troubles home. After he goes to sleep, she goes to the books to prepare surgeries and decisions for the next day. She needs help. Your suggestion will help us immensely; thank you."

"Leave it with me," said Mr. Humboldt. "Jim is the same way; he prefers sports. I am insisting that he plays the violin. Maybe we can encourage them to play together. It will be a nice match."

It happened as Jill had instinctively expected. As Randy and Jim became closer, Randy's depression progressively dissipated. He returned to his music. Charles' sports lesson became a routine and a pleasure to both. His attention to classes improved so much that his grades returned to the levels they had been before the unfortunate incident at the basketball court. Jim became his best buddy; they spent hours playing music and practicing sports together.

Chapter 14
Gamma Rays

Nothing in life is to be feared.
It is to be understood.
Marie Curie (1867-1934)

Three months had passed since Jill's decision to treat Randy's hamartoma. It took many long conversations to convince Charlie that Gamma Knife would be better than the device implanted in Randy's hamartoma. Although he had unconditional trust in Jill's decisions, the success of the pacemaker she placed in his hypothalamus, convinced him that the same approach would likely solve Randy's unexpected rage attacks. However, she ended up convincing, she pondered with him that because Randy was very young to become dependent on a pacemaker for the rest of his life a definitive treatment would be better. His brain would grow, and the electrical field of the device reach could become insufficient. There was no information in the literature about this issue. It took many weeks of explaining to Charles and several conversations he had with Dr. Hillary for him to accept the Gamma Knife safety as the first approach to treat Randy.

What Jill did for Charles was beyond any person's love for another. This delicate, intelligent, dedicated wife, and his son's mother, had already guided the family through apparently insurmountable difficulties. He knew that his work on the artificial implant would take years to lead to an acceptable form of therapy for aggressive behavior in a child. He had gone through all the hurdles of the law before he had received his own implant in his hypothalamus, which had changed his life. It had given him the freedom to have a normal life, without loads of medication. It had rescued him from a mental institution, and even kept him out of jail. He would always be at her side grateful to her and in life. Being a doctor, she was better prepared to make the best decision for Randy.

One day, Randy was anesthetized at eight o'clock in the morning, and a stereotactic device was attached to his head to guide the gamma rays and to allow the calculations necessary for the procedure. Images were obtained of his brain, and calculations were made to target the hamartoma, considering its volume, and the amount of energy required to curb its electrical discharge. These were scrutinized by a harmonic multidisciplinary team composed of a medical physicist, a radiation oncologist, and the neurosurgeon, Dr Hillary. The precisely focused gamma rays would modify the functioning of the aberrant neurons of Randy's hamartoma. Calculations were exhaustively carried out to avoid harming the normal neurons of his hypothalamus, and all the pathways crisscrossing this delicate structure. The visual pathways and hormonal cells were also to be avoided, which was a daunting task. The process was dependent on merging anatomical and functional images.

The device attached to Randy's head was clamped to a robotic machine, the Gamma Knife®, and the treatment was carried out while Randy was still anesthetized. At noon that same day, Randy was awake, as if nothing had happened. Jill took him home at the end of the afternoon, and he felt so good that he played the piano for one hour. Then he fell asleep, waking up only the next day. After the treatment, he never had another crisis. After one year, Jill considered him cured and took him off medication.

Randy became obsessed with perfectly playing the piano transcription of Bach's violin concert number 1 in E major; Mr. Humboldt had asked him to play it with Jimmy. They were to perform together at the end-of-the-year school ceremony. They set a routine to practice together for one hour every day after school, then they would go to the soccer field with Charles and practice with the school soccer team. Randy and Jim's friendship had become so tight that they were studying even the school lessons together. They spent the entire day occupied with their tasks. Their friendship fostered a close relationship between the two families.

As Randy was not taking any medication, he became highly energetic. His progress on the piano was impressive. Mr. Humboldt suggested Jill and Charles take Randy to the Los Angeles Music Conservatory, the Colburn, to perfect his performance. He believed Randy had what it took to be a virtuoso. There, he would have the chance to learn from world-renowned teachers and to see the best in the world performing, as the Colburn School is next to the major performing arts center of Los Angeles, the opera house, the Disney Music Center, and the Ahmanson theater. Mrs. Alice, Randy's piano teacher, prepared him for his audition at the Colburn.

The two boys gave a show at their elementary school recital, participated in the school choir, and played soccer together for the school team until the end of the school year. Thanks to their parent's dedication, a wonderful friendship developed out of a terrible incident on the basketball court.

Chapter 15
The Virtuoso

I know who I am and who I may be if I choose.
Miguel de Cervantes Saavedra

Randy was ten years old and already an impressive pianist. He was accepted enthusiastically by the admission board of the Colburn. Charles and Jill followed Mr. Humboldt's advice. He attended the Colburn, took piano lessons from teachers at Julliard Music School and at New England Conservatory, and from the best pianists in the world, who frequently visited the Colburn Music School. He rapidly granted admiration to the teachers who prepared him for his first recital competition. His determination, consistency, and discipline were admirable, he gave his soul to the Beethoven sonatas in preparation to play at the Disney Music Hall.

Randy took the task to heart. He started practicing ungodly hours per day. He would arrive from school and play obsessively until bedtime. His technique became flawless. His memory of music was impeccable. Jill's dedication to expanding his brain neuronal network since his fetal life worked, he had a powerful musician's brain. He amazed his teachers with his speed of learning. He prepared the Beethoven sonatas in such a way and confidence that Mr. Humboldt commented to Jill: Randy is a genius for music, a virtuoso.

Jill was impressed and pleased that he was taking piano so seriously. She was hoping that his brain would be devoted to music sensibility, a safe profession, away from any confrontations that could incite his rage attacks, which, since his Gamma Knife® procedure had not recurred.

Chapter 16
Ready for Recitals

*The only love affair I have
ever had was with music.*
Maurice Ravel

"Mom, I am scared of not performing well," said Randy. "When I played at the school recital, it was different. I knew almost everybody. Moreover, students are allowed to make mistakes; these competitions are another matter. A single wrong note is enough for the critics to destroy a pianist. It could taint my chance of becoming a concert pianist forever."

"Randy, 'stage fright' is a constant for all performers, whether they are musicians, speakers, or sportspeople. There are only two ways to overcome it. You need to be well prepared for the presentation, and then practice public performances. The first you have done; you are playing beautifully, flawlessly. The second you will acquire with time, performances, and more performances. It is natural that you feel frightened at this first quasi-professional time. It will be alright; Mr. Humboldt told me that you are a virtuoso. I have no doubt that you are. What do you say, Charles?"

"This guy is just amazing," said his father. "He has an impressive motor intelligence. You need to see the speed at which he learned to curve a football into the net. It is a difficult technique, which took me years to learn. My father would lose his patience teaching me. It entails giving the ball the proper spin, so the interaction of the ball's spinning with air makes it fly in a curve. Randy learned in less than two practices. He has perfect eye-brain-muscle coordination."

Jill said, "You see how fast he picks up the fingering of these incredibly difficult Bach's pieces. I have no doubt that he already has all these pieces in his brain's automatic regions."

"Randy, remember what I told you. When the task becomes automatic, it is time to put the art into your play. Whether it is music or soccer, the art infused in the act makes the virtuosity," said Charles

"You are ready to infuse sensibility into your music, now that you can play the pieces without looking at the score," said Jill.

"It will work for you. The recital should be a pleasure for you, like soccer always was for me. Well, it was a pleasure for me until someone fouled on me, then the game became a war. Fortunately, you will not have anybody physically opposing you on the stage, and we will be rooting for you. Audiences love to see successful children. Forget the competition with other students; you have done that so many times in the conservatory. You won so many of those. Now, it's just making music for yourself and for the audience's pleasure. That will take you where you want."

Randy smiled at his parents, reassured of their love and confidence in him.

Chapter 17
The Competition

Competitions are for horses, not for artists.
Bela Bartok

The whole family was there rooting for Randy's success, including his grandparents, Mr. and Mrs. Morales, Charles's parents, and Mr. and Mrs. Riderheim, Jill's foster parents. Jill was a Chinese orphan who had been abandoned when she was two-year-old. When couples could have only one child, parents in China would abandon the girls for the chance to have a boy. Fortunately, she had been adopted by the Riderheims, a Swedish couple who educated her in Southern California. She had all the love and intellectual support needed to become an outstanding neurosurgeon. Her parents were proud of her, and now of their grandchild at that magic moment at the Disney Music Hall.

The Disney Music Hall was packed. Randy was to play with the UCLA Orchestra, which was conducted by an assistant conductor of Gustavo Dudamel. A Venezuelan-born musician, Dudamel was a great supporter of youth, particularly young Latin musicians. He was promoting the competition to single out the best child pianist for a two-year fellowship to study at the Julliard Music School, in New York. This fellowship was the most sought-after among Chinese music students. Traditionally, they won this fellowship year after year because of their outstanding playing techniques. They were driven by a lot of pressure from their parents who sought a better life in America. They also represented a country's pride in its thriving culture, trying to show the world that Chinese people strive to be number one in any competition they participate in.

The judge's board of examiners was already accepting the idea that the Asian music students' dedication and discipline made them unbeatable. Being accepted by Julliard Music School represented the pinnacle of their efforts to study in the United States. They had first to face competition in China in order to be chosen among 2000 students, of which only 12 would go ahead and attend Beijing's Conservatory of Music. Then, they would have to win many competitions to earn the opportunity to attend a good school in the United States. However, the Beijing Music Conservatory had a corrupt bureaucracy. Outstanding students would be unfairly discarded if their parents lacked influence in the government and conservatory politics. Once in the United States, they had to win competitions facing students from all over the world to earn the opportunity to learn from some of the world's best music teachers at Julliard. The competition was fierce; to be the best student in the world was proof of talent, discipline, sensibility, and love for music.

Great Chinese performers like Lang-Lang and Yo-Yo Ma were living examples of talent, consistency, and dedication to reach success. They were role models for the last generation of Asian musicians, showing that worldwide success was a possibility for the Chinese people, mainly for those raised during the Cultural Revolution in the 1970s. The measure of success was a migration to America, a dreamland for them. The release from an oppressing regime for the arts and intellect. A hope for their parents of a better life was a huge responsibility for a child to bear. The parents dedicated all their efforts to educate their prize child, usually a boy, as girls were abandoned in orphanages because families sought to have a male son in a country where the government permitted only one child per family.

Randy was educated about the passion of the Latin blood and the amazing motor skills and dedication of Asian musicians. He was already a second-generation immigrant, without the pressure to fight for a better life. He didn't carry the pressure that the Chinese students bore. As they overwhelmingly won the music competitions with their exquisite motor skills, Randy had to beat or tie with them in motor skills; moreover, he had to infuse sensibility into his play to win the fierce competition from the Chinese students. Randy had heard of Jo Pan Jin, the phenomenal Chinese student who had never lost a competition in his life. He heard him playing the Beethoven Concert Number 4 in one of the training rooms and knew he was a real threat to him. However, Randy was at ease; his parents told him not to worry and advised him just to do his best. The whole family would always be proud of him, simply knowing how well he prepared for the competition. He went to the stage with his mom's words, "Just do your best" (Figure 7).

Figure 7:
(A) Beethoven Piano Concerto Number 3 *https://youtu.be/jX8CbP1RvJY* and (B) Beethoven Piano Concerto Number 4 *https://youtu.be/WwFxou5Iaxs*

Randy nailed the Beethoven Piano Concerto Number 3, a piano-playing marathon. He was not only flawless in his technique, but his playing was passionate and completely integrated with the orchestra. Beethoven Piano Concerto Number 3 was considered difficult for an adult, and much more so for a child. He was not only flawless in his technique, but his playing was passionate. It was such a perfect performance that he received a long-standing ovation. After he finished, exhausted, what he wanted most was to run to his mom and hug her. He was in tears; now he was relieved of the pressure he had put on himself to give a flawless presentation. Most of all, he believed he had performed to perfection, and this was the gift he had wanted to give to his mom. The audience recognized this with further ovation when he fell into Jill's arms, who was also in tears. This outstanding child needed the warmth of his mom, grandparents, and his dad. What a moment of joy he had given to his family and the audience.

He was followed by Jo Pan Jin's presentation. Jo was the favorite because of his track record and playing technique. He was able to give an incredible number of keystrokes per minute. The audience was anxious to see the presentation of this acclaimed little spiked-hair boy. He had been the first in all his competitions in Beijing and in the United States. Jo was Randy's main competition after his outstanding presentation. Although there were ten other outstanding children competing, all teachers from Colburn had already recognized that Jo would be very hard to beat; they were humbled by the musical stature of this Chinese child. Randy's teacher was hopeful however that Randy would be able to pull together the best of four cultures, as he was a mix of Mexican, American, Swedish, and Chinese, and win the competition.

Jo Pan Jin played the Beethoven Piano Concerto Number 4. He did an outstanding job; however, something amiss occurred. A touch of feeling in the presentation, such a sentimental piece deserved a flow of sensibility that did not come through in his flawless technical presentation. The audience was excited. They stood up in ovation, although the claps didn't last as long as the ones dedicated to Randy. It was noticeable. Randy won first place, and the fellowship awarded to Julliard. Jo Pan Jin accustomed to the corrupted system of the Chinese music life became furious with the judge's decision. He screamed accusing the judges of unfairness and did not accept the consolation prize, a stuffed animal. He threw the stuffed bear at the judges and walked out of the stage rapidly, crying.

Randy was stunned. The happiness of winning was compromised by his guilty sentiment at having made Jo Pan Jin, a boy he barely knew, so disappointed.

Part 3
Consequences of Success

Chapter 18
The Emergency Room

Prompt attention to detail saves lives.
Antonio De Salles

An ambulance arrived at an emergency room bringing a young boy in a coma. The rescue medical technician told the receiving doctor that he had intubated the boy that morning in his apartment because he was becoming blue with difficulties breathing. The boy's father had called 911. He described the father as a Chinese man, who was extremely anxious because the boy would not wake up that morning. It was 9 am when he called 911 with a loud and heavy Chinese accent, saying that his son had gone to bed at 10 pm the night before and had not woken up until that time. The father said his son was very tired because of his participation in a piano recital the day before. Therefore, he allowed the child to sleep late.

It was routine for father and son to get out of bed at 6 am. After breakfast, the boy would start playing piano. He would practice for five hours before lunch. The father was desperate because the child would not respond; that had never happened before. Worse, he had had irregular breathing, looking like he could stop breathing at any time. He would suddenly start again with fast breaths then progressively slow down again. He would stop breathing for a few seconds and then start again.

When the technician arrived at the apartment, he immediately recognized that the period of fast breathing followed by a short moment of apnea was Cheyenne-Stokes respiration. It indicated that the child was not receiving the appropriate amount of oxygen, and instead, he was accumulating carbon dioxide. He had measured the saturation of the latter, and it was at 45%. The technician immediately placed a tube into the boy's trachea and artificially ventilated him to provide enough oxygen. Then, the ambulance rushed him to the hospital. When he arrived, his oxygen saturation was already 99%; the technician had saved the boy's life. But he was now comatose.

The father was in such an anxious state when they arrived at the emergency room that he was unable to explain what had happened. He did not want to leave his son with the doctors. He was asked to wait in the waiting area, but he started to scream that he would not abandon his son with strangers. The emergency room security guard forcefully took him out of the receiving room. He started screaming loudly in a mix of Mandarin with a few English words. He had to be contained by two security guards, enabling a strong male nurse to sedate him, before admitting him as a patient in another room. A psychiatrist was called to help the anxious and violent man.

The boy was well-ventilated, and his blood had been collected for tests. All was calm; the father was fortunately under control. However, the emergency room doctors were still unsure what was happening with the boy. They promptly took him to the tomography area for a full body scan, hoping to find the cause of the boy's coma. After observing a completely normal scan, they decided to transfer him to a major medical center. The boy was transported to UCLA, where he was admitted to the care of the neuro intensive care unit for observation and final diagnosis.

Magnetic resonance was promptly obtained from his brain. It was also normal but with a caveat: his brain was completely occupying all the space in his skull. His ventricles were constricted, and the cerebral spinal fluid spaces around the brain were very tight for his age, a sign that he had brain edema, swelling, or increased blood volume inside of his skull. An electroencephalogram (EEG) was obtained, which showed that he was in burst suppression, i.e., periods of high electrical activity alternating with periods of electrical silence. This was a sign that he was in an inactivated brain state, caused either by a lack of oxygen to the brain or an intoxicating substance. His stomach was pumped, and the blood level of barbiturate was measured at 30 mcg/ml. This was an almost lethal level of barbiturate in the blood. Had the boy taken that many pills voluntarily? He would take a long time to wake up.

After being discharged from his local emergency room, the father rushed to the UCLA Medical Center where he found his son in the intensive care unit. The doctors got him to confess that the boy had taken a lot of pills the night before. He said his son had been distraught at not winning the piano competition, so he had given him a bottle of sleeping pills.

Without judging the man, the doctors understood what had happened and managed the patient as a barbiturate intoxication, certain that he would wake up in time. Even worse, the father revealed he had told his son he had brought shame on the family of his country and threatened to kill himself in response.

Three days later, it was possible to allow the boy to breathe on his own. Soon, he was transferred to the Pediatric Unit and discharged. He immediately started trying to practice the piano. When he played for his teacher at the Colburn Music School, it became apparent that he was not the same pianist. He had much to recover. His fingers were curling, not reaching the keys as well as before. The teacher suggested more rest and that a consultation with a neurologist was in order. Although the teacher gave the boy a period without coming to classes, the father did not accept the advice. He insisted that Jo Pan Jin keep playing, following the rigid teaching of the Chinese Music Schools. He did not take his son to the neurologist as advised.

After a few weeks of forced practice, the boy started to turn his head away from the piano; moreover, his hands stopped obeying his desire, and they would curl without any aim. It became progressively more difficult for him to play. He couldn't focus on the music scores, nor adequately reach the piano keys. The father finally gave up his rigid thinking and took Jo Pan Jin to a neurologist at UCLA. After revising the boy's records, he was diagnosed with a dystonic disease secondary to the hypoxic event he had two months before. The boy was seriously dystonic and feeling persistent muscle pain in his neck and hands, so the doctor admitted him to the hospital for pain control and exams to identify the source of the dystonia. An MRI of his brain showed a marked loss of brain tissue, specifically in the area responsible for motor control, the motor control computer[14], known as basal ganglia **(Figure 12)**. The electrical activity and contraction of the muscle were studied with electromyography (EMG), confirming the diagnosis of dystonia.

Despite high doses of muscle relaxants, Jo Pan Jin progressed to more and more contractions of his muscles. This reached all muscles of his body, to the point that, when in extreme pain, he would curl right up in bed, which was caused by massive contraction of his spinal muscles. This is a position called opisthotonos, which is present in patients with advanced tetanus. He had to be

---

[14] De Salles AA (Nov. 1996) 'Role of stereotaxis in the treatment of cerebral palsy,' *J Child Neurol.,* **11** Suppl 1:S43-50. doi: 10.1177/0883073896011001S07. PMID: 8959461.

heavily sedated to control his pain, to the point that he would spend most of the day sleeping. The neurologist caring for Jo asked the opinion of the neurosurgeons in the hope that they had an intervention that would control the dystonic movements, allowing them to decrease the heavy sedation. Jo Pan Jin was maintained in an induced comatose state due to the level of involuntary contractions that dominated his body. These contractions were very painful, and moreover, if he was left alone, he would fall from the bed because of the uncontrolled movements that the random contractions generated. His mother was brought from China to stay with him, as his dad could not bear to see the destruction he had wrought on his son. The mother, who had stayed in China working to financially help support her son's studies abroad, was so upset that she stopped speaking with her husband, Mr. Jin.

Chapter 19
Shock and Tragedy

Mournful and yet grand
is the destiny of the artist.
Franz Liszt

Mr. Jin entered a severe depressive state. He no longer went to the hospital to see his son. He had a family history of obsessive-compulsive disorder (OCD); his father had been obsessed with cleanliness and washed his hands several times during the day. He also had episodes of prolonged depression, months without getting out of the house. Therefore, he could not hold down a steady job. This was so disturbing to the family that his wife, Mr. Jin's mother divorced her husband. Mr. Jin had been raised by a mother who also had periods of depression in which she would spend weeks in bed without the desire to do anything. Mental disease was a stigma in the family; genes for mental illness had been transferred to Mr. Jin. During his mother's depressive episodes, he was cared for by neighbors. He became obsessed with never needing to receive charity from anybody. He had the traces of obsession and depression he had inherited from his parents.

He focused all his attention on getting out of poverty, relying on his son's musical talent to achieve financial freedom. It was indeed a very heavy weight he had placed on Jo Pan Jin, too much for a child. Alone with his father in Los Angeles, Jo suffered the lack of balance that his mother had provided to soften the strict treatment of his father. He missed the tender loving care that his mother always gave him while the family was together in China. Jo missed his mother immensely.

Mr. Jin was now seeing his dream of living in America, and his financial freedom falling apart. Mr. Jin had a weak personality to face America's competitive life, a country where the best brains in the world come to try life.

His despair was such, especially his guilt at destroying his son's successful career, that he lost his mind. He went to a building dedicated to research at the university complex, which was the tallest building on the university campus. He jumped from the 23rd floor to end his life. This type of tragedy, suicide, happens to approximately 15% of psychiatric patients with severe depression.

Severely depressed patients are generally misunderstood in society. They are just assumed to be lazy, and even their own families put a lot of pressure on them to do something with their lives. This behavior worsens their situation, leading these poor patients to despair. Moreover, they are the victim of the intersection of several psychiatric diagnoses in the same patient. Psychiatric patients receive the final diagnosis based on their strongest symptoms, for example, obsessions, compulsions, hallucinations, sadness, lack of sensitivity to other sufferings, and so on. As in Mr. Jin's case, obsessive-compulsive disorder, depression, and a strong family history of psychiatric symptoms added up to the tragedy of his death. It is a sad reality that happens more with men than with women, although there are more women with severe depressive disorder than men. Men are simply more likely to succeed in committing suicide.

Although tragic, the departure of Mr. Jin freed his wife and his son from the suffering afflicting the family. It did however leave a huge vacuum in their lives. His obsession had helped his son reach his dream of coming to the USA to study music but with an extreme and unhealthy discipline model. Mr. Jin's suicide and the state of the dystonia that overtook Jo Pan Jin's body shocked the classical music world. Jo Pan Jin was already well-known in Los Angeles, heavily sought-after on social media, and admired for his exceptional achievements at such a young age and the promise of success he represented.

His dream of studying in New York was now out of reach. The doctors at the University Medical Center were not coming up with a solution better than keeping the boy heavily sedated to abate his pain and prevent him from falling from his bed due to the sudden strong contractions. These spasmodic contractions could even cause him bone fractures and joint dislocations. Mrs. Jin decided to stay in Los Angeles, where she would have more support, not only from the Chinese community but also from the Colburn community where her son was well-known. She expected support from Jo Pan Jin's teachers from the Music Conservatory, the Colburn. She hoped for her son to stay at UCLA Medical Center to continue his treatment, as she knew it would be a long and difficult road she and her son had to endure. She had hope in the possibility of gradually decreasing the sedation and getting him back to his studies. She expected that his passion for music would free him from his dystonic suffering. Was it possible?

Chapter 20
Mom Action

God could not be everywhere; therefore, he made mothers.
Rudyard Kipling

The UCLA neurosurgeons were called into the case. Jo Pan Jin's contractions were beyond the control of oral medications. The boy could not spend his life on intravenous sedation in an intensive care unit. Two months had passed without any sign that the sedative doses could be decreased. Dr. Hillary and Jill were called to give an opinion. Dr. Hillary promptly mentioned his experience in a similar situation.

"I saw 'dystonic mal' like this in a two-year-old child here in this ICU approximately 20 years ago. The neuropediatric ICU staff wanted me to do something. Then we were treating dystonic patients with lesions in the pallidum, a region called basal ganglia (**Figure 12**); with a specific group of cells we call 'the brain crossroad for motor modulation.' These cells were known to be very hyperactive in dystonic patients; only heavy sedation would silence their spurts of electrical discharges, disturbing that poor two-year-old girl. After an electrophysiologic exploration of the region, I decreased the cell's hyperactivity with graded heat using radiofrequency. Interestingly, two years later, the patient's mother came to my office just to show me the results of my work. The child was an active 4-year-old running around, speaking, and talking normally. It was an amazing feeling, one of those moments that show you how wonderful it is to be a doctor. All my efforts to become a doctor were rewarded by a single case."

"Jill, do you have a suggestion?" He asked.

"Sure," said Jill. "There are at least three procedures we can do to help him besides the type of radiofrequency lesion you just described, which is a heat-generated coagulation of the tissue, a measure which is irreversible. We can implant an old-fashioned deep brain stimulation (DBS) device, which may stop the firing of the cells by overwhelming their activity with electrical high-frequency spurts. We can test using high-frequency focus ultrasound (HIFU) to make the coagulation under functional imaging in the Magnetic Resonance Machine (MRI), tailoring it only to the rapidly firing neurons, or we can use low-frequency ultrasound (LowFU), trying to stop the hyperactive neurons, also under MRI guidance. The problem with the LowFU approach is that it is not permanent, so we will have to keep repeating the stimulation periodically to keep the dystonic contractions under control."

"Well, Jill, which of the three do you prefer?"

"As you know, Charles has developed a device capable of recording neuronal firing and selecting the group of cells needing to be stopped. The device is all wireless and can be directed in a magnetic field inside the MRI, positioning it in a proper way. It can also be repositioned if needed to adapt to the disease progression or improve its effectiveness. Seeing this boy, the same as I feel about my own son, I would like to provide him with a solution that we can adjust as need be, providing him with the opportunity of one day returning to playing the piano. In fact, there are only two of these MRI devices in the world. One is here at UCLA, and the other one is at Columbia University in New York. Charles got a grant from NIH to bring this machine to UCLA. Taking care of this boy is a great opportunity to prove that we can modulate a group of cells in the brain with an intelligent device. We can enhance existent networks and develop new ones that can not only treat the diseased but also maintain the complex network of the brain, providing the individual with the chance to follow his dream."

"Jill, what you are proposing is an experiment, not a proven therapy," said Dr. Hillary thoughtfully.

"Yes," she continued, "but we did a similar experiment on my own husband's brain, and now he is helping humanity, bringing resources to the university; moreover, he is a great father and companion for me. I am very proud and grateful to you, this university, and the Institutional Review Board (IRB) for allowing me to use all my studies to help my family and the man I love." She finished with tears in her eyes.

"Well, Jill, you convinced me that we need to move in this direction. It is crucial that we do this as soon as possible to relieve this boy and his mother of their suffering. We need to organize the team for the task. You will have to take the leadership."

They invited Jo Pan Jin's mother for a conversation, as there was a lot to explain. She would have to work with her son for months or years to see him able to play the piano again. Although they believed it was possible, they had no idea how they would achieve it. They needed support from a whole team, including a neurologist, neuroradiologist, medical physicist, bioengineer, anesthesiologist, and the physiotherapy department. It was a great undertaking. Jill promised to assemble the team and organize a meeting to listen to everybody's opinion so she could write the protocol for the project. She left the ICU full of hope on her way to meet Mrs. Jin in the hospital cafeteria to discuss the procedure's risks and costs.

***

When Jill described the course of treatment to Mrs. Jin, she promptly said, "But I don't have money for all this."

"Don't worry about money. I will be able to have this all done inside the budget of a study we are performing. I want you to know that the surgery I am proposing for Jo has never been performed before in the world. It is a completely new approach to treating severe dystonia, like the one your son has. I want you to know that my husband has developed a device that has not been used in humans, which we will be trying for the first time with your son. Therefore, the whole treatment and the surgery will all be covered by resources obtained from the American Government. Additionally, I plan to organize a group to acquire funds from donations to help us provide all the care necessary for Jo. It is important to help your son. Rest assured that we will do our best to cure him so he can go back to his piano studies. It may take several years, but if you accept what I am suggesting and help us stimulate him and fight against this disease, we will succeed. I am sure that technically, we can do all that is necessary.

"I am planning to do the surgery in two months. I will try to control his dystonic movements with a non-invasive technique we developed here at UCLA. We will stop the hyperactive neurons in his basal ganglia, a specific site in the brain called the pallidum (**Figure 12**), with focused ultrasound [15]. It is a completely safe way of doing it; although it is reversible, it means that the dystonic movements will return if we stop repeating the applications. He will receive a series of applications trying to take him out of deep sedation. This stimulation therapy is not final; however, it was repeated by Jill. He cannot spend his life depending on applications that only cause temporary improvement, without freeing him completely from this taxing disease. I want to provide him independence and get him ready to enjoy playing his piano at full speed. What do you think about this proposal?"

"Dr. Morales, this is my dream," said Mrs. Jin.

"I also want you to value the relationship Jo has with his music. You saw his life being organized around the routine of a concert pianist. You and your husband used all the natural brain plasticity since his toddler years, preparing him for a musical career. His brain is totally wired for music development. He is music!

"We must take advantage of this during his recovery. We will silence the hyperactive neurons at this point, then take advantage of the dominant music-related pathways in his brain to achieve his cure, a modulation we neuroscientists still do not understand well, but that we know exists. Sad music makes us depressed, sad, and quiet. Happy music makes us dance and want to socialize. Although there is still a lot for us to understand, we will study his brain connectivity through advanced images demonstrating his state at rest, with traces of improvement.

"Once we identify the progression of his brain pathways[16], we will intensely stimulate specific areas with ultrasonic waves; music will show us where to do it. You will be very important in this process of stimulating his brain pathways and nuclei, as you know the nuances of the effects of music on your son. Count on me to be with you on this challenging, beautiful task we

---

[15] Mulgankar AP, Singh RS, Babakhanian M, Culjat MO, Grundfest WS, Gorgulho A, Lacan G, De Salles AA, Bystritsky A, Melega WP (2012) 'A prototype stimulator system for noninvasive low intensity focused ultrasound delivery,' *Stud Health Technol Infor.*,173:297-303.

[16] Misaki, M., Mulyana, B., Zotev, V., Wurfel, B. E., Krueger, F., Feldner, M., & Bodurka, J. (2021). 'Hippocampal volume recovery with real-time functional MRI amygdala neurofeedback emotional training for posttraumatic stress disorder,' *Journal of Affective Disorders*, 283, 229-235. doi:10.1016/j.jad.2021.01.058.

will accomplish together. Now, you are one of the most important components of our team. We need you immensely."

"Dr. Morales, I don't have words to express my gratitude for your interest in helping Jo," she said passionately.

"You can be assured I will treat him as if he were my son; there are many similarities between Jo and Randy," Jill said.

"Great. I will arrange a meeting with some pianists who have won their battle against dystonia so they can mentor him. There is a great Brazilian Maestro who I am sure can help Jo. He fought his dystonia for over 70 years and has extensive experience using music to control the disease."

Mrs. Jin was skeptical about Jill's explanations regarding her plans to return Jo to his piano dreams. She was however ready to go along with any plan that would get her son out of the intensive care unit. She was spending her days sitting at his bedside, feeling completely powerless to help him. It had felt like she would be tending to someone like a baby for the rest of her existence. Without a job, without any entertainment, and without any hope, she had been falling into despair. Jill's promises were her only hope. She would take any suggestion to take her and her son out of the predicament that her crazy husband had left them in. She was so distraught by the situation, and so resentful of the late Mr. Jin, that she hadn't mourned his death. Jill's work with Jo was her only hope.

"Dr. Morales, please do your best. This situation is unbearable. I even thought about going back to China. There, I can find a job and pay someone to help me care for Jo. The problem is that he will not have the proper medical care there. Medicine there is not at the same level you have here at UCLA. I am very grateful to the nurses; they have been marvelous and accommodating in letting me stay here with Jo in the ICU. I see their dedication to their work; they treat the patients with love. I also see the physiotherapists coming and stimulating Jo's muscles every day. They hook him up to a lot of wires and apply electricity to his muscles. He shakes all over with their stimulation. They say that it is to prevent his muscles from becoming atrophic. Also, the bed rotates all the time so that his skin remains supple. I have never seen one of these in China."

Chapter 21
The Protocol

First, to be a good human being,
then a good doctor,
then a good surgeon.
Gene Stern

Jill assembled a team of experts to collaborate on Jo's care. Dr. Hillary was to be the advisor of the surgical team. Moreover, with his influence in the hospital's admiration, he would be able to gather resources to help with the costs. Dr. Robert Howard, a neurologist, was to be responsible for the pharmacotherapy to control Jo's muscle contractions. Dr. Michael Wolf, the anesthesiologist, would have to choose the proper medications, to avoid modifying the pathological function of the neurons during the surgery. The implantation of the device Charles developed had to be precisely where the pathologically firing cells in Jo's brain were located. The neurons are highly sensitive to the medications used in anesthesia; therefore, the proper level of sedation was essential, a challenging task for the anesthesiologist. An excess of anesthesia, even when using the best-chosen drug, would completely hamper the quality of the images and the micro-recordings dedicated to identifying the firing rate of the sick neurons.

Dr. Wilson, the neuroradiologist, and Dr. Mallory the nuclear imaging specialist, would advise on the best magnetic resonance sequences they should use to obtain the images and the molecular markers to obtain the positron emission tomographic (PET). Jill set a meeting for them to discuss her plan of work and to learn from the team the difficulties they would have to face, as well as the feasibility of her plan.

The meeting started with Jill's presentation of Jo's medical history. She recounted how the boy had been allowed to take a large number of pills by his father, the reason why he had the brain injury. She stressed that it was secondary to the hypoxic period he had endured. Immediately, Dr. Howard suggested that they should also have a psychiatrist in the group, as the boy had clearly been emotionally abused by his father for a long period, not only this time that had ended up in such a tragedy.

"He must have a trauma beyond the muscle reactions we see. In fact, all patients who present dystonic movements have some psychiatric trace woven into the disease, even if it is difficult to pinpoint," he said.

"I agree," commented Dr. Hillary. "We know from the organization of the brain that the structures related to behavior are very close to the ones related to motor control. In the basal ganglia, the neurons, and relay fibers representing the wiring coming from the most anterior portion of the brain, are responsible for the person's mental make-up. These are closely related to the neurons that modulate the motor function in the pallidum. All cortical areas send axons that converge in the basal ganglia, a packed area of neuronal relays modulating intellect, emotions, and motor function. It is important that we have psychiatric support for Jo. As he gets out of this motor conundrum, the mental disturbances may become apparent."

"Dr. Howard," said Jill. "I will invite a young psychiatrist I met recently, Dr. Paul Wronsky, who is very interested in the association of movement disorders and the behavior of these patients. There are some interesting psychological findings on these patients, as is the case for Tourette's syndrome patients."

***

They organized all the imaging studies for as soon as Jill could control the violent contractions Jo was having, without relying on sedation. An RM was obtained under the orientation of Jill and the support of Dr. Wolf and Dr. Wilson. He was anesthetized in such a way that the dystonic movements would not corrupt the quality of the images. Dr. Wilson obtained the functional sequences, demonstrating the area where Jill knew the active neurons were present. This image was necessary for her to use a technique called neuronavigation. This technique allowed her to pinpoint precisely the LowFU waves into the posterior ventral pallidum region (PVP), the portion of the brain-computer responsible for controlling the dystonic movements. Her plan was to use the ultrasound low-frequency waves to control the violent contractions Jo had been having when the sedation was abated. Using these images, she was able to calculate the pathway of the ultrasound waves throughout Jo's brain in the direction of the PVP, the precise target required to control dystonia (**Figure 12**). This region was known to control dystonic bursts in several diseases, including Parkinson's disease, generalized and focal dystonia, and Tourette's syndrome[17].

Every morning for a week, Jill went to the ICU, and, with Jo still sedated, she applied the navigation device to Jo's head and precisely sent the low-frequency ultrasound waves to the calculated target, bilaterally. This was done without difficulties or reactions from Jo's vital signs, as he was being fully monitored in the ICU, including continuous electroencephalogram (EEG). At the end of the week, she asked for the ICU team member to decrease the sedation while he was hooked up to the navigation device. Amazingly, he only had a few dystonic movements in his right hand. She immediately applied another bout of LowFU, controlling his hand dystonic movement, as well. She thus confirmed that the PVP site was indeed important for the control of his violent contractions. She became overjoyed, she knew now that she would be able to help Jo. It was just a matter of proper coordination of the team, and the successful construction of Charles' magnetic guided 'porcupine fish' device. She knew that Charles was capable of constructing the stimulator. The question was if they could successfully guide it into the brain.

She called Dr. Hillary to give him the news. He came to talk to her at Charles' laboratory. They were delighted with the success she had achieved with the LowFU. Now, it was just a matter of completing the treatment flow. Dr. Hillary suggested that they should try the device on pigs before going to Jo's brain. The size of the pig's brain would allow them to try the surgical procedure, so they would have no doubt that they could successfully position the smart stimulation device in Jo's brain. They took this advice. They were eager to implant the device successfully. Besides wanting to help Jo, they also had an interest in developing the device and a spin-off company based on their technology. They had patented the concept of the device, as well as the methodology of the surgical procedure through the University Patent Office

---

[17] Altenmüller E, Jabusch HC. (Mar. 2010) 'Focal dystonia in musicians: phenomenology, pathophysiology, triggering factors, and treatment,' *Med Probl Perform Art.*, **25**(1):3-9. PMID: 20795373.

(UPO). They hoped the device would help millions of people, and certainly give them financial freedom to support Randy's studies.

***

The following Monday, Jill went early to the ICU. Jo was again completely sedated. She promptly asked the ICU team why.

"Well, Dr. Morales, he was well until last night, then he started to contract his right hand, and suddenly started shouting that he wanted to go home. I had to sedate him; he was becoming very agitated with a strange gaze, dilated pupils, and almost a nystagmus, his eyes wandering in all directions. I really didn't know what was happening. Moreover, his blood pressure went up, and his heart rate also increased. It looked like he was fearful of something. When I saw his systolic blood pressure reaching 170mmHg and his heart rate at 130 bpm, I had no doubt that I had to sedate him. He was sweating heavily, too. It looked like a neurovegetative reaction. Was he having a severe neurovegetative crisis? What do you think, Dr. Morales?"

"What is your name?" Jill asked the young doctor, as she had never seen him in the ICU before.

"Patrick Nolan, nice to meet you, Dr. Morales. I just started this ICU rotation. I am a first-year general surgery resident. I am not used to neurosurgery patients; sorry."

"Patrick, no stress, just call me Jill," she said. "We will work together to help this little genius concert pianist when he wakes up from the sedation."

Indeed, Patrick got right to the point. Jo was remembering the moment that his father forced him to ingest an ungodly number of pills and threatened to kill himself. It is a very severe trauma, an abuse of this poor child. They would have to treat not only his motor violent involuntary contractions but also his mental distress. Jo had a crisis of Post-Traumatic Stress Disorder (PTSD). This is a very difficult disorder to treat. It is a devastating psychiatric disease that is managed with intense behavioral therapy and medications. It causes severe disturbance in the patient's life. Before the Vietnam War, there was a major gap in the psychiatric diagnosis of these patients, as they were labeled as having the most inappropriate diagnoses before; for example, they were thought to be schizophrenics. Therefore, they were wrongly treated with drugs that didn't apply to this incredible state of severe anxiety, a disease on its own[18].

"Patrick, please remove the sedation. I will come in the afternoon to stimulate his posterior ventral pallidum (PVP) and perhaps his lateral amygdala with low-frequency focus ultrasound (LowFU). I will discuss this with Dr. Hillary, Dr. Howard, and Dr. Wronsky. Dr. Wronsky, the psychiatrist, may be able to help us with medication to calm him down when he wakes up."

"OK," Patrick said. "I will call you as soon as I notice that he is waking up. I don't want to have to sedate him again. I feel sorry for this little boy; what a story! I can't imagine what was going on in his father's mind when he sedated him. He was a crazy man, so it's no surprise that he killed himself. What a path of destruction he left behind. Do we have a destroyed musical genius here?"

"Patrick, don't get despondent; we will cure him. You will see," said Jill, and left the ICU.

---

[18] van der Kolk B. A. (2005) 'Developmental Trauma Disorder: Toward A Rational Diagnosis For Children with Complex Trauma Histories,' *Psychiatric Annals*, **35**, no. 5: 401-408.

Chapter 22
The Protocol Music and Touch

The power of music and the brain's plasticity go together very strikingly, especially in young people.
Oliver Sacks

Jill was able to gather Dr. Hillary and Dr. Wronsky for lunch at the cafeteria. Dr. Howard, the neurologist, was not able to join them. She promptly gave them the news that she thought Jo was suffering from PTSD secondary to the abuse he received from his father. She explained the terrible face and the agitation that Patrick had described to her.

"The good news is that the series of LowFU in the PVP has improved his violent dystonic contractions. The bad news is that we will have a difficult psychiatric situation. I thought about applying LowFU in his basal lateral amygdala (**Figure 12**). We did experiments in the laboratory that showed that we can control rats' fear of electrical shocks when the lateral amygdala is stimulated[19]. I thought we could try since we can reach anywhere in his brain with the Navigation RM we already have. What do you think, Dr. Hillary?"

"We cannot do it without permission from the Institutional Review Board (IRB). You are jumping from rats to humans without the proper proposal and protocol. If we encounter a reaction to LowFU that we don't expect, we will not be in a good situation with the IRB. I suggest that you write a proposal for treating him in this way. First, we should ask Dr. Wronsky for his suggestion. Do you have any way to help him?"

---

[19] Langevin JP, De Salles AA, Kosoyan HP, Krahl SE (Dec. 2010) 'Deep brain stimulation of the amygdala alleviates post-traumatic stress disorder symptoms in a rat model,' *J Psychiatr Res.*, **44**(16):1241-5. doi: 10.1016/j.jpsychires.2010.04.022. Epub 2010 May 26. PMID: 20537659.

"Yes, the treatment of PTSD involves trying to block the bad memories, impeding them from surfacing, avoiding the torment that recalling a past traumatic event is created in the patient's mind. It is interesting that these traumatic memories come to the patient's mind as if they were happening at that moment. They don't feel them as a past event but something that is happening at that very moment. That is why they have all the vegetative symptoms, sweating, rise in blood pressure, tachycardia, and true diaphoresis," explained Dr. Wronsky

"Yes, it's nice to know that fits my diagnosis; however, if I cannot just apply LowFU and we don't want to sedate him to block his flashbacks anymore, what can we do?"

"I have an interesting suggestion," said Dr. Wronsky. "UCLA has a very active music therapy department. They have achieved wonders when appropriate songs are played to patients[20]. I wonder if we should try music therapy for him first, before directly stimulating the depth of his brain. He is an outstanding musician. His brain is full of music. Music is probably associated with some good memories that might calm him down. We just need to find out the ones that bring the best out of him."

"Great idea, Dr. Wronsky. I will ask for help from the music therapy people. Mrs. Jin will instruct us on the repertoire we should use. He won many competitions, which must have brought a lot of happiness to him and his family. She will guide us. Thanks, Dr. Wronsky; this is helpful."

Dr. Hillary looked concerned, however. "I think that the concerts he participated in, except for the recent one that he lost for Randy, must have brought him a lot of anxiety as well. These competitions take a lot of effort, and I am sure that he will remember his father putting a lot of pressure on him. When music is offered, it is better that you be prepared for an anxiety, panic, or even aggressive reaction. I would suggest that you start with the lullabies that his mother sang to him when he was a baby. Ask her to sing for him if you plan to calm him down."

"You may be right, we will talk with the experts, the music therapists; we know so little about it. It is a new specialty that is becoming very popular. Many aspiring musicians who are in the process of being recognized but need

---

[20]Magee WL, Clark I, Tamplin J, Bradt J. (2017) 'Music interventions for acquired brain injury,' *Cochrane Database of Systematic Reviews*, Issue 1. Art. No.: CD006787. DOI: 10.1002/14651858.CD006787.pub3.

a job are going into the music therapy profession. There are however dedicated ones taking the specialty very seriously. They must acquire a good knowledge about the brain and music, which they already bring to the table when they choose music as their career. For example, it is well-known that Parkinson's disease patients can improve during their freezing episodes[21], i.e., stop paralyzing during the gait if they are humming a familiar song. Also, Alzheimer's disease patients can be tranquilized if the music they enjoy is played to them[22]. Music's healing power is becoming well studied; it all makes sense; it touches plasticity. Moreover, it stimulates the brain through many angles—rhythm, memory, hearing, and motor—if the patient decides to dance to the music, which is almost an automatic reaction when one listens to music. Indeed, listening to music is a very broad stimulation of the brain[23], without mentioning the feelings music brings to us: happiness, sadness, religious trance, and bursts of energy to dance."

**

Jill left the cafeteria and went directly to the ICU. Jo was waking up; his face was serene. Mrs. Jin was at his bedside. Jill immediately asked her to sing lullabies.

"Please sing the lullabies you sang to him when he was in your womb. I hope it will be soothing to him."

"Sorry, Jill, I didn't sing to him. It was not a custom in our region in China. We were in a very small city close to Shanghai. Jo only had contact with music when my husband decided to move to Shanghai to educate him as a musician,

---

[21] Machado Sotomayor MJ, Arufe-Giráldez V, Ruíz-Rico G, Navarro-Patón R. (2021) 'Music Therapy and Parkinson's Disease: A Systematic Review from 2015-2020,' *Int J Environ Res Public Health,* 18(21):11618. Published 2021 Nov 4. doi:10.3390/ijerph182111618

[22] Hsu MH, Flowerdew R, Parker M, Fachner J, Odell-Miller H. (2015) 'Individual music therapy for managing neuropsychiatric symptoms for people with dementia and their carers: a cluster randomised controlled feasibility study,' *BMC Geriatr,* **15**:84. Published 2015 Jul 18. doi:10.1186/s12877-015-0082-4

[23] Aalbers S, Fusar-Poli L, Freeman RE, et al.(2017) 'Music therapy for depression,' *Cochrane Database Syst Rev.,* **11**(11):CD004517. Published 2017 Nov 16. doi:10.1002/14651858.CD004517.pub3

hoping to bring us to America for a better life." Mrs. Jin seemed somewhat ashamed to confess that her husband put so much pressure on their only son.

"Don't worry, just tell me what kind of music he listened to in his early years," asked Jill.

"Initially, my husband always played Beethoven; he always mentioned that it was well structured and would help Jo to like music," said Mrs. Jin

"OK," said Jill, and she looked for a Beethoven piano concert on her cell phone. She promptly found Randy's recording of the Beethoven Piano Concerto Number 3. She started playing it close to Jo's right ear without thinking twice.

Immediately, he started to become agitated, his pupils became dilated, his blood pressure went up, and he started with contractions of his whole body, developing opisthotonos. Mrs. Jin started crying; Jill promptly turned the music off. The nurses and Patrick came running to Jo's bedside. Jill immediately ordered the nurses, "Let's give him midazolam."

Once the medication was administered, Jo immediately fell asleep with regular respiration. His blood pressure returned to normal, and all vital signs stabilized. The oxygen saturation hadn't fallen. Therefore, no harm was done. However, Mrs. Jin was crying nonstop. Jill hugged her, asked Dr. Nolan to keep an eye on Jo, and took her to the doctor's lounge room in the ICU.

"I am so sorry, Mrs. Jin. I didn't expect such a reaction to this Beethoven Concerto. It is so beautiful and soothing that I felt that would bring him early childhood memories. But apparently, we brought out his recent memories of the competition. Clearly, he suffered the anxiety of the moments when Randy was playing. We will have to find music soothing to his brain. We have experts here at the university to help us. Please try to remember the music that calmed Jo and the pieces he played for fans. He never played these pieces at concerts but at home for himself. Happy music he played when the family was harmonious and proud of him. This will help us a lot in his care."

After Mrs. Jin stopped crying, Jill went to find Dr. Hillary to discuss the effect of Beethoven's Piano Concerto Number 3 on Jo's brain.

***

Jill found Dr. Hillary in the corridor going to his office.

"Do you have some time for an embarrassing conversation?" She asked.

"Sure, I am waiting for an operating room to be ready. I will be taking a meningioma out of a 36-year-old woman's frontal lobe. It is a huge tumor, but we should be able to take it out easily; do you want to help me?"

"If you really need me, yes, but if you already have help from the residents, I prefer to work on Jo's case. I just made a basic mistake in the ICU, which I would like to apologize for and discuss it with you. I need your opinion on how to proceed. Nothing major, but was an important lesson for me, and, I believe, for all of us.

"I'd prefer to go to the cafeteria and have something to eat. I don't like to start a long surgery like the one I am facing without eating. You probably have seen people fainting during surgery. Usually, it is because they didn't eat properly before and had hypoglycemia. When the stress mounts during the surgery, the brain eats glycose. Let's eat something and discuss your situation," said Dr. Hillary.

Once they had bowls of soup in front of them, Jill said, "I just did what you told me not to do; I am sorry. When I asked Mrs. Jin to sing lullabies, she told me that she never sang to him. She cuddled him to sleep, and he would fall asleep without difficulty. When his father started to play music to him, it was already classical music, mostly Beethoven. Then I did exactly what I was not supposed to do: I turned my cell phone on to play Beethoven's Concerto Number 3. The very one Randy played against Jo in the competition. It was a disaster, as I should have expected! He had the fight or flight response: his pupils dilated, his blood pressure rose, he had tachycardia, and became very agitated. I had to sedate him promptly."

"A subreption finding, it was an experiment without permission from the IRB, and against my advice. Unintended, but you showed the power of music in his brain. There are specialists at the university to help you, so you shouldn't have been nonchalant about the effects of music on his behavior. You know that his brain is very powerful in music. Fortunately, you were in the ICU with all the resources at hand to fix your blunder. Your tentative was bound to fail. You need to be more careful, Jill; we need to learn more about PTSD treatment before we try every suggestion we hear."

"Sorry, Dr. Hillary, it was the desire to help him with Mrs. Jin's information."

"Actually, you learned something very important from Mrs. Jin about touch therapy."

"There is a psychiatric movement using touch to help people with PTSD. Dr. Kolk, from Harvard, wrote a book in which he dedicates a chapter to touch. As you know, he is one of the most knowledgeable psychiatrists on PTSD[24]. He is open to medication, music, and touch therapy. I just never heard of him being favorable to surgery. In fact, there is very little written about PTSD and neurosurgery. This is a devastating disease that needs a definitive therapy. Again, as in most of these psychiatric diseases, drugs and behavior therapy fail in about 15% of the patients. Suicide is prevalent among these patients, and it is common for them to abuse their families when they lose mental control. It happens often; they have terrible nightmares. The worst thing is that these nightmares are real for them; the terrible tragedies they experienced are really happening in their minds, when, in fact, they are hallucinating. These poor souls frequently resort to recreational drugs and/or alcohol. It is a major disease with social repercussions that are likely to be passed down through generations, as they themselves can be abusive to their children. It is history repeating itself; see the relationship Mr. Jin had with Jo."

"There is a huge population of these patients in the Veterans Administration (VA) hospitals, I saw a lot of them in the VA Hospital here in Los Angeles. It was in the VA Hospital in Boston that Dr. Kolk got his experience, helping to introduce the PTSD diagnosis in the DMS-III [24]. Because of the PTSD resistance to the medical and behavioral treatments in a substantial number of patients, we needed a better solution.

"Mental diseases, in general, are of difficult treatment, the reason why we developed studies in our laboratory trying to find ways to help these patients with neuromodulation."

Dr. Hillary was excited by Jill's interest in the subject; he continued, "As with neurological and psychiatric diseases, we surgeons are the last resort. The reality is that there is a substantial population who aren't recovering through all the non-surgical approaches, including the 'Integrative Medicine Approaches,' which have grown in the major universities, such as our own here in the West, and at Harvard University in the East [25]. Seven percent of the US population suffers from PTSD every year, and approximately eight million

---

[24] Bessel van der Kolk, M.D. (2015) *The Body Keeps Score. Brain, Body and Mind in the Healing of Trauma*, Pinguin Books.

[25] [https://www.hsph.harvard.edu/magazine/magazine_article/halting-the-legacy-of-ptsd/1].

adults need help. We don't have ways of getting this statistic for children, as they frequently do not report, or even do not understand they are being abused. See the example of our patient Jo. We only learned the intensity of the abuse he was going through because of the tragedy it led to. Studies of non-invasive neuromodulation, through what we call the USB of the brain, are ongoing here in our university for children, with Food and Drug Administration (FDA) approval. We hope somehow to be able to rescue this population of PTSD patients who do not benefit from the non-invasive approaches. Surgery is always a more direct way of delivering neuromodulation. Your work with us and with your husband shows why we should trust both, non-invasive and invasive neuromodulation."

"Well, Jill, I am just being called to the operating room. Would you please search at the university Integrative Medicine Department for ways we can help Jo with music and touch? Please don't do anything on your own. They have a website[25]."

"Sure, I will contact them. Thanks for your orientation and this exhaustive lecture on PTSD," said Jill.

Chapter 23
The Touch and Music Experts

*I can't understand why people
are frightened of new ideas.
I'm frightened of the old ones.*
John Cage

Jill called the 'Integrative Medicine' department asking for help and received a positive response. Young volunteers and well-trained professionals promptly got to work evaluating Jo's situation. When she told them her experience of playing Beethoven to Jo and how he reacted, they started laughing.

The chief of the department asked, "What do you think about us trying to open his skull to touch your patient's 'brain music center'?"

"As a matter of fact, this center does not exist," answered Jill. "That is the beautiful part of the work I am asking you all to do. Music is everywhere in the brain. I believe it will stimulate all of Jo's senses. I apologize for my intrusion in your specialty; however, I experienced the power of music on Jo's behavior, and the potential for us to help him with music. He is all about music; his father forced music into his brain when he was a toddler. He forced it on him in such a way that it became a kind of abuse. This boy won all the piano competitions in China and the US until the last one, which led to his father losing his own self-control. He overdosed the boy with sedatives, leading him to respiratory insufficiency and brain damage. The man became so disturbed by his brutal behavior and the tragedy it had led to that he enhanced the disaster by committing suicide.

"Mrs. Jin, his widow, is distraught, but eager to help us. She is a wonderful mother, ready to collaborate with us on taking her son out of this predicament and returning him to his piano studies. His reaction to the Beethoven Concert Number 3 was completely unexpected to me, although Dr. Hillary advised us to be very careful with which music we presented to Jo. I understand why now, but I never imagined that the power of music would be so strong over him.

"We will review his music tendencies and choose the appropriate therapy. It must be very gradual, with weeks of light and disciplined music introduction. Also, we will learn from Mrs. Jin what she did throughout his childhood to soothe him. Chinese culture is knowledgeable about 'Integrative Medicine'; in this respect, we are beginners compared to them. They come to our country to learn our medicine, but we have a lot to learn from them. Our health care is more and more integrating their techniques with our therapeutic arsenal. Cuddling babies without music is a common attitude among them, and even in our own culture. Touch also works; we will recruit our 'Touching Therapy' group to help. Our medicine is too bogged down into drugs and surgery, forgetting that we are sensitive beings who have developed a love for sounds and touch since primordial times.

"We are getting some amazing results with long-term coma patients. Some are unresponsive to all stimulation, including the presence of their families. However, when music is brought into the context, in a few weeks, they open their eyes, respond to light touch, and start to speak. We have all experienced memories coming up when a familiar song is played. It can be sad or happy memories, and the happy ones in particular are believed to stimulate the immune system. It takes away the trauma that brought them to the state of hopelessness, bringing an aura of happiness and a desire to live. We see this amazing turning point for patients who underwent traumatic events, such as car accidents, mugging, rape, and other horrifying experiences, and can often reduce medication due to improvement in the patient's mood.

"The experiments have told us a lot about the state of despondence. It is one way that antidepressants are tested. Hopeless rats who are dunked into the water without the possibility of swimming out of it are the experimental models. They finally give up swimming in a state of hopelessness; then drugs are given to get them swimming again. This is one way the drugs are proven effective for depressive states. The problem is that drugs are being abused in our society; patients become completely dependent on them, many times accepting side effects that could be avoided with other forms of treatment. Important side effects include a foggy mind, lack of libido, dry mouth, and so on. These kinds of side effects destroy the quality of life. That is what we are working on in our research. How can we decrease medication doses and even their need for it?"

Jill was grateful the university could provide this support to Jo and Mrs. Jin. She did agree with them that the abuse of medication left many people incapable of working and excluded from the simple pleasures of life. She had seen it happening with her husband until she had liberated him from drugs with the implant of electrodes in his hypothalamus. It had really been lifesaving for him and for their marriage, allowing them to concentrate their work on a dream project. Jo would be the first to benefit from Charles' years of work in his laboratory, developing a completely wireless device capable of modulating specific areas in the brain. This promised to have an efficacy that drugs or external neuromodulating devices would never achieve. It is impossible to completely abolish the side effects of systemic medical therapy.

Chapter 24
The Colburn Community's Heart

Music is the movement of sound to reach the soul for the education of its virtue.
Plato

Jill continued giving the LowFU stimulation to Jo's PVP. She was amazed at the effect of this stimulation on his dystonic movements. The only muscles she was not getting complete control were the fine muscles in his right hand. He had difficulty moving the three medial fingers. The thumb and the second finger were normal, but the third, fourth, and fifth were very curled. Another frustrating thing was that every morning when she came to neuromodulate him, he had contractions in his neck and shoulders as well. She had to apply the LowFU for half an hour before she could gain control of these sites. The music and touch people had done an amazing job. He was always serene listening to music with earphones. She asked Mrs. Jin which music was having such an amazing calming effect on him. She promptly answered, Chopin's Nocturne Opus 9 Number 1.

"Amazing," said Jill. "How did you decide that Chopin's Nocturne Opus 9 Number 1 would calm him down?"

"Simple; my husband didn't like it. He always thought that it was not impressive enough to the audience for Jo to incorporate it into his repertoire. I never agreed as I love Chopin's smooth sound. His piano compositions are so much like Jo's manners. They fit with his mild personality. I think that the Heroic can raise any audience when played with passion, which my son has had for music since he was a baby. So, when my husband was not at home, I played Chopin's Nocturne Opus 9 Number 1 for Jo. Usually, he was playing with his toys, away from the piano. He was always very happy at these moments. I could talk with him, cuddle him, and have a mother-son relationship. I loved those moments as well.

"When I played Chopin's Nocturne Opus 9 Number 1 when he was five years old, he would run and hug me, it was so cute. When his father arrived, it was just tension and him making Jo play the piano nonstop. I felt sorry for Jo; he was so young, but I followed his father's ways, as he made me believe that it was the best for his future. Indeed, he was an amazing technical pianist. It's just that, with some of the pieces he played, he didn't have feelings for them; it was an obligation. I am sure that if he starts to play Chopin, he will be a great success.

"We will get there; trust this team of wonderful people; we want to help him. First, we need to find a way to pay for his treatment. Our secretaries checked Jo's student insurance from the Colburn. They will only pay for the procedures that are proven to be effective in traditional medicine. Therefore, they will not pay for all this 'music and touch' therapy, as well as the experimental treatments such as the LowFU, and the surgical procedure we are planning. I will have to find funds to proceed with these treatments. I rely on you to reassure us that what we are doing is in fact helping your son. Your support will give me the strength to ask for help from donors. They will have to feel we are doing is effective. I am planning to have you speak to the audience to convince them to help your son. Is it OK?"

"Don't you worry, Dr. Morales, I am with you all the way," Mrs. Jin said emotionally. "You got my son out of a coma. Now, he is capable of communicating with me, squeezing my hand, starting to use his fingers, and most of all, smiling. Count on me; Jo has a life ahead. I will fight for a successful career for him."

"I have a plan," said Jill. "What do you think about a charity walk for Jo Pan Jin to fund his treatment? It will be promoted through the Colburn, with a concert at the end of the walk at the Disney Music Hall. I am sure we will touch The Colburn Community's Heart. Jo was already admired and loved there. I have researched the artist who could give the concert and discussed it with Dr. Hillary. He thought that the whole thing was a great idea. There are two icons in the history of pianists with dystonia who can have an impact. Leon Fleisher and João Carlos Martins. Unfortunately, Fleisher passed away at age 92 during the Covid-19 pandemic."

João Carlos Martins was a famous and loved Brazilian conductor dedicated to helping young musicians and dystonic patients. He was a successful concert pianist for years until the dystonia of his right hand started limiting his work. He persisted, however throughout his career playing the piano with the left hand, having several surgeries to recover his right hand, and even surgery in his brain because of his love for music. To make his situation even more complicated, Maestro João Carlos was the victim of a head injury while traveling for a concert tour through Eastern Europe. However, he believed that his dystonic symptoms started at the age of 16 to 18 years old, again due to excessive practice. Leon and João Carlos are examples of discipline, resilience, and trust in medical treatment, as both were able to achieve continuous success helped by medicine and their determination. Moreover, both were able to reinvent themselves as conductors of remarkable success, proving that music is in the brain and not only in the hands.

"When music occupies the brain, it is an asset no one can take away. Jo has his brain full of music; you and Mr. Jin gave him this asset."

Maestro João Carlos followed Leon's advice, shifting his career to be a conductor. Leon knew João Carlos had what it took to be a successful conductor. Although Jo was young and still had much to learn, his brain was wired for music in his early years. We must figure out how to damp down these hyperactive neurons that are disturbing him. We have a lot of tools to achieve that, and music is one of them. People who love music and have talent like these two world-famous musicians testify that Jo can rely on his music as a future profession. Both conductors kept themselves at the apex of their profession despite significant physical difficulty.

"Excessive practice may be why Jo's right hand resists the ultrasound stimulation. Leon Fleisher believed the dystonic disease in his right hand was caused by excessive practice, the well-described focal dystonia, or 'Musician's Dystonia.' He practiced seven to eight hours per day. He tried any treatment he heard about to maintain his piano technique. He went through psychotherapy, rehabilitation therapy, repetitive muscle shock treatments, hand anesthesia, and even botulin toxin (Botox)[26]. This last one allowed him

---

[26] van Vugt FT, Boullet L, Jabusch HC, Altenmüller E. (Jan. 2012) 'Musician's dystonia in pianists: long-term evaluation of retraining and other therapies,' *Parkinsonism Relat Disord.*, **20**(1):8-12. doi: 10.1016/j.parkreldis.2013.08.009. Epub 2013 Aug 30. PMID: 24055013.

to play the piano with the right hand again and even allowed him to record an album[27]. He was in so much despair during his fight against dystonia that he considered suicide, a decision common among artists[28].

"João Carlos Martins also experienced such despair [personal communication], and he also considered suicide at the age of 26. We don't want this to happen to Jo. You must be aware of this danger since he has a history of suicide in the family[29]. His family could be considered dysfunctional, as your husband and your son had a tough relationship[30]. Moreover, you were not present with them for long periods while working in China to support them financially here in America. Do you know of any other suicide in his or your family?"

"Yes, one of my husband's brothers also killed himself. I don't know why he did that, but in China, people do it, usually due to government persecution. He was a good family man. He left one daughter and his wife. They were beneficial to me during my time working in China alone."

"Well, Mrs. Jin, life will be easier now; we will find the right support for Jo and you."

---

[27] Sussman J. (Aug. 2015) 'Musician's dystonia,' *Pract Neurol.*, **15**(4):317-22. doi: 10.1136/practneurol-2015-001148. Epub 2015 May 28. PMID: 26023204.

[28] [https://www.nytimes.com/2020/08/02/arts/music/leon-fleisher-dead.html].

[29] Jones JD, Boyd RC, Calkins ME, Moore TM, Ahmed A, Barzilay R, Benton TD, Gur RE, Gur RC (Jan. 2021) 'Association between family history of suicide attempt and neurocognitive functioning in community youth,' *J Child Psychol Psychiatry.*, 62(1):58-65. doi: 10.1111/jcpp.13239. Epub 2020 Mar 30. PMID: 32227601; PMCID: PMC7529718.

[30] DeVille, Danielle C.; Whalen, Diana; Breslin, Florence J.; Morris, Amanda S.; Khalsa, Sahib S.; Paulus, Martin P.; Barch, Deanna M. (2020) 'Prevalence and Family-Related Factors Associated With Suicidal Ideation, Suicide Attempts, and Self-injury in Children Aged 9 to 10 Years,' *JAMA Network Open*, **3**(2), e1920956–. doi:10.1001/jamanetworkopen.2019.20956.

Chapter 25
The Walk for Dystonia and Music

To send light into the darkness of men's hearts,
such is the duty of the artist.
Robert Schumann

Jill contacted the professors at the Colburn, explaining her desire to promote a concert at the Disney Music Center as a fundraiser for Jo Pan Jin's treatment. She was received with great enthusiasm. The school was following each victory she was having with Jo's recovery. She dedicated herself to Jo's care because she felt sorry that her son's competition victory had caused so much suffering for Jo's family. Indeed, the teachers at the Colburn had noticed that Randy was very withdrawn during recess. The tragedy touched everyone who knew of Jo Pan Jin's talent, and Randy Morales, in particular; they were colleagues at the Colburn. They often saw each other at the auditions and concerts at the Disney Music Hall.

Randy was a compassionate boy; he would rather have lost the competition than feel that he was the cause of so much suffering for Jo and his family. He went through this gilty feeling with Jimmy when he pushed him on the basketball court. He entered into a depressive state, which only improved after he befriended Jimmy and understood that he had not caused significant damage to his colleague.

Jill was helping Jo not just because she was worried about how Randy was feeling, but also because she felt compelled to care for such a beautiful and talented child, who had suffered so much from the pressures of fame and his father's obsession. Unfortunately, neither the son nor the father was prepared for life's disappointments. The destruction of two lives because of a piano competition and a music scholarship, even for the most prestigious music school, such as Julliard, was not justified. Jill had even generously told Mrs.

Jin that when Jo got better, she would give Randy's scholarship to Jo. If Randy decided to go to Julliard, it wouldn't be difficult for Charles and her to afford his studies. Her relationship with Mrs. Jin and Jo was already tight, and Randy heard so much about Jo's recovery at home from Jill's conversation with his father that he learned to like Jo. Out of his good heart, he wanted to befriend Jo and help him at school.

There was not a single professor who didn't know what had happened with Jo and his father. The story had been in the *Los Angeles Times*, as it was so dramatic that the whole classical music community was dismayed by the tragedy. Therefore, it was highly receptive to the 'Walk for Musicians Dystonia.' The famous Brazilian pianist and conductor João Carlos Martins, who fought throughout his life with his dystonic hands, therefore very sympathetic to Jo's difficulties, was touring with his Brazilian Bachiana Philharmonic SESI-SP in the United States. He was also scheduled to perform with the Los Angeles Philharmonic, with which he was already familiar as he had performed several times with the Orchestra as a pianist. Once with Indian conductor Zubin Mehta and another memorable presentation at the Hollywood Bowl with the famous composer and conductor Aaron Copland." He offered to conduct the concert to help raise funds for Jo's treatment. The Walk for Dystonia and the Concert were publicized throughout the city. The advertisement was sponsored by Disney Music Center management. Banners with Martins' photo were displayed on Wilshire Boulevard and Hollywood Boulevard. The administration of Colburn School and Disney Music Hall gave their full support to the event. Jill was sure that she had already secured the necessary resources, as the event was so well received by everyone that even the university was advertising it.

The heavy promotion helped Jill obtain permission from the Institutional Review Board (IRB) to accept the surgical intervention as the assurance that the IRB supervised the procedure costs and the society's acceptance of it. There was no doubt about the procedure's ethical nature and need. Jill's proposal breezed through all the university regulators. The hardest thing was getting approval for the 'porcupine fish,' a revolutionary technology. The induction of energy with radiofrequency, an old and well-accepted technology, was used to power the device; this helped to authorize it. She believed that the influence of the electrical pulses should cover all the harmful neurons due to the device's shape and spikes. The influence of the electrical field generated by the device could be expanded by infusing more and more energy into it. A miniaturized computer inside the device could record cell activity and send the recordings via Bluetooth to a remote observation and data mining station at the university. This information would be analyzed continuously, and the device would emit pulses when demanded, informing the scientific team 24/7 of Jo's neurological behavior.

The stimulation was needed based on cell activity in the PVP to correct any abnormal cellular behavior. If the harmful cell activity was not damped naturally by the patient's physiology, the device should suppress it. Stimulation and suppression were, therefore, to be modulated by the device. Given the nature of the patient's disease, the idea was for the device to be a security pod for Jo's brain, capable of avoiding undesirable cell firing or dormancy. The device had already been tested in animals, as had all the procedure steps. Charles completed the tests two weeks before the fundraising event.

***

Jill went to Los Angeles Airport (LAX) to meet João Carlos Martins. She was amazed at how easygoing the man was. For someone so famous, he had no self-importance and was a pleasant, humble man. The same was true of his wife. The couple were completely in tune with each other's energies, despite Martins' advanced age (he was over 80), the heavy tour schedule in the USA, and the 14-hour flight from São Paulo to Los Angeles. They immediately asked how Jo was faring. They had heartily accepted the invitation to help the boy. Jill could feel their natural sympathy for the boy's hurdles. It was also an excellent opportunity for them to bring awareness of their work with the Dystonia Foundation. Although they did not expect a reward for their participation, the foundation's director told Jill they might appreciate a donation if she succeeded with the fundraiser.

The event organizers had already budgeted for the event, as well as the costs of the surgery and the production of the device to be installed in Jo's brain. Additionally, expenses were to be generated by the music therapy and touch therapy. Jill was very grateful to them for the fantastic results they had obtained with Jo's PTSD crises. She became convinced to help the development of this therapy for her patients. It was amazing how they had made music permeate through the depths of Jo's entire brain, warding off the harmful memories and protecting him from the traumatic events he had been through with his father[31]. She would not have to worry about PTSD at this point, leaving only the motor symptoms to be managed, as they were the only factor hindering Jo from returning to his piano.

On arriving at the hotel, the Martins said they wanted to visit Jo, although they wanted to rest the next day before they went to the hospital. Maestro Martins also needed to get acquainted with the LA Philharmonic. He had one week to work with the musicians and rehearse Randy with the Orchestra. He wanted them to play a piece they needed to become more familiar with. A Brazilian neurosurgeon had composed music for the buffalos suffering in the Bad Lands of the USA, dry lands in South Dakota (Buffalo Gap[32]), which strongly resembled the dry lands of the northeast of Brazil, from where the composer had migrated to the USA. It was a beautiful, sentimental piece, showing a lot of happiness and sadness at the same time. It was perfect for Jo's situation, a great tragedy with a whole community fighting for recovery. He knew the piece's orchestration would be beautiful for the occasion, exuding suffering, resilience, and redemption. It would suit this alliance between Brazil and the USA to help Jo, a Chinese music genius: three countries brought together by music's universality.

---

[31] Thaut, M. H. (2015) 'Music as therapy in early history,' *Music, Neurology, and Neuroscience: Evolution, the Musical Brain, Medical Conditions, and Therapies*, 143-158. doi:10.1016/bs.pbr.2014.11.025

[32] https://www.youtube.com/watch?v=tRYiRy_2lu8

Buffalo Gap

Asfora & De Salles

First Part G+

Introduction

I go, I go, I go, go, go
In the beauty of love, I go
In the beauty of the earth, I go
Lands on-the-go, we go

In the strength of bull, we go
With the strength of love, we go

With the speed of horses, we go
In the beautiful dry land, we go
Completing love, we go
In the earth with bounty, we go

Seeding our love, we go
Harvest your love, I go
Fruits of us lovers we give
Forever in this earth we seed

***Second Part* G-**

The buffalo gap in seeds
Seeding and grazing through
buffalo love, buffalo gap
To the end of times, we see

Strength and mighty, we see
The bounty the earth gives, we see

Buffalo gasp, Buffalo grasp, Buffalo gap
Buffalo finds hope,

The life, the bounty,
The green in the dry land

The life, the bounty,
The green in the dry land
We go, we go

***

    The walk progressed from UCLA to the Disney Music Hall, 16 miles: four-hours of a crowded and happy walk. It started at 8 am from the Bruin Bear Square, in the center of the Campus. The crowd invaded the whole square and beyond, invading the campus gardens. There were over 5,000 people. Each paid $20 for registration for the event. However, the real income would come from the concert, which had sold 2,000 tickets at 50 dollars on average per ticket, making an additional $100,000. Jill was also waiting for donations from her patients and possibly a billionaire who had decided to embrace the cause. She hoped for a significant donor to finance the laboratory and implant projects. They had scraped together all the funds Charles had obtained with his RO1 NIH Grant to complete the animal experimentation and build the unique device installed in Jo's brain. Although they would be treating Jo's motor violent contractions and fine movements, the potential applications of the device were vast in neurodegenerative diseases, including Alzheimer's disease, Parkinson's disease, epilepsy, and others.

Chapter 26
The Fundraiser

I was obliged to be industrious.
Whoever is equally industrious will succeed equally well.
J.S. Bach

The crowd's arrival at the Los Angeles Music Center (LAMC) was a happy event. There were several food trucks in the area, and classical music from several groups of students played at different corners and in the square of the music center. The Walt Disney Concert Hall can seat 2265 people, so less than half of the crowd would be attending the concert. Although it was prepared with large screens to forecast the concert in this fabulous Los Angeles tourist site, visiting the marvelous work of the architect Frank Gehry in collaboration with Dr. Yasuhisa Toyota, an acoustician, was worthwhile. The amazing metal structure was built outside the music center and in front of the Colburn. The location concentrates a wealth of performing arts pavilions dedicated to opera, theater, and the music school.

The project to bring the Walt Disney Concert Hall to the LAMC area started in 1987 with a donation by Walt Disney's widow. Her generosity supported music and provided resources to help sick people worldwide, without counting the years of music entertainment it provided to Los Angeles and visitors worldwide since it was inaugurated in 2003, a 16-year building project.

The auditory was packed with very informal people; many of them had walked 16 miles to be there at the concert; they were wearing sports clothes, although there were also very important people dressed appropriately for a great event in the music hall. The concert started for the surprise of all with Randy Morales playing Chopin's Opus 9 Number 1. As it was an event to help Jo Pan Jin, Jill felt it was important for Randy to play the piece that pacified his friend in the intensive care unit. For Randy, now 11 years old, it would be a good memory that would take away his resentment for winning the competition, bringing Jo to the predicament he was suffering. The conductor, João Carlos Martins, had prepared Randy for the concert opening. The next piece was the Beethoven Concert Number 3, again in honor of Jo Pan Jin. The second half started with Wilson Asfora's 'Legend of the Buffalo Gap', a Brazilian-American composition bringing the two countries' friendship to help the young Chinese genius.

The Concert ended with Maestro João Carlos conducting Beethoven's Symphony Number 4 (Figure 8), a piece so well performed by Jo. Once again, remembering that Jo was the reason for the fundraising event. Surprisingly, after each piece there was applause with the audience standing up. An encore, again in honor of Jo Pan Jin, Randy played the first prelude of the first volume of Bach's Well-Tempered Clavier. Martins, who had been giving recitals with his left-hand for years because of his right-hand dystonia, wore his supporting gloves. It drew attention to reinforce the reason for the fundraise, touching on the generosity of the donors. A second encore was kindly granted by Maestro João Carlos, the Gand Cadenza from Ravel's Left-Hand Concerto. The audience insisted on another encore, which they received with Randy and the Orchestra playing the Tico-Tico in Fubá. It was a happy and successful concert ending.

A  B

Figura 8:
(A) Beethoven's Symphony Number 4 https://youtu.be/PDiDnp4aztA and (B) Bach's Concert for 2 Pianos in C minor https://youtu.be/gvvqBGcx4OE.

The concert raised more than enough funds for Jo's care during hospital admission and rehabilitation. Jill and Charles were delighted with the effort. It was far more than they had been counting. Also, unexpectedly, they received a donation of $2 million to be applied to dystonia research. This was to be divided between Charles' laboratory and the Dystonia Foundation. The donor was interested in electronics and genetic research. He was from a family with the DYT1 gene, and one of his children had severe generalized dystonia. Therefore, he needed an immediate solution for his son's suffering and to spearhead long-term genetic research that would take care of the DYT1 gene defect. Additionally, several medical companies sponsored the event, granting further funds.

Both João Carlos Martins and Jill were extremely proud of their efforts. Maestro João, as he was called in Brazil, promised to instruct Jo through his return to music. Jill had told him she was having difficulty controlling the dystonic movements of Jo's right hand with the LowFU applications. She feared the same problem could recur with Charles' smart deep brain stimulation device. It was difficult to pinpoint the neuronal network responsible for the pinky, ring, and middle finger, as their representation in the brain cortex is minute, compared to the representation of the thumb and the index finger in humans. This is probably why these fingers fail when they are overworked by a virtuoso's piano practice, as they have no cortical reserve.

Martins greeted Jill and said, "Please let me know if you need my help with Jo. It will be a pleasure to come to Los Angeles and spend time here to help him. I want to dedicate this period of my career to helping musicians suffering what I endured for so long without finding people who knew how to help me. Medicine was so primitive during my youth. I learned my tricks the hard way; I want to pass them along."

"Maestro, I don't have words of gratitude for your efforts, generosity, and desire to help Jo. The Los Angeles music community will always be grateful and proud to receive you here. Count on me to promote your help for Jo and the dystonia cause, too."

"It will always be a pleasure," said Maestro João. He, his wife Carmen, and the Bachiana Orchestra followed to New York for a concert planned at Carnegie Hall as they completed their USA tour. From there, they would leave for Brazil, as they had a commitment to their philanthropic affairs, management of their orchestra, and a deserved rest.

Part 4
Doctors, Musicians, and Dystonia

Chapter 27
Scientific Plan

*The best life is not the longest,
but the richest of good deeds.*
Marie Curie

Jill called a meeting with the team to plan Jo's surgery. Jo was already in the ward with the dystonia controlled by the daily LowFU application. Neither monitoring nor sedation was no longer necessary, as stimulation was effective. She went early every morning to his room and spent 30 minutes stimulating his PVP. She was not going on Saturdays and Sundays, but she did this purposefully, as she wanted to evaluate whether leaving two days without stimulation would make the generalized dystonic movements return. He didn't have violent contractions, but his hands were more dystonic on Mondays, especially the right hand. She confirmed he needed the surgery soon, as the LowFU effect was very short-lived. It would not be enough to alleviate his dystonia throughout his life, and much less keep him healthy playing piano, which was his dream and her medical and scientific challenge. She presented this issue to the group; it was unanimously agreed that the surgery should be done as soon as possible so Jo could go home and return to school and his music. He had already been in the hospital for three months, including two months in the ICU, before Jill had controlled his generalized dystonia with the LowFU.

As she had all his preoperative exams ready, and Charles was more than ready with his device, they planned the surgery for the following week. They reserved the MRI room for Tuesday morning; ten hours of surgery were expected. During the procedure, imaging, calculations, electrophysiology studies, and Jo's physical exams would take a lot of time. Additionally, they would have to take him out of the MRI for the electrophysiological studies to avoid the interference of the strong magnetic field on the neuron's manifestations, then introduce him back to the machine to obtain new images for adjustments of the device in his PVP; this would all take hours. The device spikes had to be properly directed to the region of the hyperactive neurons using the magnetic field.

This was a first for them, although Charles was well-trained at managing devices in the magnetic field, as he had performed the surgery on many animals. This maneuver was delicate, technically challenging, and demanding of complex calculations and time. He taught Jill the procedures, and she participated in many experiments with him. The surgical steps, like the common neurosurgical procedures, were already in her automatic moves in the operating room. The challenge the whole team had to face was not in their routine work. The stress was at another level when operating on humans, especially a high-profile child-like Jo. The procedures were not second nature for them yet, so they required intense concentration. Dr. Hillary was to help Jill during the surgery.

Dr. Wolf, the anesthesiologist, knew he could only use drugs with temporary effects, as he would have to wake Jo several times during the studies. This was important; otherwise, the team would be waiting for the drugs to wash out from Jo's body before the recordings from the targeted neurons became reliable. Also, images of Jo's brain had to be obtained in the proper steady state during tasks, and he had to be unconscious when any surgical pain was anticipated during the procedure. Now all the details were planned, Jill spent more time organizing the MRI sequences that would be necessary to identify the nervous fibers and the cluster of neurons to be studied and modulated. The MRI physicists and Dr. Wilson helped her choose the sequences and the tasks for the functional MRI. They also planned the volumetric images to ensure they could visualize the target and the structures to avoid during the surgery, like blood vessels. After many hours of discussion and pondering, they felt ready to obtain Jo's brain images.

They planned to have all the images acquired two days before the surgery, as they wanted time to study Jo's brain. It involved unavoidably complex statistical analyses to ensure the reliability of functional images, correlation of the diverse modalities, and planning the target so this hard part of the procedure could be ready, avoiding delays during surgery. These images would be merged with a set of images acquired during surgery, having fixed a localizer to Jo's head. He had to be under anesthesia to fix the localizer. Additionally, the earlier images, obtained without anesthesia, would provide information about the steady state of his brain while performing challenging motor tasks, such as using his right hand on a keyboard. They had to localize the 'key neurons' to be modulated while he was playing, the cluster of neurons acting up, making his hand curl.

***

Jill brought Jo to the MRI scanner two days before surgery. He was very cooperative, staying still during the image acquisition. He performed tasks with the keyboard, he sang, wrote, and identified objects during the imaging. These images were immediately placed in the hospital system for analysis by Dr. Wilson, Hillary, Jill, and Howard. After their analysis, it was concluded that they also needed images with molecular information, as expected; these images had to be planned with the nuclear imaging specialist. Dr. Malory was asked to acquire these images using a very special protocol, demanding very thin cuts, as the hypermetabolism expected in the PVP was very difficult to detect due to the small volume of the PVP. It was a group of cells encrusted in the middle of each brain hemisphere. They expected to glimpse the group of cells in glycolytic metabolism, confirming the location of the most active neurons during the manual tasks. They needed to do this individually, for the right and the left hand and each of the ten fingers, which was a very difficult imaging acquisition protocol.

Dr. Malory pondered the request, suggesting that the studies should look at glycolytic metabolism and blood flow using fMRI or PET O_2. Due to the short life of the tagged O_2, PET O_2 was too laborious to obtain; therefore, functional MRI (fMRI) would be a better technique for correlating the two fuels used in the brain. Combining these two fuels used by the neurons, O_2, and glucose, would help define neuronal hyperactivity[33]. It was, therefore, decided that the two scans, FDG-PET and fMRI, would be added to the planning.

---

[33] Hahn, A., Gryglewski, G., Nics, L., Rischka, L., Ganger, S., Sigurdardottir, H., ... Lanzenberger, R. (2017) 'Task-relevant brain networks identified with simultaneous PET/MR imaging of metabolism and connectivity,' *Brain Structure and Function*. doi:10.1007/s00429-017-1558-0

Chapter 28
Surgery and Recovery

*A surgeon knows all the parts of the brain,
but does not know his patient's dreams.*
Richard Selzer (1928-2016)

The big day arrived. Jill and Dr. Wolf met with Jo and Mrs. Jin in the ward to review all the procedure's steps, the risks, and the immediate recovery after surgery. Jill stressed the risks of intracranial hemorrhage, brain damage, infection, and failure of the procedure to help Jo. She also stressed that any of these unlikely occurrences could have severe consequences, such as death, a prolonged coma, cognitive deficiencies, and neurological deficits for life. Dr. Wolf went through the risks of anesthesia, repeating some of the ones Jill had stressed and adding the ones inherent to anesthesia, including hypoxia with worsening of Jo's current symptoms. He knew that his current state was due to hypoxia caused by heavy sedation, the very state that they would be returning Jo to several times during the planned studies, which were necessary for the proper installation of the device to control Jo's dystonia.

All this just increased Mrs. Jin's anxiety. Jo listened with courage and the desire to get better. His hope of returning to being a normal child, studying piano, and meeting with his friends at school made him strong. His trust in Dr. Morales had increased immensely through the close relationship they developed during the LowFU applications. He experienced her compassion and competency as a medical doctor. He had observed her care for Randy at the competition and during the functions at the Colburn. His mother also spoke highly of her after she left their hospital room every morning. For him, these were assurances that all would go well. During the weekends, Jill visits Jo in the hospital and frequently brings Randy to see him. It was part of her plan to show Randy that Jo was recovering well and that he would soon be at Colburn.

They usually played a game of chess and talked about their schoolteachers and friends. Jo loved it when Randy came. They built a tight friendship. The weekend before surgery, he came to wish Jo good luck and told him that the whole school was rooting for him.

Jo remembered Randy's words that Sunday. "Be confident, Jo. My mom and dad don't spend a day without talking about how excited they are about helping you. I am confident that soon we will be playing piano together. I will see you next weekend. I bet I will win the chess game next time." Randy hugged his friend tightly and left smiling with his mom. Randy's visit gave Jo a lot of confidence.

After a routine preamble before surgery, Jo was taken to the operating room, where Dr. Hillary, Charles, and a resident were already waiting for them. There was only one resident to help with the surgery because Jill had asked to limit the number of people in the operating room to decrease the risk of infection and the danger of distraction. While Dr. Wolf took Jo to the operating table, the others went to the computer of the MRI operating room to manipulate images, finalize the plans, and discuss the best approaches. Charles had prepared two devices, as Jill had insisted that she wanted to install them in both brain hemispheres. Dr. Hillary had raised the possibility that the right hemisphere was just on the borderline of its neuronal reserve, barely maintaining the left hand normal. The hypoxia to which Jo had been subjected during his sedated comatose state had reached his whole brain, so there was no reason to think that the right hemisphere was more resistant than the left one. Except for the motor disturbances in Jo's neurological examination, no deficit had been detected in his cognitive and musical ability. Mostly, his right hemisphere, which was responsible for his abstract and music love and preferences, had not been affected.

Music was affecting Jo positively. He didn't know about his dad's suicide yet, as his mom decided to only tell him after he left the hospital. She didn't want him to have another trauma or develop a guilt complex while he was still so mentally fragile. She told him Mr. Jin was in China working to support them. This actually gave him relief, as he preferred the love and tender care his mother provided him to the harsh and demanding Mr. Jin's manners.

Dr. Wolf asked Jo to think of some music while preparing the anesthetics. Jo asked him if he could play some music.

"Sure," said Dr. Wolf, who always brought his small boom box to the operating room. Many surgeons loved music during surgery, and Dr. Hillary and Dr. Morales always asked for music during their surgeries.

"Jo, what kind of music do you want to listen to?" Dr. Wolf asked.

"I love classical music, as you know. Please just don't play Beethoven."

"So, I will play Franz Liszt. What do you think about La Campanella in G-Sharp Minor, played by Lang-Lang.? It is happy and difficult; is that OK with you?"

"Great," answered Jo. "I love Liszt. It starts so mild and builds up to energetic and mild simultaneously. Played by Lang-Lang, it is even better. Please play it."

At this point, Dr. Wolf had already inserted a catheter into Jo's arm vein and was ready to inject the propofol. La Campanella was still playing when Jo serenely fell asleep. The nurses came and finished placing all the catheters and a Foley for urine collection. The surgery would be long, and Dr. Wolf had to balance Jo's fluids tightly. All intake and output from Jo had to be closely monitored, as children become dehydrated easily, and any volume of blood loss is highly significant for a small child. Children's anesthesia is very challenging; everything happens so fast; they enter into shock and/or hypoxia very easily. Dr. Wolf also held Jo's ventilation steady; trachea intubation is difficult in children.

Dr. Hillary entered the operating room and commented on how much he loved La Campanella on G-Flat Minor. "Did it have any effect on Jo?" He asked.

"Yes," said Dr. Wolf. "He became very serene, and when I injected the propofol, he smiled. He is a remarkable kid. He seemed to be completely cooperative through the whole anesthesia induction. Lang-Lang had a great calming effect on him."

"Well, it is a great piece for him, as it starts with a slow right hand and builds up afterward, demanding high dexterity. If he starts playing it, it will be a great exercise for his right hand. Liszt has some great mild right-hand pieces, such as Romance in E-Minor, Libestraum No. 3 in A-Flat Major, etc.," remarked Dr. Hillary.

"Dr. Hillary, I didn't know you knew so much about Liszt and piano," said Dr. Wolf, looking surprised. "Amazing, where do you find time to keep up with music and still be a scientist, a professor, and a surgeon?"

"The three professions you mention are the triple threat of an academic surgeon! We are not promoted if we don't master them all. The university demands publications, teaching, and making much money, clinically and/or in grants, or perish! However, music is a pleasure; my mom made me study piano until I was 13. Then I became a rebel, decided to play soccer, and, worse, found the girlfriends and abandoned the piano. What a terrible decision, now I am just a listener. Classical music does help my writing, though. I believe it stimulates the whole brain and arouses it into a creative mode, as it incites all our senses. We see it so strongly with Jo; his brain has a wealth of stored music. I bet we can find music pieces to stimulate different areas of his brain. You found Liszt's La Campanella to help with our surgery. I will remember to suggest it for the music therapy group. They will have a major role in his rehabilitation."

"Yes, they will," agreed Jill, while working on Jo's head's antisepsis and asepsis. "I imagine me playing for him and Randy together. I want them to get closer; it will be good for both. I will mention that to the music therapy group. Well, let's keep the good music going. We will need a serene environment when we wake him up for the test. If he was smiling with La Campanella, we should play it again when we wake him up. It will probably continue the music in his mind, as he was interrupted by propofol-induced sleep."

"I don't know if he was interrupted; he probably continued listening when he was sleeping; let's also monitor his EEG during the entire procedure and sleep-wake periods to learn how music controls his brain waves. We know so little about it, and music has been lifesaving during his agitations and dystonic crises. Conversely, it can also be a trigger of so much agitation and aggressivity when the proper ones are not chosen, and he enters into his PTSD mode. What an interesting, powerful effect music has in his musical brain!" said Dr. Hillary

"Yes, what an interesting lesson this boy has taught us on music-brain interaction. I always thought that music's effects on the brain must be powerful, even though it hasn't fully worked for Randy," said Jill while positioning Jo's head in the stereotactic localization and holding device.

"Well, Jill, music is a global brain modulator," said Dr. Hillary. "With Randy, you were expecting that a group of neurons encrusted into the smallest and most eclectic portion of the brain, the hypothalamus, could be controlled by music. Music penetrates in places related to feelings, memory, rhythm, and motor functions, but not in the middle of the hormonal headquarters of the brain. At least if we were talking about the hippocampus, the highly epileptogenic brain structure, which is also highly affected by music and feelings, and one of the largest structures of the limbic system, it might have worked. But I suspect the effects of music on the hypothalamus must be weaker, as it is so busy with so many internal functions of our body."

"I disagree," said Jill, "since we found that music works so well for Jo's rage behavior, it must have a strong effect in the hypothalamus, the crossroad of human behaviors. Indeed, it has already been found that cortisol levels are decreased in the blood of patients undergoing anesthesia and listening to music."

"Good point; I will think about this remark, read it, and return to this interesting subject with you. Someone must have studied the effects of music on the rat's hypothalamus. I will look for those studies and get back to you. But now it is better we concentrate on this complex surgery."

After fixing the stereotactic device to Jo's head, they wheeled him to the RM to obtain the localization image that was to be related to the previous functional images obtained. This one would be the base for all the precise calculations to reach the targets, as the device would be visible.

***

After a complete analysis of all images, the surgery started. The location of the two small incisions in Jo's frontal region was identified. This allowed for minimal shaving of his head and a minute opening in his skull of 6 mm diameter. A few drops of blood were lost, but the hemostasis was easy. All vessels throughout the trajectory of the brain were visualized by the images and avoided until the target, permitting the safe conduction of Charles's 'porcupine fish' device. A special conducting probe was delivered to the desired site. They operated on the left side first to improve the most troubled hand, the right hand. The right side followed promptly; this was done smoothly and without difficulty. Once the devices were in place and adjusted inside the magnetic field, the monitors started to detect the effect of the electrical stimulation on Jo's motor function.

Dr. Howard, the neurologist, had already arrived for the detailed examination necessary to ascertain the proper device location. This was achieved through microelectrode recordings performed throughout the trajectory of the delivering probe, locating the hyperactive neurons in the target. Now, Dr. Howard would confirm if the stimulation induced by the device would indeed cause the desired effects and define the thresholds of stimulation that would lead to side effects. When broad stimulation was performed in the left PVP, inactivating all device spikes on the left, Dr. Howard immediately noticed that the muscles in his right arm and hand became tense. Also, Jo, who was already completely awake from the anesthesia, said that he had flashing lights in his vision.

Dr. Howard asked, "On the left, or right?"

"Both sides," Jo answered.

"OK, what can be done?" Dr. Howard said and looked at Jill.

Charles answered, "It's not a problem. I will turn off the lower spikes, and the flashing disappears. I can also increase the tension of his hand muscles if you want. We have it all under control. What do you want me to do?"

"I would like to see you stimulating only the superior ones first. Let's check if we control the scotomas' flashing lights in his visual fields. His responses are very reliable, so it will be the best way to confirm if your device is smart, like you say."

"Sure, I will show you." Charles activated his remote control and turned off the lower spikes, the ones close to the visual tracts, the most central ones in the PVP. Bingo, Jo confirmed the flashlights had disappeared.

The same trial was done in the right brain. Charles continued the test, activating spikes of the device in all directions, right, left, upper, down, and diagonally, while Dr. Howard and Jill examined the stimulation's effects on Jo's muscles, thoughts, vision, and vital signs. Jo was very cooperative. Sometimes, he said that his speech was difficult, and his hand or his face were tight; indeed, his motor capabilities were being completely controlled by the device at the will of the programmer. Charles became increasingly excited as his device was working perfectly.

"Amazing," said Jill, "we never saw such a fine directional stimulation as you are achieving, Charles. Apparently, your device is a success."

"Sure," said Dr. Howard, "I am satisfied with the examination. A lot of work will be done to program this device properly, but what I have seen until now is very encouraging. Congratulations, Charles."

"Thanks, Dr. Howard; it took the work of several graduate students throughout the years to achieve this completely wireless and intelligent device.

We can also record the activity of the PVP cells if you want to see that before we take him for the final MRI confirmation."

"Yes, by all means," said Dr. Hillary. "I believe that this is the most important development of your device, as we will use these recordings to program it, and as you already explained to me, smartly, this device will be turned on and off by the analysis of these recordings, and the need of specific function, correct?"

"Yes, I would like to test this capability before we take Jo to the MRI," said Charles. "Is it OK, Dr. Hillary?"

"Sure, what do you think, Jill?"

"Yes, I am just a bit worried about the time. It is already 5 pm, and we still have a two-hour wait for the MRI scan, but indeed, this test is a must."

"It will take less than half an hour," assured Charles.

Dr. Howard was ready to ask Jo to perform specific tasks while Charles was recording the field potentials and promptly analyzing them. Based on Jo's hands-demanded activity, he had previously programmed the device to turn it on and off. The keyboard was placed over Jo's chest so he could play it. His right pinky curled when he tried to play with the right hand at the beginning of La Campanella. He started playing again with a certain frustration, but at his and all present amazement, the playing of the right hand was smooth. The device was active, as confirmed by Charles. There was an ovation in the room. The ones with surgical gloves and the ones without gloves clapped, congratulating Jo.

Jo started crying emotionally and said, "Yes, I must practice playing La Campanella as Lang-Lang plays. I'm sorry I'm not playing it well."

"You will have your life to do so, Jo. You will have all our support, be assured," said Jill, also with tears in her eyes.

She forgot she wore a sterile gown and hugged Charles, thanking him. It was a beautiful moment because Charles also had tears in his eyes.

He hugged her tightly and said, "I have to thank you all for giving me the opportunity to try the device and help Jo. This is an exultation feeling that we don't have in the laboratory. I know it is a feeling you all have every time you help a patient, as Jill has described it to me so many times. It is, however, different from being here in the operating room and living in this moment. It is never to be forgotten and craves to be repeated countless times. Now I understand why Jill is glued to the hospital and the operating room. It is addicting to be able to help someone to this extent. Thanks, thanks to you all!"

"Dr. Wolf, please put Jo to sleep; it is time for him to rest. Now we go to the RM to check the device and see if we can move it by the magnetic forces, as Charles advertised to us," said Dr. Hillary.

"Do we need to move the device?" Dr. Howard asked anxiously.

"Not necessarily, as you confirmed with your examination that the position is perfect, but we need to know if it is possible; we may run into difficulties in the future. Charles planned for that; it is in the surgery protocol," said Jill.

Dr. Howard said, "OK, but I am living. I am not prepared for these crazy hours you impose on yourselves. Do not forget that I am a neurologist. I did not become a neurosurgeon just to avoid your craziness, Jill. Good luck," and left.

The placement of Jo in the MRI took a few minutes. The images obtained showed the perfect position of the 'porcupine fishes.' Charles rotated them slightly by manipulating the magnetic field, first on the right hemisphere, then on the left. He confirmed that they had returned to the precise place before the manipulation; if necessary, Charles sighed in relief, considering himself satisfied with the possibility of using this capability. He knew of the importance of this feature, as he had a device implanted in his hypothalamus himself, and he had some strange memories and sweating when his stimulation was turned high. His already ancient device, implanted eight years ago, was completely obsolete by today's standards. He couldn't even enter the high-power magnetic field of an MRI without damaging his device. Well, old technology that he and his father developed, which gave his life back. In his mind, another surgery to implant a modern device in his brain was out of cogitation.

Jill and the helping resident closed the two wounds in Jo's frontal region while Charles tested if he could charge the device at a distance. It was done by placing the inductor over Jo's forehead, under the surgical drapes. He was able to induce a charge on both sides at once. It would take Jo approximately one hour weekly to keep his device charged. A very easy and reasonable task, as it can be done while reading, watching TV, and even sleeping. He just must be quiet and serene for one hour per week.

***

Jo was transferred to the ICU and was already awake. He talked calmly and listened to 'La Campanella' with his earphones. It was becoming evident that Franz Liszt would be in his repertoire soon. Jill went to inform Mrs. Jin of the surgery's success. She was thrilled to give her the details. She described every step Jo had been through, his cooperation at every moment, his improvement during the stimulation, and his precise information about its effects. She was also very proud to relate that the devices were perfectly positioned, as checked by the MRI performed at the end of the procedure. She also stressed that they could correct the position if it became necessary. She described the device charging procedure when Dr. Hillary arrived in the patient's family information room close to the ICU. He had certified that Jo was well, being monitored and awake. Dr. Wolf had told the ICU staff about the ins and outs of the liquids and medications used during the procedure. They were ready to pick up the torch from the anesthetist and the neurosurgeons to continue with Jo's care in the step-down unit.

"Congratulations to Jo and the whole team, Mrs. Jin. The surgery was a complete success. Jill probably gave you all the good news already; it was marvelous. I didn't know that Jo liked Franz Liszt. La Campanella helped with the anesthesia induction and throughout the examination period when he was awake. I believe it will be his favorite piece in his concerts in the future," said Dr. Hillary.

"Yes, Jo always listens to the series recorded for Sony called Lang-Lang, Liszt my Piano Hero with the Vienna Philharmonic by Valery Gergiev, the controversial Russian conductor. He loves Lang-Lang's happy personality, as well as his life story. I read it to him when he was six years old. Lang-Lang inspired Jo throughout his studies. He is a hero for the youth in China. He achieved the dream that all young Chinese musicians have: to become famous and travel worldwide to see life in the West. Jo has always dreamed of this because of the stories I have read about famous and successful Chinese musicians such as Lang-Lang and Yo-Yo Ma. I always thought that I should tell him stories that encouraged his ambition. It worked, but Mr. Jin pressed Jo too hard, so my poor son didn't have a childhood. My husband was too unstable himself to provide stability for Jo. He couldn't transmit stability to any of us. I hope I can offer him peace of mind to develop his talent from now on. I am anxious to see his recovery."

As expected from a young boy, Jo breezed through his one-day ICU period, went to the ward, and again breezed through there as well. After the type of music that calmed him down was identified, his management became easier. Since the surgery, he hadn't once needed sedation. The physiotherapists and music therapists came every day to cheer him up. Jill planned to keep him in the hospital for five days, then discharge him to return 14 days later to program the device. It was left off during this period of recovery in the hospital. Jill would recommend that he did not insist on playing piano too much. However, after five days without stimulation, his right fingers did start to curl again. Mrs. Jin called Jill, sounding disappointed.

"Dr. Morales, I am worried. Jo has been listening to Franz Liszt all the time, but I am noticing that he is becoming agitated and impatient anyway. Do you think he needs medication to calm down? Will you really send him home today?"

"No, I hope he will not need medication for his dystonia. He is without any medication for his brain at this point. He is taking only the antibiotics I prescribed. Now is the time to turn on his device with very low energy. Apparently, he needs a little bit of stimulation. We will see if we can send him home soon. I want to observe him here for two days with low stimulation before letting him go. Did you notice what agitated him and what calmed him down?"

"Oh yes, for example, Hungarian Rhapsody No. 2 in C-Sharp agitates him, while La Campanella, Romance, Libestraum (Dream of Love), Consolation calms him down very much. I know how to manage him with music, but he needs to manage himself."

"OK, I will call Charles and schedule a time for us to come here this afternoon and turn his devices on. I know you are anxious for us to do it so you can go home. Please be patient; we may need some adjustments. His brain is still a bit swollen because of the manipulation of the brain tissues to implant the 'porcupine fish.' It is normal for his brain to experience instability during this acute stressful period."

"'Porcupine fish' what is this?" Mrs. Jin asked sounding doubtful.

"Oh, it is the name Charles gave to the device because it looks like a porcupine fish in its shape and spikes. Have you seen a porcupine fish?"

"Yes, it is that small white fish with a thin tail and a large head, with the whole body full of spikes."

"Yes, each of the spikes is a stimulating contact, especially the spike located at the end of the fish pointed to the back, to the most posterior part of a structure called the pallidum, in the PVP. This structure, almost in the center of Jo's brain, is part of a group of cell clusters called basal ganglia, also known as the modulatory computer of the brain. For example, if we stimulate the tail of the device, we know we will cause contractions in Jo's face. Each of the spikes is directed to a portion of the posterior ventral pallidum (PVP) to modulate the brain's central computer to make his hand work. We can also take care of the agitation if needed. We can stimulate the most anterior spikes of both devices, on the right and left. That way, we can modulate his behavior and a cognitive portion of his pallidum, where we have cells related to the frontal portions of his brain, responsible for anxiety, depression, self-control, judgment, and mental equilibrium. As you can see, this device gives us an immense opportunity to help Jo."

"Thanks, Dr. Morales. You have such a calming effect on him and me. Jo is lucky to have you as a doctor and friend. Thanks for all your efforts."

***

Jill and Charles arrived in Jo's room at 4 pm to program the device to control the initial contractions in his hand. He sat calmly in a comfortable chair, listening to music with his earphones. When he saw Jill and Charles, he smiled. Apparently, he had no bad memories of the piano competition with respect to Randy's parents. Music had influenced his memory for the better. Charles didn't know him well, as his closest contact with Jo had been in the operating room. He had seen him playing Beethoven's Concert Number 4 and loved his performance. But Charles had not known how he would react to seeing him. The forthright smile touched him, although he knew that Jill's presence could cause Jo to be happy to see them arriving to help him.

It became apparent that music therapy had done a world of good, as he was calm and cooperative. It had not, however, been able to control Jo's motor system. There was no medication that could help him without a systemic effect on his body and brain[34]. One measure that could possibly help was an injection

---

[34] Devlin, K., Alshaikh, J. T., & Pantelyat, A. (2019) 'Music Therapy and Music-Based Interventions for Movement Disorders,' *Current Neurology and Neuroscience Reports*, **19**(11). doi:10.1007/s11910-019-1005-0

of botulin into specific muscles of his right hand. Conversely, this would decrease his right hand's dexterity, and he needed the muscles to function perfectly to play the piano well.

Jill was convinced that working on the underlying cause of the disease would be better than any kind of palliative therapy, such as damping his muscle function with paralyzers or suppressing his brain with drugs. She believed music influences the brain, as she studied how it reaches its multiple sites and pathways. She had found several publications disclosing how pathways in the brain were enhanced by specific tunes and rhythms. However, they were more speculations than scientific evidence. Functional imaging and tractography were starting to demonstrate the power of music to promote brain plasticity in patients with brain injury[35].

Jill knew how much plasticity music could induce, especially in a young brain like Jo's. Charles had developed the solution she had been dreaming of[36]. She and Charles started programming the stimulation to improve Jo's right hand. After trying the spherical electrical distribution, having all the spikes on and reaching all directions in the PVP without satisfactory control of Jo's dystonic hand, they decided to target the neuronal cluster responsible for controlling the medial fingers. They were in the upper lateral quadrant of the PVP, as had already been demonstrated by a German anatomist in the 1960s. The homunculus of function in the brain, imitating Penfield's brain mapping[37], was upside-down[38], justifying their trial. High-frequency stimulation in the region promoted complete control of his right-hand dystonic movements, including the three stubborn smallest fingers. Their study of this right-hand control suggested that stimulation of the left hand, albeit at a lower intensity, should also help Jo's piano skills. They turned the device on the right side to a

---

[35] Barnes, M., Good, D. (Eds.), 2013 *Handbook of Clinical Neurology. In: Neurological Rehabilitation*, vol. 110. Elsevier, London.

[36] Alves-Pinto, A., Turova, V., Blumenstein, T., Thienel, A., Wohlschläger, A., & Lampe, R. (2015) 'fMRI assessment of neuroplasticity in youths with neurodevelopmental-associated motor disorders after piano training,' *European Journal of Paediatric Neurology*, **19**(1), 15-28. doi:10.1016/j.ejpn.2014.09.002

[37] Penfield W, Boldrey E. (1937) 'Somatic motor and sensory representation in the cerebral cortex of man as studied by electrical stimulation,' *Brain*, 60(IV): 389-443.

[38] Hassler, R. (1982) *Architectonic Organization of the Thalamic Nuclei*. In Georges Schaltenbrand and A. Earl Walker. Stereotaxy of the Human Brain, Thieme; New York. pg. 161.

much lower strength but with the same frequency and field of stimulation, encompassing the same cluster of neurons it had encompassed on the left cerebral hemisphere. By the time they finished their work with Jo's brain, it was already 10 pm; they had spent six hours probing the wireless devices until they found the perfect point for stimulation.

Charles turned on the device's recording mode. The computer it was linked to in the room would transmit Jo's brain field potentials to his laboratory over the next 24 hours. Charles wanted to analyze Jo's need for stimulation during these 24 hours. This baseline data was essential for the long-term planning of Jo's therapy so they could teach Jo and Mrs. Jin how to control the devices.

Mrs. Jin followed them to the ward's corridor and hugged them, crying and saying, "I don't know how I ever will pay you for what you have done for my son. I don't have an expression like your 'God Bless You' in Chinese, but I wish you all happiness in this world, health, and success for Randy."

"We are not doing more than we would do for any of our patients; it is our work. You cannot imagine how happy we are to see Jo better, ready to pursue his career. Count on us to facilitate his studies at Julliard. We will send Randy, too, as he desires to go. We promise you that we will find a way to send them together. Let's finalize Jo's rehabilitation and plan for their time in New York."

Chapter 29
Music Power and Pleasure

*Music has real health benefits. It boosts dopamine,
lowers cortisol, and it makes us feel great.
Your brain is better on music.*
Alex Doman

Jill continued studying the effects of music on neuronal networks. She wanted to observe Jo's recovery in depth and restore his musical career. Their next task was to publish the results of the therapy they developed for dystonia, as the disease still didn't have a definitive treatment. They discovered a viable surgical prosthetic solution: an inconspicuous wireless computer implant for the center of the brain capable of modulating it. The reality was that the musician's dystonia still didn't have a complete pathophysiologic explanation.

It was believed that musicians who had a dystonic person in the family had a genetic predisposition to acquire a musician's dystonia. Approximately 200 genes have been related to the various forms of dystonia. It was also known that the basal ganglia circuitry, responsible for the modulation of fine movements and mental nuances, is generally dysfunctional in dystonic patients.

Victims of a traumatic lesion, vascular lesion, drug toxicity, or a hypoxic event like Jo's can develop either generalized or focal dystonia[39]. When there is a triggering factor, as in Jo's case, through overuse of the fingers, the disease appears in that location, probably due to a problem with those neurons in the network responsible for the repetitive fingering movements. Jo did not have

---

[39] Preibisch C, Berg D, Hofmann E, Solymosi L, Naumann M. (2001) 'Cerebral activation patterns in patients with writer's cramp: a functional magnetic resonance imaging study,' *J Neurol.*, 248:10–7.

classical musician's dystonia but suffered a consequence of generalized hypoxia, which had made the basal ganglia deficient. Charles's device was an implant and not a direct cure for the disease, although it is becoming scientifically proven that brain stimulation generates plasticity, which, over the years, leads to a healthy brain. In other words, neurons are recruited to perform the demanded function. Music can also provoke this demand in the neural networks, although it is not as robust as direct deep brain stimulation.

In fact, Jill was observing the sum of two modulation techniques to improve Jo's dystonia. The first was the pallidum stimulation, specifically in the PVP hand receptive field and motor areas of this site. She had initially accomplished this with LowFU, which had got him out of the dystonic crisis. This was followed by the bilateral surgical installation of the implants. The second approach was Jill's insistence on influencing the brain nodal network with music neuromodulation. This effect was far broader than the electrical stimulation, affecting the more primitive portions of the brain with the rhythm and the more developed brain through the nuances of tunes. It seemed a mild way to affect all the sensory, motor, and circuits related to mental well-being. She hypothesized that music affected dystonia through sensory inputs, sound vibration, and feelings generated by the music, which brought memories and effects in the pleasure circuitry of the brain, namely dopamine-dependent neurotransmission.

"When she talked to Dr. Hillary about this theory," he said. "It is quite possible that music can control several types of dystonia with its broad effect on the brain. I had a patient with a terrible generalized dystonia who was completely normal when she was dancing. A famous physiotherapist in Toronto, Canada, helps patients through music and dance therapy. Jo's love for music must be helping him. I believe you are on the right track, Jill."

"Yes, I have been studying the brain pleasure pathway as the surrogate for dystonia control," she said. "The ventral tegmental area (VTA) in the brainstem has connectivity with the nucleus accumbens (NC). This frontal lobe pleasure bundle, or tract, anatomically and scientifically known as the 'Foreway Bundle,' is an addictive dopamine-dependent pathway connecting the VTA and the NC. It is triggered by pleasure feelings caused by recreational drugs, gambling, and other addictive elements. Music can activate this circuit. I am afraid that these complex pathways through Jo's brain, now affected by a man-made computer, might confuse his normal behavior, judgment, and drive to study."

"I don't think so. I'd expect that the stimulation being applied to his pallidum will strengthen the circuitry responsible for Jo's movements, a phenomenon already described in the literature, although it is yet to be proven."

"I understand your concern, though. This 'Foreway Bundle' is a confusing pathway for any doctor dealing with addicts. The human addiction to pleasure is difficult to curb, as the addict persists in wanting to feel that bliss, especially when it is the only thing they have to live for, the pleasure of the dopamine rush. Patients who went through traumatic experiences that caused PTSD often end up reliant on this 'Foreway Bundle' pathway to forget their suffering. Therefore, science needs to find a surgical solution to these patients' predicament, as their number is increasing."

Jill had been fascinated by the control of addiction since her studies as a graduate student with alcoholic primates. She wondered if Charles's 'porcupine fish' could be activated in the strategic brain region when the patient first started craving their addiction.

"We are dealing with a neurotransmitter and a hormone," continued Dr. Hillary. "Dopamine is involved in important features of human lives, such as motor function, memory, behavior and cognition, attention, sleep, arousal, mood, learning, lactation, motivation, and pleasurable reward. Its discovery was worth a Nobel Prize[40]. It probably has a key role in dystonia. There exists a Dopamine Responsive Dystonia (DRD), in which patients improve when they take L-Dopa, the same medication taken by Parkinson's disease patients to improve their motor symptoms. It's worth bearing in mind that dystonia symptoms go beyond the visible and embarrassing muscle deformation and contractions patients suffer."

"Yes, Dr. Hillary, I have observed that patients with dystonia have a peculiar psychological make-up. It places them in a unique mental state when compared to that of normal people. This abnormality worries me in relation to Jo, as he had every reason to develop a psychiatric disturbance."

---

[40] Iversen SD, Iversen LL (May 2006) 'Dopamine: 50 years in perspective,' *Trends Neurosci*, **30**(5):188-93. doi: 10.1016/j.tins.2007.03.002. Epub 2007 Mar 26. PMID: 17368565.

"Yes, Jill, as besides the dystonia, he comes from a family with a history of psychiatric diseases and suicide. We must carefully observe his behavior in the next few months until he can be left alone. As long as he is with his mom, I don't believe it will be a problem, as he is so young. He must get back to his piano as soon as possible, taking advantage of the power of music to influence his brain."

Chapter 30
Music Healing

Music can heal the wounds which medicine cannot touch.
Debasish Mridha

Jill sent Jo home. He was completely out of danger with respect to his respiration, so he no longer needed to stay in the hospital. His dystonia was completely controlled without medication. The devices implanted in his pallidum were turned on when triggered by the signals that he would move and use his muscles. This was completely independent of Jo's volition, triggered by brainwaves generated by the thought of performing movements. It was enough to keep his dystonia under control in daily life. She also suggested that Jo restart his piano lessons, which she believed would be good physiotherapy for him and boost his and Mrs. Jin's mental status. Jill saw Jo every week to support him and his mother psychologically and check that his dystonia was not returning. What she was noticing, however, was that she had to progressively increase the electrical pulses delivered by the devices to keep his dystonic movements in check. Fortunately, the device was rechargeable wirelessly by induction; therefore, energy would not be a problem in keeping Jo's dystonia away.

The main problem was his right hand. His littlest three fingers would curl when a task was challenging, such as playing the piano. It was immensely frustrating for Jo. Especially when he was trying to play Liszt's Grand Galop Chromatique in E-Flat Major. Although the music was very cheerful, he would stop when the demand increased on his right hand. He ended up crying at the piece's most exciting passages. Mrs. Jin didn't know what to do. She became distraught along with him at those moments and felt hopeless. She was so worried and despondent that she asked Jill if it would be necessary to prescribe a medication to help the brain devices, which were active at those moments.

Jill could see from the recordings that the energetic drain in each device was incredible, especially the one implanted in the left side of his brain, controlling the right hand.

However, she didn't want to prescribe Jo medication for this. Why sedate his whole brain to treat a very local symptom? She also didn't want to inject botulin toxin into his hand muscles, as it would decrease his fingers' ability, compromising his playing and probably leading to depression and despair. So, she insisted on increasing the stimulation and recommended Jo practice with the right hand more and more. She asked Dr. Hillary if he agreed with this approach; she was at a loss. She was not seeing any improvement in his fingers' curling, even when the electric current through his pallidum was very high.

"Why don't you ask the Maestro João? He lived through this anguish for years; nobody knows more practical measures for dystonia than him. He was a very successful concert pianist for years, dealing with identical dystonic episodes, curling of the same fingers as Jo."

Jill told them about Dr. Hillary's suggestion the next time Jo and Mrs. Jin came to regulate the devices. Maestro João lived in São Paulo, leading a very busy life; while he was more than 80 years old, he had a very packed touring schedule with presentations every week and charitable activities for children's schools and slums throughout the country. His music teaching kept children on the right track, away from the streets. Besides, he had his own orchestra. Although busy, he always had time for needy children; Jill hoped he would lend some time to help Jo.

Jill contacted Maestro João asking for help. He was very receptive; so receptive that he invited Jo to spend time with him in Brazil so he could teach Jo tricks to improve his right hand. He would spend his summer vacation in Brazil dedicated to piano lessons. Jill promptly took advantage of the invitation and included Randy as company for Jo. They were now very close friends; Randy was a great emotional support for Jo. They became real buddies; Jill very much stimulated their friendship. It would be good for Randy, as she felt dedicating himself to Jo's improvement was useful. Randy was very touched by all that happened to Jo after the day he won the piano competition for studies at the Julliard School.

Jill also felt bad about the occurrence, and beyond the medical interest in helping Jo with his dystonia, she also had a scientific interest and a good education for Randy. She stimulated his solidarity with his friend, and knowing

Randy, she knew he would be a good influence on Jo. It was settled that Randy and Jo, supervised by Mrs. Jin, would be in Brazil during their summer vacation. Jill arranged an apartment with Airbnb. She was planning to accompany them to São Paulo, ensure that they were close to where they would be studying, and in a city's safe location.

Chapter 31
Motor and Sensory

When music hits you, you dance.
Lailah Gifty Akita

Jill was fascinated by how the finger curling was overriding the deep brain stimulation she had pinned her hopes on. After that complex surgery, the implant had effectively started controlling his dystonic crises. He no longer needed the daily HiFU stimulation. It was a worthwhile and liberating operation. She had been able to abate a 'dystonic storm,' all the involuntary contractions induced by Jo's brain, which were causing severe pain. From the intense spasms he had suffered at the peak of the crisis, she had concluded it was an abnormality in the brain's motor area, anterior to the central sulcus, which represented the frontier between the sensory and the motor cerebral areas. This motor and anterior part of the brain, largely responsible for his volition, would trigger the fine movements necessary to play an instrument, whether a keyboard, strings, or wind. This anterior portion of the brain also brought emotion to his playing. The connection of the limbic system with motor function is modulated by the computation of motor movements that control the vehemence or the mildness of his finger strokes.

Jill was really at a loss to explain why her treatment was now failing. She had the implant precisely located in the PVP, the motor area of the pallidum. The scans she had obtained in the post-operative period showed the perfect localization of the devices and their spikes. She had tried all possible combinations, but Jo could not play the difficult pieces with his right hand. She dug into the literature, trying to find a solution.

The basic physiology of the movement, muscle tone, contraction, and modulation had been studied in detail by a Swedish neurosurgeon, Dr. Lars

Leksell[41]. He described the muscle spindles which give information to the spinal cord and the brain. His studies were key to understanding why some muscles relax and others contract in harmony, allowing our fine movements. Agonists and antagonists balance to give us the amazing finesse of movement, permitting modulation of the information going to the fingers' muscles when activating the keyboard, the string instrument, or the vocal cords when playing the wind instrument or singing. It is a very complex interaction of sensory and motor functions. This intrinsic and amazing integration is beyond the capability of any gadget devised by humans.

She gathered another intriguing finding from the scientific literature. Enrico Caruso, the famous opera singer who lived at the beginning of the last century, had facial surgery during his career. His voice became more moderate as a result. This fact was studied by a French scientist, Dr. Tomatis[42]. Caruso had two periods of singing, from 1896 to 1902 and from 1903 to 1921, when he died. During the first period, his voice was considered excellent until he had his face surgery, which presumably damaged one of his Eustachian trumps, the connection of his inner ear with the pharynx. He lost part of his sound perception, mostly the decibels that could be perceived by his cochlea. (This organ inside our ear transforms the sound waves of diverse frequencies into electrical impulses.) These travel through sensory pathways toward the sound interpretation part of our cortex. This is located in the temporal lobe, where we interpret speech and music inputs.

Dr. Tomatis further discovered that one can sing only in the frequencies one can hear. Therefore, Caruso could not sing at very low frequencies below 2000 Hz. He could, however, sing at a slightly higher frequency than most of the singers; he could reach 8000 Hz, while singers usually go to 7000 Hz. These descriptions from Dr. Tomatis, taken together with Dr. Leksell's studies, led Jill to conclude that, possibly, Jo was not receiving the proper information from the spindles of his right medial fingers. So, she had to study the outputs from Jo's fingers. This was probably the key to the puzzle of why her stimulation was not proving as efficient as she had expected.

---

[41] Lars Leksell, ed. (2022) *Brain Fragments: Daily Notes and Reminiscences*. Dan Leksell, trans. Ekerlids Forlag, ISBN: 978-91-86,323-53-7.

[42] Doige Norman, M.D. (2007) *The Brain that Changes Itself. Stories of Personal Triumph from the Frontiers of Brain*, Pinguin.

She realized that Jo's fingers were indeed obeying the instructions of his intellect. In other words, the impulses from his brain going to his fingers were correct; what was incorrect was the integration of this information with the necessary information returning to his brain from his fingers. The agonists, in other words, the muscles responsible for the contraction, were being informed and received the information. The antagonists, the muscles responsible for relaxing harmonically with the ones that contract, were not relaxing. The brain was not informed of the need for the antagonist's relaxation. So, there was a lack of communication between agonists and antagonists, but why? She went to Charles' laboratory to explore the problem of the incoming impulses about Jo's muscles' position. The integration of these two items needed to be precisely coordinated to create the smooth movement she was hoping for from Jo's three right-hand middle fingers **(Figure 5)**.

"Charles, do you know if your device receives information from Jo's muscles?"

"No," answered Charles. "This is not programmed in the device's software. We programmed it to send impulses based on the patient's volition, not his fingers failing to move properly. It's like the device you implanted in my brain; it is turned on when I have the urge to become angry. It is the same algorithm. Jo's device emits signals when he decides to use his fingers."

"Well, Charles, unfortunately, the harmony of the human body is way more complex than a single direction of information. There is a harmonic integration between sensory and motor information, which we must contemplate. It is the connection of the sensory cortex, which is not integrated with his brain's anterior part. It is in the anterior portion, the frontal lobe, where the motor, cognitive, and sentimental part of the brain lies. You will have to think about how to solve this information mismatch. This harmonic integration is key for our smooth, purposeful, and emotional movements. After all, Jo is an artist. Based on all his perceptions, his sensibility must be considered so that he can play piano flawlessly and sentimentally. Do you think you can manage this without the necessity of another surgery on his brain?"

"I need time to think about this; we thought we had to take care of the motor aberrant output, and we blocked them, so much so that he is back home and starting to play the piano. Now, you tell me I need input from his sentiments and muscles to make him a virtuoso. This is challenging. You really are demanding the best of my abilities. I hope I can fulfill your expectations."

He looked at her thoughtfully. "It is easy to love you, but it is not easy to work with you. Your thoughts are too complicated."

"My thoughts are not complicated," said Jill, "but the brain is too complex. Since I implanted the devices in your hypothalamus and made you smarter, I expect you to follow my brain. You stopped using your muscles as a famous soccer player and became a scientist good enough to win the Nobel Prize. Let's solve this puzzle."

"If one day I win a Nobel Prize, it must be given to both of us; this device you placed in my hypothalamus really linked our brains together in a very harmonic way, almost like the harmony we see among violins and piano in an orchestra. As the device is roughly oval-shaped, I will use the anterior spikes to gather the cognitive sentimental and the middle for motor outputs, while the posterior spikes will receive information from the posterior portion of the brain, where the sensory information is received. Jo needs all these senses perfectly integrated to play piano; we must figure out how to integrate it into our device. If we solve this puzzle and make a virtuoso of Jo, I believe we deserve the Nobel! I accept the challenge."

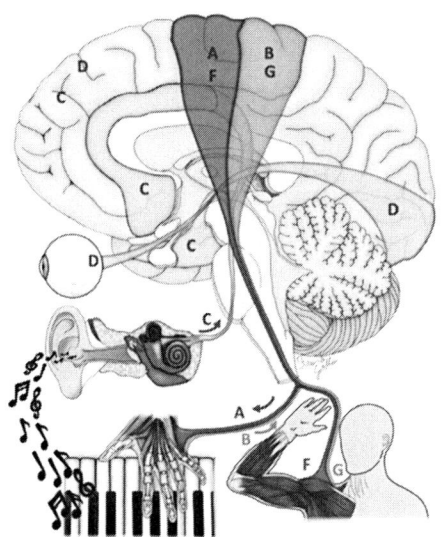

Figure 5: *Simplified integration of motor and sensory functions*
*Simplified integration of motor **(A)** and sensory **(B)** functions to control the fingers' movement. Fine motor control is based on hearing **(C)** and sensory **(B)** information of the hand position in the piano. This information is used by several brain centers occupying a very complex network. This network integrates hearing (**blue**), touch*

*and proprioception **(brown), and** vision **(yellow)** to control the fingering with strength (motor) and feelings, the musician's sensibility. Notice the vision (yellow) in the visual cortex **(D)**. This integration generates the delicate fingers' automatic commands, elaborated in the basal ganglia **(not shown here; see Figure 12)**.*

*The limbic system modulates the inputs to control the muscles that command the fingers, allowing for artistic interpretation. Major muscle groups, as represented by the pathway from the supplemental motor, motor, and sensory areas to the deltoid **(F and G)**, are easier to modulate using electronic human-made devices than the fine fingering muscles activated to play the piano as a virtuoso **(A)**. Although represented by the pathway coming from the same supplemental motor and direct motor cortical region **(A and F)**, the fine movements take more cortical space. The representation of these outputs from the brain is not proportional to their importance in the figure.*

*The inputs to the brain coming from the muscles and joints are necessary for the integration of delicate movements **(B and G)**. The true electric-chemical modulation integrating the incoming (afferent) and outgoing (efferent) information occurs in the basal ganglia, represented in **Figure 12**.*

Chapter 32
Boys Success

No one was near to confuse me,
so, I was forced to become original.
Joseph Haydn

Both mothers and boys arrived in São Paulo to work with Maestro João. They left the Guarulhos International Airport at 9 am. The size of the city was overwhelming to them. The language and the costumes were totally foreign to Dr. Morales and Mrs. Jin. They would need a guide to organize the boys' stay to make it productive. They arrived at the hotel and stayed until they took the Airbnb. Hotels are always the easiest way to orient one to an unknown city. Once at the hotel, they promptly called the Maestro. The sweet voice speaking clear English who answered the phone with a friendly welcome and promised to help them was the Maestro João's wife, Carmen.

"Don't worry," she said. "I will send our driver to bring you here tomorrow for lunch. You will meet our secretary, Vilma; she will be your guide in the city. Then, we will organize your stay in the Airbnb. I was there checking it out. It is a very nice three-bedroom apartment. As you requested, it has a large living room and a piano."

"Mrs. Martins, thank you very much for checking it out for us. I believe we will need your help; we are amazed at the size of this city. The traffic from the airport to the hotel was overwhelming. It was a 14-hour flight, so we were very tired but will be better tomorrow. Then we can organize the boys' stay in São Paulo. They will be ready to meet Maestro João the day after tomorrow."

"No stress," said Carmen. "João has a concert tonight, and tomorrow, he is busy with a school we support. In the meantime, take the time to get acquainted with the city. Although São Paulo is an immense city, has a modular organization; within four blocks, you have all your basic needs in terms of commerce. You will enjoy life here, it can be easy and practical, as long as you don't have to travel long distances. Mrs. Jin, we have a large Chinatown if you miss China."

"The problem is the language. Neither I nor Mrs. Jin understand Portuguese. Do you think it will be a problem?" Jill asked.

"Yes, it will. In the streets, only a few young people will be able to help you if you don't understand the language. But don't worry; Vilma will help you until Mrs. Jin becomes acquainted with the surroundings. Vilma can also go to Chinatown if she needs some special Chinese supplies," said Carmen.

***

As they were jetlagged because of the five-hour time zone gap between São Paulo and Los Angeles, they went to bed at 3 pm and woke up late the next day. Jill couldn't find Randy in bed, so she got all worked up and called Mrs. Jin, who woke her up. When she asked if Randy was there with Jo, Mrs. Jin said they were not there. The two left their rooms feeling desperate; where would those boys go in this crazy city without knowing the language? The only language they had in common with these people was the language of music.

They ran to the hotel lobby, where there was a crowd surrounding a piano. The boys were playing, enjoying themselves, and being acclaimed. They took turns showing off their incredible skills. The mothers smiled and joined the crowd. Jo and Randy began playing Chopin's Prelude in D major Molto Allegro. Randy played the right hand and Jo synchronized played the left hand of the piece, while leaving the other two hands resting on the bench, thus preventing the crowd from noticing that Jo's right hand was missing. They continued happily alternating some Preludes and started playing Schubert's Fantasy in F Minor for four hands[43]. The mothers were amazed and proud, they didn't know their sons could play the Preludes so well. They joined the crowd in the ovation.

"I didn't know you could play Schubert's Fantasia," Jill said.

Mrs. Jin confessed that when Randy went to play with Jo at her home, she felt very confident that she could leave them alone in the apartment and take advantage of the opportunity to go shopping. Sometimes, they played piano together when she arrived, but she didn't know they were studying all these

---

[43] https://www.youtube.com/watch?v=UyjzqPPXDcw

pieces to play together. They studied Mozart's Four Hands Piano Sonata in C Major K521[44] and some pieces by Brahms. Their teacher at Colburn probably told them to do so. Sometimes Jim, Mr. Humboldt's son, who played the violin, would come to our apartment, and the three played together. They spent hours filling our home with the most beautiful music. She just didn't know that Randy could give rest to Jo's hands by alternating Preludes with him.

"Randy and Jo, it was very nice of you to alternate the Preludes," said Jill.

"Nobody told us to study the Preludes, but I knew Jo liked them. They calmed him down. I suggested that we play it together when we were at home, said Randy happily."

"Yes, I love Chopin's Preludes. A few of them are very difficult for the right hand. So, Randy and I alternated playing most difficult for me. It's fun to play together. We will show the Maestro some Preludes demonstrating the synchronization of our brains, as well as asking for advice on how to improve my fingers, of course," said Jo.

***

The meeting with the Maestro João was a revelation for the boys. They met him during the rehearsal of the Bachianas Orchestra, as the Maestro was conducting the Brazilian Bachiana Number 5, composed by Villa-Lobos. The soprano singing, Leticia Santos, a beautiful teenage girl with dark skin, had the purest voice they ever heard. Immediately, Maestro João stopped the rehearsal and introduced Jo to the orchestra. All were receptive and encouraged him to play the piano then so they could get acquainted with the famous spiky-black-hair boy's talent. They greeted Randy, who was already their colleague from the Concert at the Disney Hall, to raise funds for Jo's treatment. Maestro had announced to them that he expected all orchestra members' support to overcome the limitations dystonia was imposing on him.

The boys saw two Steinway Grand Pianos waiting for them side by side on the stage. They were invited to play four Preludes of the Well-Tempered Clavier by Bach and four preludes by Chopin, in three of which one played the right hand and the other the left hand so that the orchestra could listen to them and get to know boys' talent, in addition of the synchronization of the right hand and left hand between them. The orchestra noticed that they were in front

---

[44] https://www.youtube.com/watch?v=Pmofd2euA-8

of two child prodigies. They almost repeated the same presentation they had done in the Hotel Lobby.

Surprisingly, the whole orchestra didn't notice any of Jo's fingering failure. The boys completed the 24 preludes seamlessly. Only Maestro João noticed Jo's discreet difficulty with the right hand's three middle fingers. Although it was a fine presentation, Maestro knew they had a long way to go to give Jo's security to play for audiences without Randy providing him with the alternate rest. They applauded the boys as though they were old fellow orchestra members. Maestro João had already prepared his staff for the work they had to do to enhance Jo's self-esteem.

Then, the boys sat in the audience, and the soprano continued her rehearsal with the orchestra. Randy enjoyed the singing, but Jo was completely taken by the emotion of the aria. As the soprano sang the Bachiana n. 5, his eyes filled with tears. It was the first time he heard that heavenly sound. Unfortunately, until the tragedy, he had played, driven by discipline, to develop a perfect technique. For his stern teachers, the technique was all that counted, not the enjoyment of the music and its true sentimental meaning.

Thanks to this, he had become almost a robot. He was capable of performing music but regrettably not allowed to feel the pleasure of it. Old-school Chinese music teaching was done by a master who provided the opportunity for the student to learn his expertise by imitation. The student would observe the master playing and then try to imitate his performance rather than learning through solitary discipline.

Perfection demanded from the performer of Western composition is acquired by mastering the piece, and playing becomes second nature. It is true that music requires impeccable playing, as a single misplaced note destroys a performance. However, feeling the music and loving it makes the artist dedicate hours and hours to achieving perfection. Humans thrive when they give their best, noticing the collaboration of all, with recognition and gratitude for their efforts and talents.

The artist dedicates so much time to playing with a perfect technique because of the zenith one reaches with music interpretation. It is the height one reaches when jogging or even with drugs. It is a rush of endorphins. The feeling that music provides explains the hardship the artist endures through their impeccable discipline. In fact, the technique must be secondary, practically automatic, as it belongs to the human primitive brain, the automatic brain, what the neurologists call the extrapyramidal nervous system. As a musician perfects the technique, the modern brain, which elevated the primitive human to homo sapiens, with enlarged frontal lobes and extensive connections to the limbic system, takes over. The connections bringing external inputs into these most developed parts of the brain overwhelm the musician in his interpretation of the feelings the melody provides. The sublimation of the technique is married to the perception of the beauty and the essence of human existence brought by the power of music over the brain, which is combined to excite the virtuoso in his performance.

The boys could see such feelings personified in that young girl when she sang the Bachiana Number 5. The Maestro could make that young soprano an instrument of his orchestra. Leticia was not only an instrument producing a heavenly sound; she also inspired inexplicable feelings. The boys were astonished by the art of such quality being presented in this simple and happy environment introduced by that affable Maestro.

When the aria finished, Maestro João asked, "What do you think about this music? Do you know who composed it?"

"No," answered Randy.

"I never heard anything so beautiful," remarked Jo, still with tears in his eyes.

"It was composed by Heitor Villa-Lobos, a Brazilian composer who lived at the beginning of the last century. He translated the beauty of this country, the birds, the forests, and the nostalgia of those times to music. His rhythm is unique, combining Bach's structure with Brazilian street music. It is unique music coming from Brazilian folk songs, as is the case with many classic compositions. For example, the romantic composer Franz Liszt (1811–1886) found inspiration in Hungarian folk songs. Villa-Lobos reached more recognition worldwide, in Europe and the USA than in Brazil during those years. This goes with the saying that *it is easier to be recognized by foreigners than by your countrymen.*

"The aria, Bachiana Number 5, was sung by the most famous sopranos of the last century, like Kathleen Battles, Maria Callas, and others. Villa-Lobos became known as the composer who brought Brazilian music to the world, mostly because he was able to assimilate popular Brazilian folklore with European classical music. Maria Callas sang this aria perfectly, amazingly supported by a single accompanying guitar and voice making divine music.

However, most sopranos perform the Bachiana Number 5 supported by eight violoncellos, as suggested by Villa-Lobos. The person who really spread the true meaning of Villa-Lobos's compositions throughout the world was the Brazilian opera singer Balduína de Oliveira Sayão, known as Bidu Sayão, who was able to take the soul of Brazilian music to the major theaters in Europe and the United States, from La Scala in Milan to the Met in New York.

"I am training Leticia to sing this aria, supported by eight violoncellos from our orchestra; she is one of the most talented young artists we have found in our travels throughout our country. She is from Manaus, in the middle of the Amazon Forest. This search for artists is part of a program supported by the Bachianas Foundation. It seeks to bring music to the children of the poorest populations throughout Brazil. I will connect you with our young musicians coming from this effort during your vacation here. We will allow you to see this country's major cities.

"Manaus is known for its beautiful opera house, which was built during the Brazilian rubber boom at the beginning of the last century. Rubber trees grew naturally in the Amazon Forest, where the rubber was first collected for industrialization. It became a major Brazilian export during the first half of the last century. It brought wealth to the construction of the opera house in Manaus. This was until English explorers took the rubber tree to Malaysia, where the equatorial climate resembles the Amazon. They organized rubber tree plantations that permitted production on a large scale, overcoming the 'Seringueiros' slower amateurish production. Manaus is now over two million inhabitants harbor city at the junction of two rivers, the Amazon and the Negro, where the color and temperature of the waters coming from the two rivers famously do not mix for miles, a true marvel of natural beauty.

"Boys, I am sure you will quickly pick up the language and learn Brazilian music in depth, as music is a language you already understand. It is an authentic melting pot. The music will allow you to gather the real flavor of this country, which is completely different from that of the USA, Europe, and China. Our classical music reflects a mix of European, Latin Culture, and African feelings and rhythm, all embellished with the rigor of Western classical music. The soprano Ana Maria Martinez from Porto Rico and Gustavo Dudamel from Venezuela, conducting the Berlin Philharmonic Orchestra, reached the soul of our classic music performing the Bachiana n.5. I will make sure you love this country and its music."

Chapter 33
Boys and Maestro

Our greatest weakness lies in giving up. The most certain way to succeed is always to try just one more time.
Thomas A. Edison

After the rehearsal, Maestro João gave the boys full attention. He started the conversation by saying that he noticed Jo's right-hand fingers failing and how prompt Randy's entrance to help his friend had been. He continued, "It is a great opportunity for us to have you here; you have much to add to our efforts to help children. As you probably already know, besides my dedication to music and directing the Bachianas Orchestra, I am also dedicated to helping children use the power of music. Music keeps children out of the streets, introducing them to serious discipline. It prepares them for a wonderful music profession when they have the talent. When someone feels the thrill of the audience's gratitude for a high-quality performance, that person is forever hooked on the exhilarating feeling. My intention is to give youths this thrill at least once, and then the dedication comes naturally. You had this today when our orchestra recognized you as talented. I am sure that today's feelings will be forever imprinted in your memories.

"Once children are hooked, music enters their brain with its marvelous influence, developing the cerebral connections that make a musician. It is not only cerebral development but also correction through the plasticity of the personality of physiological brain defects. This is all thanks to how music penetrates our brain, which is extremely powerful during a child's development. It becomes like the automatic behaviors found in all animals' brains, the automaticity of flying for birds, running and walking for mammals, swimming for fishes, and all insects' complex movements. Music integrates with the human cerebellum, brainstem, and forebrain, driving motor skills, sentiments, and creativity. Music plays a central role in brain development. I help over 4000 children with my music throughout this country.

"Jo, I observed your difficulty with Chopin's Prelude 5. It is indeed challenging in the right hand. This is especially true when you have gone through the four previous ones, as the first is not easy either; the anxiety of presenting for the first time to our orchestra was obvious. The resting Randy was providing to your hands alternating the preludes helped, as your mind must also be at ease knowing he is there to support you. I saw in your right hand what I felt throughout my entire career. I have literally got first-hand experience with musician's dystonia. When you entertain audiences with your musical talent, the world will be at your side. The obvious discipline, love and feelings expressed through music will win the audience to your side. We will start with Chopin's 24 Preludes and Bach's 24 Well-Tempered Clavier Preludes and Fugues, because you have already shown that you feel them and have dedication to them. Plus, you and Randy clearly have fun playing them".

"First of all, I want to hear each one playing alone, anything you feel comfortable playing."

Randy played three Chopin preludes, and Jo played three Bach preludes. After that, the Maestro announced that his wife had arranged a second piano in their home so the boys could start practicing side by side under his supervision. "We will work with the discipline of athletes and the soul of poets. Being in my home, I will have enough time to bring both of you to perfection.

"Carmen also has learned that a neighbor living five floors below us, in the building where we have our condo, will be out of the country on a business engagement for six months. He is our friend, has a piano and offered a place for you to stay there during this period you will be here in Brazil. He loves music and is sympathetic to our efforts to help Jo and the musician's dystonia cause. Carmen already told your moms they would cancel the Airbnb reservation so that all of you could move from the hotel to our building in the next three days. I expect you two to practice on their piano for the assignments I will give you and have three hours every morning at my home practicing side by side for my observation. We will have a fun and productive period for you here in Brazil. Carmen and I certainly will do all in our power for you to have an unforgettable period with us."

Chapter 34
The Maestro's Story

I am hitting my head against the walls,
but the walls are giving away.
Gustav Mahler

"Let me tell you my story, which was full of difficulties and exhilarating happiness," said Maestro João Carlos Martins. "I want you to understand that resilience is important in difficult moments. I would say this not only in music, as it is also true in any field of life. I was a sick child; I had some loss of consciousness between three and five years old. During that period, I also had to undergo surgery to correct my esophagus. Fortunately, I came out of those difficult years well. My family had some difficulties as well. My mother played the piano and had some involuntary closing of her hands; she developed Alzheimer's disease as she aged. My father, who wanted to be a concert pianist, lost part of his hand in an accident, so he had to accept that playing piano was an impossible dream for him.

"He was, however, a successful businessman who could buy a piano for his family. He fomented our music development, living well and healthily until his death at 102. My son has involuntary movements of his hands when he speaks, as I do. This suggests that I may harbor some genetic dysfunction with hand movements; a genetic predisposition for this difficulty is already described in the literature[45]. This predisposition showed up when I stressed my hand muscles to the maximum. It started with the busy fingering in the right hand, then spread to the left hand.

---

[45] Bäumer, T., Schmidt, A., Heldmann, M., Landwehr, M., Simmer, A., Tönniges, D., … Münchau, A. (2016) 'Abnormal interhemispheric inhibition in musician's dystonia—Trait or state?,' *Parkinsonism & Related Disorders*, **25**, 33-38. doi:10.1016/j.parkreldis.2016.02.018.

"When my father bought a full grand piano for the family, I was 8 years old. At that time, I don't remember having any difficulty with my playing technique; playing piano came easily. Soon, I was dominating the most difficult pieces, becoming a concert pianist and thus fulfilling my father's dream. At 12 or 13, I was already playing very difficult pieces. My father used to give me Benzedrine, then a drug popularly used to improve performance. It was believed that the drug increased disposition and resistance to sleep. Moreover, it also improved people's intelligence and prowess. The effects attracted the general population, and students and soldiers fighting in World War II were eager for a miracle pill. In the late 1960s, drugmakers sold billions of these pills annually.

"I grew up in this environment of excelling, high performance, and acquiring more and more admiration from classical music aficionados. Success in high-level classical music requires perfectionism and complete immersion in its technical and sentimental aspects. I did so intensely that at age 18; my teachers probably noticed that I had some fingering difficulty, as they advised me to elevate my hand and hit the keyboard with force and commitment. As my objective was my presentation at Carnegie Hall sponsored by Roosevelt, I don't know if this was helpful or prejudicial, as I had developed a secure way to support my hand with my thumbs, which was working for me. The reality is that I started to develop pain in my forearms and tiredness in my hands and fingers. I started to exchange the night for the day, sleeping hours before my concerts and spending part of the night excited after the extraneous demands on my hands during the concerts and exercises. This permitted me to continue my success throughout the world, including exhilarating moments, such as my great success at the Carnegie Hall in New York.

"Between 20 and 22 years old, I worked very hard, with an obsessive perfectionism, as I recorded seven albums in the USA. I became so exhausted and with so much pain in my arms that I had to soak in a warm bathtub after my concerts. I now believe that this excessive demand on my muscles was physical and detrimental to my brain connections. Music demands an extensive integration of the cerebral neuronal network[46]. I was suffering from a failure of this integration in listening, feeling, seeing notes, interpreting them, and sending messages to arms, hands, and fingers. My hand's two most

---

[46] Daniel J. Levitin (2007) *This Is Your Brain on Music: The Science of a Human Obsession*, Plum/Pinguin.

cumbersome fingers gave up first, the pinky and the ring finger of the right hand. Interesting that these were the same fingers that failed for Leon Fleisher, who became my friend. We used to exchange experiences, advice, sorrows, and ideas to reinvent ourselves. We became conductors when playing the piano was an impossible strain on our hands. Leon became a great teacher and successful conductor until his recent death in Baltimore. He was still mastering pieces for the left hand at 92.

"I developed a new way of playing, practicing slowly and using alternate fingers, index, and thumb to compensate for the lack of dexterity with the three others. This worked for me for a while. At 24 years old, my two stubborn fingers on my right hand started to have a life of their own. They started with involuntary movements, completely out of my control. Coincidently, around then, I fell over a stone in Central Park in New York while playing a soccer game. As a Brazilian at heart, I had joined a group of Brazilians playing in the middle of an improvised soccer field. I saw the game from the window of my apartment and ran to the park.

"Perhaps I was subconsciously looking for an accident to explain my difficulties with my right hand on the piano. It happened; I hurt my right ulnar nerve that fall. My difficulty with my right hand worsened, triggering a series of surgeries to work on my stubborn fingers. I had my ulnar nerve transposed by a famous American neurosurgeon, Dr. Joseph Ranselhoff. After injections, a course, of heavy physiotherapy for my fingers, and the use of steel finger protectors, I could continue my career for two more years. That took an incredible effort, but I could hide it with my resilience, determination, and love of music. This effort took me to a major depression, which almost drove me to suicide. At that point, I realized music was running away from my hands like a lover was abandoning me.

"I persisted with my obsession for my love, music. I had devoted my life to that career; I could not abandon my piano. I forced my right hand as much as possible, spreading my right thumb and index finger to an extreme. I played with my thumb and index finger with such force that my other three fingers, the sick ones, improved somewhat after two years but also started to fail. This was noticed in one of my concerts, leading to a critic publishing a review saying that I was no longer the same virtuoso. I became so distraught that I abandoned the performance trail. I could not listen to classical music for at least three years, trying to forget my destiny. I stopped playing the piano professionally for almost seven years. Instead, I became a businessman in Brazil.

"I started promoting a famous Brazilian professional boxer, Éder Jofre. He was a champion at featherweight and bantamweight. This incredible athlete taught me that resilience has no end. He returned to boxing after a loss and became world champion for the third time, all under my tutelage. This lesson touched me immensely, so much so that I went back to being a concert pianist. If he could return to fight, I could return to the piano. My hands had had seven years of rest. As a fighter, I challenged myself to record the complete Bach piano compositions.

"Well, for today, I have spoken enough, but I want you to keep in mind, Jo, that you must never give up; you are capable of anything you want to do. The human brain is limitless as long as intelligence is used; one can always take advantage of one's natural talent and the knowledge one has acquired. When people are connected in thoughts, the force increases exponentially. Look at the force of an orchestra, the achievement of going to the moon, or the culture of art, religion, science, and the constant progression of the homo sapiens to a better civilization to enforce your belief that all is possible.

"Ingenuity in any field of knowledge enhances human life. Tomorrow, I will continue telling you my history after we rehearse for your presentation. I will teach Jo how to control his right hand. Now, I leave you with three human characteristics that move civilization toward continuous and solid progress. The leapers are like Einstein, Newton, and Jobs, who create new paradigms, leap ahead of the crowd, and lead to real progress. They change the course of humanity. The sleepers are the teachers in general. They pass accumulated knowledge to new generations, firmly establishing progress. They propagate the achievements of the leapers. The keepers refine the leaps of knowledge the geniuses make; they redo experiments on well-understood phenomena. They are the guardians of the scientific truth. All these personalities are of extreme importance for humanity's progress. You must decide where your personality will thrive, excelling in your talents, creating, teaching, or performing with quality."

Chapter 35
Plasticity Revolution

*Music can put a baby to sleep
or inspire a soldier to war!*
Kenny Werner

Jill was talking to the Maestro, "Now we know how to manipulate neuronal networks for our advantage, with music, electrical stimulation, magnetic stimulation, ultrasound, intellectual pursuit, and mental or physical exercise. This ability to affect neurons with multiple types of energy allows medicine to improve people's quality of life in diverse situations. We know it can help with dystonia, but also a myriad of neurological diseases, neurodegenerative or not, for example, essential tremor, Parkinson's disease, epilepsy, obsessive-compulsive disorder, depression, and severe chronic pain. Jo is a perfect example of how technology can suppress a disease to the point of taking someone who was handicapped and suffering from severe muscle pain, and restoring them to a productive life.

"Unfortunately, we can still not control the finer movements as successfully. The networks responsible for the extremely fine movements, like the fingering needed to meet the challenge of playing an instrument as a virtuoso, are way more intricate than the ones controlling large muscles **(Figure 5)**. Muscles related to natural skills, such as those responsible for walking or basic daily functions like drinking and writing, are easier to control. Although we can reinstall function satisfactorily for a normal individual, returning someone to being a delicate surgeon or a virtuoso musician is still a major challenge.

"The brain circuitry is too complex, comprised of 100 million neurons spreading their connections, the axons, like main wires, and additionally billions of dendrites, secondary wires interconnecting the neurons. It is virtually impossible for artificial electronics to imitate the massive connectivity of the brain. The brain developed over millions of years of evolution and adaptation. Therefore, we need your help penetrating Jo's brain and its intricate minute organic wires using music, helping in ways that our electronics cannot. Music can change the nuances of brain electronics, following the performer's physical demands. The neuronal network develops plasticity when a specific repetitive task is performed. I believe that, with the proper use of different unique networks, it is possible to use the chemical-electrical interaction induced by music to modify, correct, and improve the brain's capacity. I hope you can help Jo with your experience of years fighting dystonia. I must return to Los Angeles as work awaits me there. You will have the boys for a sufficient period to help them. It is a privilege for them to spend time with you, as I know you will greatly help them with music and advice."

"I will do my best, Jill," answered the Maestro. "I learned how to modulate the brain with music, at least in my own case. I did it during my fight against dystonia for over 70 years, maintaining an acceptable career as a high-performance musician. It was demanding that I record the complete Bach music production, which forced me to succeed. It obliged me to develop strategies permitting me to be the only concert pianist to achieve this feat. It combined the resilience of a fighter, to whom flaws are recoverable and acceptable, and the determination of a musician, where flaws are not permitted. I had lived over 70 years with no flaws permitted. However, once I participated in the training and success of a boxer, I saw that the real champion has to recover from a fall to become stronger.

"A musician is not allowed to have flaws. Even when you don't make mistakes, but one performance was not the same level as previous ones, the critics can be severe to the point of leading a musician to suicidal thoughts, which I experienced myself. Fortunately, I didn't kill myself. After that most disastrous moment in my career, I eventually recovered to enjoy an entire professional life of achievements and happiness with music."

Part 5
Tours and Concerts

Chapter 36
Boys Bach's and Chopin's Preludes

Chopin's Preludes are compositions of an order entirely apart...
they are poetic preludes analogous to those of a great
contemporary poet, who cradles the soul in golden dreams...
Franz Liszt

Maestro told the boys that they should rest 30 minutes after every 15 minutes of practice. This would prevent too much strain on their brain-hand command and develop a pleasant work discipline.

"Randy and Jo, we will use your friendship to make you two world-class classic piano interpreters. Also, I was amazed that you could play the 12 first Chopin's Preludes together on a single piano. However, this approach is not a reality for us to recuperate Jo's abilities, nor a reality for you two to play together pieces of other composers. Many pieces would be challenging, or even impossible, to have both of you on the same keyboard. We will have you playing together but with two pianos and four hands. Yes, you can complete each other, but on the second piano, you both have the freedom and opportunity to shine independently. Life is long, and you will not be able to spend your lives together; I want you both to be secure in each other's rights.

"As you started playing Chopin's compositions spontaneously for fun, they will be our development exercises with two pianos in four hands. They are very prone to what I will suggest as a strategy to improve Jo's right hand and, simultaneously, give Randy the opportunity to hone his skills. Randy playing in parallel with Jo the most difficult moments of the right hand in each piece will confidently facilitate Jo's return to music, knowing that if he stops, Randy will be playing. It will sometimes be difficult but productive for Jo's right-hand improvement, which is our main challenge while you are here in Brazil.

"If you achieve good quality playing together, it will be a novelty worldwide. Moreover, Jo will look at Randy's right hand while playing and imagine that he is seeing his own hand, a technique known as the mirror hand. A Spanish neuroscientist, Pascal Leon, has shown that the brain develops cortical areas when thought is applied to doing motor tasks in a mirror. The amplification of cortical brain areas was documented not only through the improved skills of the trainer but also by a technique called transcranial magnetic stimulation (TMS). Moreover, it was evidenced by magnetic resonance image (MRI) of the specific cortical areas[47].

"It will be easier for you to start our tour throughout Brazil when you open the concert by playing Bach's and Chopin's Preludesm before the Orchestra appears in the stage. As you have already mastered them, all the stage fright and initial anxiety at the beginning of the concert will be lessened. They are well-known and loved by the audiences, and they are independent and short compositions that touch audiences' feelings deeply. They will demand a variety of technical challenges from you using both hands. We will carefully choose the ones Jo will play and the ones Randy will play. You will play as a unit. I will arrange the recital script to achieve seamless performances.

"Two facts are important in this effort. Firstly, because you play three of the eight Preludes with Randy with his right hand and Jo with his left hand, completely synchronized. Secondly, It will be intense therapy for Jo's right hand, because I want to make sure Jo feels the music and listens carefully to Randy's right-hand movements when he plays alone, and when you play together. Jo, you will play mentally, recruiting cortical areas in your brain so that you can eventually perform the parts played by Randy without difficulty (Figure 6)."

---

[47] Doige Norman, M.D. (2007) *The Brain that Changes Itself. Stories of Personal Triumph from the Frontiers of Brain*, Pinguin, Chapter 38.

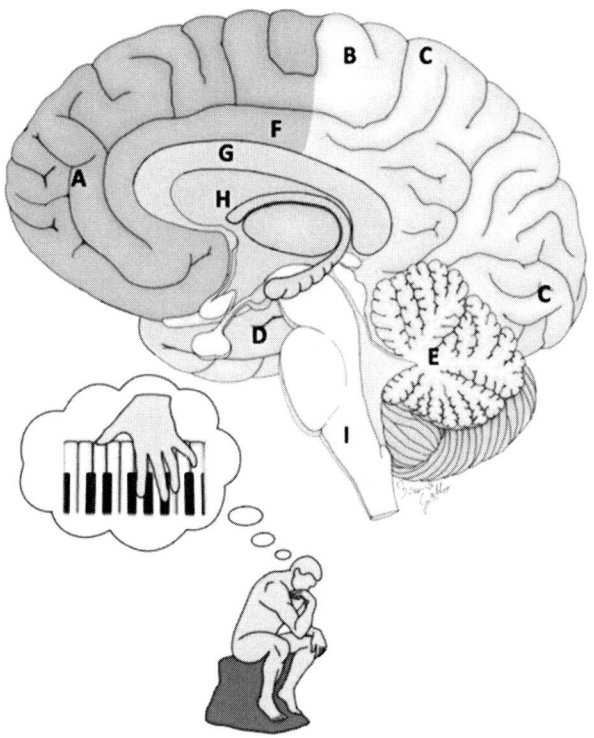

Figure 6: Thinking is brain exercise
Thinking is brain exercise. When the fingering fails, what fails is the area of the brain responsible for the integration of the movements, the elaboration of the command, not the fingers' muscles. The area of the brain is sending wrong signals and deficient signals to command the muscles. The muscles are there; the problem is that the demand is too overwhelming for the brain. Activation of the dormant areas, either with thoughts, electrically or magnetically, may improve deficits. Muscles increase and strengthen with exercise; the same happens with the brain. Most of the brain is recruited by thinking of playing music. Areas A, B, C, D, E, F, G, and H are activated when playing only with thoughts. The brain stem (I) is not activated because the message is not sent to the fingers to play.

"Now, here is our script for the Brazilian tour. We will begin working on our repertoire with you by playing as follows: Jo starts the concert playing Bach's Prelude in C Major playing alone. Then Randy plays Chopin's Prelude in C major alone, giving Jo's right hand a rest. We will continue with the Chopin's Prelude in C minor, which Jo, now rested, continues playing alone. Bach's Prelude in C minor Jo plays with his left hand and Randy with his right hand. This prelude is key, you will demonstrate your hands and your brains, in general an unprecedented feat in concerts. We will follow this first performance with Bach's Prelude in G major with Jo playing the left hand and Randy playing the right hand, insisting to the audience that you are capable of brain-brain and your hand-hand integration. Having demonstrated the challenge of playing together, Jo continues with Chopin's Prelude in G major. Randy will play Bach's Prelude in D major alone. You will then again play together the Chopin's Prelude in D major with Jo using his left hand and Randy using his right. I illustrate it for you in the presentations (Figure 9).

Figure 9:

Bach's and Chopin's Preludes in C major
(A) https://youtu.be/B9tZfxfbObk, and C minor
(B) https://youtu.be/reK-iNLRbQ8, in G major
(C) https:/ /youtu.be/ym6RCTaE4jk, in D major
(D) https://youtu.be/h8HyvWMzokI. João Carlos Martins as a child around Jo's and Randy's ages.

Next we move on to something more conventional, playing the Concerto for Two Pianos in C Minor BWV 1060, movement III by Bach (Figure 8). We will take a 20-minute break. In the second part I will conduct Beethoven's Symphony number 4 and play the Grande Cadenza from Ravel's Concerto. The encore will be "Tico-Tico no Fubá" by Zequinha de Abreu and Aloysio de Oliveira with an orchestration I made for you two to play with our orchestra. The Berlin Philharmonic played this piece as an encore, and it was a great success in Germany, said the Maestro enthusiastically[48]. This Concert will last approximately 1 hour and 30 minutes, with an interval of 20-30 minutes. The

---

[48] https://www.youtube.com/watch?v=PEZtTmVGdQw

first part will be to highlight you playing solo piano and Beethoven's Concert number 4. What do you think?"

"Maestro, you know what is best. We are here for you to teach us," Randy said, Jo nodding in agreement.

Prelude in C major is difficult for both hands, I want to demonstrate to the audience that Randy has a superb piano level, like what Jo had just demonstrated with Bach's C major, establishing the audience's admiration on you two. You will have impressed the audience right from the start of the concert. It will be another great practice for integrating your brain hemispheres, as it will be Jo's turn to pay attention to Randy's hand movements. A practice for brain motor function during the concert, and for musical sensation integrating your four cerebral hemispheres, preparing you for the challenge of playing Bach's Prelude in C minor together."

Jo will play the Chopin's Prelude in C minor showcasing his gorgeous piano sound. The Bach's prelude you will play together with Jo using only his left hand. Chopin's G major Prelude is a vivace, fast in the left hand, excellent for Jo to play alone. So, you understand how I organized the Preludes, providing opportunities for both of you to have your own presentation, but insisting on the integration of your skills.

"Maestro, don't worry. We learned not to disturb each other on a single keyboard; imagine that it would be easier with two pianos. We have trained to play these preludes together for fun so often that we skip notes on purpose, knowing the other will play them. It is the part of the fun and our integration playing together," said Randy.

Figure 8:
(A) Beethoven's Symphony Number 4 https://youtu.be/PDiDnp4aztA and
(B) Bach's Concerto for 2 pianos in C minor
https://youtu.be/gvvqBGcx4OE.

"Well, now, we will identify other difficulties with two pianos. Mastering a piece is tricky, mostly when integrating two brains, actually four cerebral hemispheres, into play. We will work on our rehearsals until you can get the most out of these wonderful Preludes by Bach and Chopin. It will be fun. I would like to play the parts Jo will do and then have Jo playing the right hand with me. I am up to this challenge. I want to play like you two have shown possible," said Maestro, smiling and continuing.

Commenting on the last Chopin Prelude that you will play together, the one in D major, you will again play as if you were one person, Randy plays his right hand leaving his left under the keyboard, while Jo plays his left hand leaving his right hand at the seat. In this Prelude you will demonstrate to the audience again the complete integration of your brains, what you achieved with two Preludes by Bach, you will also demonstrate the same challenge with this one by Chopin.

"Maestro, thanks for the example with these first four of Chopin's Preludes for the concert. I am sure that after the first part of the concert, the initial anxiety will be over, and the remainder will be without problems. I am sure that after the first part of the concert, we will be ready to integrate with the Orchestra.

"Do you agree, Randy?" The Maestro asked.

"I agree with Jo. We have played these Bachc's and Chopin's Preludes so many times that I have no doubt that we will do well. We already excel with them in a single keyboard, as we demonstrated at the hotel lobby. It was seamless; having two keyboards as you are orienting it will be 'a piece of cake.' Will the orchestra enter at any moment while we are playing?"

"Not during the preludes, but to accompany you in Bach's Concerto for two pianos in C minor. In the second part we will complete the concert with the Bachiana SESI-SP orchestra playing Beethoven's fourth symphony. I intend to have you as soloists in the concert, an attraction for the public, as the Orquestra Bachiana SESI-SP is already well established here in Brazil. It will help you become famous in our country. Initially with the Bach's and Chopin's Preludes and the Bach's Concerto. When we march into the world tour, I'm planning to keep the same program, going only with small exceptions. Here in Brazil, I want you to play with the Orchestra to give you an experience of our work culture. We will prgress one step at a time. Furthermore, my concern is much more about recovering Jo's right hand and giving him confidence as an interpreter. For you, Randy. I want you to be comfortable in front of any audience, your mother asked me to focus on this with you."

"Thanks, Maestro. I am sure that with your orientation, we will be able to help Jo, and at the same time, I want to develop my skills. My mother will be happy. She has done so much for me already. I want to reward her efforts to have brought us here to be educated," said Randy seriously.

"How I see the challenge she posed to me is that we will have a lot of fun making beautiful music, enjoying our time together and our audiences. Count on us to develop a concert that you will be proud to have played for the rest of your lives. This complete combination of four cerebral hemispheres in these smooth, rhythmic and feeling pieces is magical. Although this combination of preludes will take a little over 16 minutes, they will give you the opportunity to show the audience how feelings flow through the innermost part of your being in a complete integration between the of you. It will be your most unique asset to perform these together in a novel manner, presenting these preludes. Young performers like you can do this before each of you gets settled on your own way of thinking and playing," said the Maestro.

"Randy, your mother talked a lot about brain plasticity, asking me to work with you and Jo, mostly on Jo's recovery. I plan to use music to work with brain plasticity; the novel concept of complementary function when deficient brain areas need aid from the wider cerebral networks is challenging. It will be interesting to see how you help each other with the difficulties. I am particularly curious about the motor tasks required to play an instrument. We know that plasticity is the explanation for why intense physiotherapy recovers patients from neurological deficits, which until recently were considered beyond hope. It takes a new approach to combined cerebral power. We know that brainstorming, a community of ideas, or the mental effort of a team is far more powerful than a single person's thinking. The power of an orchestra is a live example of how brains coordinated by a conductor create amazing results. It is an interesting musical concept having you two summing your brains.

"You may believe that I am trying to protect Jo's right hand with less demanding rapid fingerings," said the Maestro, looking at Jo sympathetically.

"The real strategy makes him so comfortable with the left hand that, when he plays these pieces alone, he will only have to think about the right hand, as the left hand will be completely automatic. Once rested, the areas of Jo's left cerebral hemisphere commanding the right hand will recruit neighboring cortical neurons in the proximity of the motor strip that we didn't challenge, as they were not being challenged when the left hand was being developed. I used this strategy by giving concerts only with the left hand. There are many pieces that were developed for the left hand only, such as Maurice Ravel's Concert[49]. During that period, I rested my left brain, which permitted me to return to playing with both hands. I hope this works for Jo."

"Thanks, Maestro. Yes, I still have much to improve. Sorry," Jo said, putting his head down.

"It is not a problem, Jo," reassured the Maestro. "We are here to achieve a complete recovery of your right hand, but it can't happen overnight. It is just a matter of time and hard work. Resilience and the help of your friends, us. We will do the job.

"You will seal your mark with your coordinated efforts. I am sure the audience will admire this collaboration between young buddies who show solidarity. Certainly, in the program for the concert, we must inform the audience of the woes you went through and why you are here in Brazil playing together under my orientation.

"The country knows all about my work, my difficulties with dystonia, and the disasters during my career," said the Maestro. "Now, at an advanced age, I have dedicated my time to teaching our youth resilience, hard work, and generosity. I believe I have been achieving it, as my social media is largely followed by young people. It has been a wonderful time when I worry less about my technique and more about what I can give back to others. What is amazing to me is that I am still improving in my own technique. The power of brain plasticity is remarkable and, in my opinion, infinite. Your mother will be able to tell you that, Randy."

"She tells me about her ability to improve brains all the time," said Randy. "My father exemplifies her dedication, resilience, and ingenuity. I admire them both; I often think of following in her footsteps for a career. I am torn between music and science; what do you think, Maestro?"

"Don't worry about that right now," said the Maestro, "you are too young to make the most important decisions in your life; just do what you love for now. You will have the opportunity to see enough science at school and at home with your parents to make a well-informed decision when the moment

---

[49] https://www.youtube.com/watch?v=KJTUUKAdZDU

comes, so it is a bridge to cross when you arrive at it. At the right time, you will naturally tend one way or another; your sensibility will help you decide between science and music, as both need sensibility. The musician is a lonely soul who makes millions happy in audiences, and his recordings are now spread digitally through cyberspace. A doctor creates happiness family by family, person by person, while the scientist can reach millions like the musicians with his discoveries and teaching. Both professions will bring you extreme happiness and a wide positive impact throughout humanity. I have reached it professionally; I am sure your mom and dad feel it in theirs. Work well done always brings happiness."

Jo had his head down while this conversation was going on. Randy noticed and signaled to Maestro João, who also noticed Jo's sadness. After a pause, like the pause we see in music for a prompt, vigorous start, he directed his words to Jo.

"Jo, I want to help you understand something. Your parents made an extreme effort to prepare you for music. They depended on you for their dreams to come true. In other words, they didn't have the opportunity to develop their dreams because of the limitations imposed on them by the tough system they lived in before they came to the USA. Your father was not ready to face a completely different culture, not only in terms of the way of thinking but also the way of speaking. He was too stern not only with you but also with everyone around him. He could not adapt to a life of complete freedom when he never had experienced it before. It is like a bird that has always lived in a cage; it will die if left out in nature. This is in spite of the fact that when it is in the cage, the bird sings, longing to have its freedom. Your father was a victim of the stark policies of Chairman Mao Zedong. Freedom is now progressively reaching your country.

"Improvement sometimes takes harsh decisions. China endured a great famine from 1958 to 1962; farmers were obliged to work in iron plants, while intellectuals were forced to work in rural areas. It was a famine, causing 50 million people to die. For example, the province of Anhui, the most affected by starvation, lost approximately 9 million people. Today, it is an example of the Chinese people's ingenuity and resilience, as it is one of the fastest economies in the country, and it is based on electrical car manufacturing. China has come a long way in caring for its people. You here, showing the world your talent, is an example of the freedom arriving in China.

"Arriving in the USA was the completion of your father's dream, which was also the dream of two generations of his family. It was what he dreamed of for him and what he dreamed of for you. He could not imagine returning to life away from the complete freedom he experienced here in America. Moreover, he could not understand living a less harsh life than he had endured. This explains his attitude to the end, especially when he thought he had harmed your career forever. It was too much for a man who loved you so much to suffer. Now you have your mom caring for you, and she has you to care for her, as you are still so young. Remember her happiness and your own is your goal."

Jo did not fully understand what Maestro was talking about. As he was taught at school, he thought China was a perfect country. He also didn't understand what the Maestro said about his father's destiny. His mom said that his father had returned to China to work. When discussing China and his dad, he would ask his mom what the Maestro meant. It was too much for the young boy to digest; Maestro had talked like an adult.

"Randy's parents had a different situation. They had the chance to realize their dreams because the country they lived in gave them the freedom to become whatever they dreamed of being. Randy's father, Charles, had become a soccer star and a brilliant scientist, thanks to his parents and his mother's resilience and dedication to their love."

The Maestro also talked to Randy about this, saying, "The book written about their lives is very impressive, a heartbreaking example of the love and dedication of soul mates. Great professionals always have these qualities; be sure to keep up with both. Success will come in unexpected hours, as the American poet Thoreau said in the nineteenth century.

"Jo and Randy, your friendship has the two ingredients needed to create success. You have demonstrated love and dedication to each other, admiration, and resilience in your work. You have learned not to compete and instead joined forces to win together. It is like the force of an orchestra. A completely new outlook on your lives. You are a man who will bring happiness to millions with your music. Jo, you have a beautiful future ahead of you, and for sure, for your mom, as she will realize her dreams through you, a dream she and your father cultivated since the day you were born. Count on all of us to be at your side. Together, we will *cradle the audience's soul in golden dreams.* In the preludes, Randy stays with the right hand and Jo with the left hand (**Figure 9**)."

Jo smiled timidly. "Thanks, Maestro. You have our work cut out for us! I understand your plan of giving me rest for the right hand and, at the same time, making me think about using it while Randy plays. However, is it possible I will lose more dexterity and disassociate my right hand from my left?"

"As you will be thinking as if you were playing **(Figure 5)**, you will be exercising your brain's left cortex, which is related to your right hand, while integrating music through your whole brain. You will not stop using the muscles of your right hand, as you will be playing several Preludes using it. I chose some very challenging pieces for you. I don't want you to become frustrated and insecure if you fail. You will notice that the portions that Randy will initially complete for you will later come naturally to you without the need for him to pitch in when we are settled and done with our training. While playing together, you will feel at ease playing, and your right hand will naturally regain dexterity as your middle fingers improve**)**.

"Success is exhilarating; your internal strength will increase, Jo, to the extent that you will overcome all difficulties. Count on me to help you; I have been through what you are experiencing many times. After each success, I felt an injection of determination and the desire to overcome whatever obstacle I met. You are young and talented, and you have loved ones supporting you. The audiences will be rooting for your success; audiences love children. Nothing generates more sympathy than seeing a prodigy child playing while the audience knows they have faced struggles. Now, let's work!

"Randy, I will discuss this plan with your mother. I want to be sure that my assumptions on the treatment I am giving Jo through music are scientifically sound."

They dedicated many hours a day to the script that the Maestro designed for them. The four-hand pieces were played from 7 to 10 am. Then they would go up to Maestro's penthouse, where he would review the progress of the entire script. After lunch they worked on Bach's and Chopin's studies as a general practice until 4 pm. Then they went to play in the auditorium with the Bachiana Orchestra. After a month of this intense work, Maestro felt that they were ready for the first concert, which was scheduled at the Manaus Opera House, located in the State of Amazonas, in the north of the country.

Chapter 37
True Science and Music

Music is the only means of understanding among birds and beasts.
Kenny Warner

"The boys are amazing," said the Maestro excitedly.

"Jill, I need to know if my proposal for their time in Brazil will improve Jo's fingering. Additionally, I need to know what you expect me to offer Randy. I sent you the script for the concert I planned, starting with the Bach's and Chopin's Preludes that they already master. I want to make sure I'm not negatively impacting Jo's hands with demands on his participation in the concert. Over the years, I have read a lot about how to improve my right hand. I made many mistakes because I never dug into the scientific understanding of brain development, as I should have done. I read that there is little one can do to recover a lost portion of the brain.

"I observed an important decline in my playing after I had a brain trauma walking in the streets of Bulgaria. I became desperate many times with the regression I saw in my ability to play pieces that were very familiar and common in my repertoire. Moreover, the critics were so hard on me when I didn't perform as expected, given my fame as a concert pianist. It happened after one of my New York performances; I told the boys that I even thought of killing myself. I recovered over the years from that deep depression. I don't want to lead the boys down the difficult path I traveled through in my career. I need your criticism based on your neuroscientific mindset and your knowledge of brain plasticity. Did you read the script?"

Jill was in Los Angeles listening to Maestro João through a video call. "Maestro, I read it and made some notes. I loved it; I just have some points to stress. Some of my remarks are for you; others are for Jo's mom.

"First, decrease Jo's body movements while he is playing so that no dispensable movements compete with the brain cortical areas required to control the fine movement of his right hand.

"Second, ask them to visualize playing the difficult passages mentally. Jo needs practice visualizing the constant use of his right hand. Visualizing musical pieces that demand the most of his right hand will help him. When he does this, the cortical neurons will work as if he were, in fact, playing. There will be a recruitment of the peripheral cortical areas related to the motor control of the right-hand fingers, specifically the ones he is having difficulty using. Because he is only thinking and not moving his body, talking, or seeing, the cortical areas responsible for these functions can lend some neurons to the playing. The act of thinking will also call blood supply to the regions.

"This increase in blood supply to areas demanding more glucose and oxygen can be detected by a functional MRI (fMRI) using a technique called Blood Oxygenation Level Dependent (BOLD). MRI can be manipulated using different sequences to stress anatomical and functional markers. This powerful MRI capability is often used to diagnose a variety of diseases, as well as to explore brain plasticity.

"The computerized axial tomographic scan (CAT scan) is very limited in this way, dependent on the absorption of x-rays by the head tissues, including bone and brain; it has great limitations when analyzing brain function. That is why PET-CT (Positron Emission Tomography CT) is widely used. It creates a molecular image fused to a Computed Tomography (CT). In fact, we learn about brain function and plasticity through the correlation of all these images. The plasticity we are trying to stimulate in Jo's brain is starting to be identified by pooling together all these images.

"It is simple to understand that we are fostering plasticity in children's brains from birth. A mom stimulates the baby with language, vision, motor, and sensory cues when communicating with him or her. Those are powerful inputs, organizing the section of the brain that will make that child a specific adult. School is another huge source of plasticity for homo sapiens. Through this amazing capability of our brain to adapt to situations through repetitive tasks, we dominate all earth's species. We need to keep track of Jo's brain function as he deals with the demands we impose on him. This must be done with periodic brain imaging with techniques focusing on different aspects of his brain anatomy and function. I will monitor him and let you know if we need to make any adjustments to the script, Maestro.

"Third, make them memorize the pieces. Memory is kept away from the motor cortex and even the hippocampus when it is completely established by repetition of a task or study. It goes to different brain areas needed to integrate all senses to automatically establish knowledge. That is why, when one loses the hippocampus depository, short-term memory suffers the most. The hippocampus stays in the medial part of the temporal lobes **(Figure 5-D, See also Figure 12)**, connecting to the whole brain, principally to the frontal lobes **(Figure 5-A)**, a great depository and integrative region of memory. It harbors intellectual knowledge and integrates it through the limbic system.

"The command necessary for playing the complete memorized pieces will flow from distant areas of the brain until it arrives at the motor cortex **(Figure 5-B)**. It arrives in the motor cortex after modulating the information in the basal ganglia **(Figure 12)** and cerebellum **(Figure 5-E)**. The neuronal population in the motor cortex and its vicinities will be free to work only in transmitting the already elaborated messages going to the fingers to execute the piece. Therefore, the motor cortex is freed to act as a simple relay of messages to control the fingers and is, thus, able to recruit neighboring cortical areas to perform its motor message task. This message is missing in Jo's left side of the brain.

"The sensory cortex **(Figure 5-C)**, lodged just behind the motor areas, receives input from the hand regarding the fingers' position. This message is integrated through the music circuit of the brain for the continuous and harmonic performance of the music piece. In fact, it is a complete circuit of sending orders and receiving information about the fingers' position, which is connected to the most intellectual areas of the brain. Music requires all our circuits, such as memory, sentiments, proprioception, hearing, and coordination. The perfect integration of all these circuits leads the performer to command the direct motor pathway to play the instrument, whatever it might be. We need to sharpen all these circuits in Jo's brain, for that matter, the circuit of all your musicians in the orchestra and Randy's. Maestro, as the conductor, you must integrate the circuits of all your people together; what a task!

"Recruiting and preserving enough 'motor cortical real state' for Jo's third, fourth, and fifty right-hand fingers is our objective. We will be working on the creation of synapses and neuron recruitment in order to integrate them with the development of a robust dendritic network. It requires myelinization of the novel dendritic branches and a buildup of brain-supportive cells, known as glial cells. We will be working on a true process of brain construction through repetition, which we know is dependent on a factor recently discovered called brain-derived neurotrophic factor (BDNF).

"Additionally, local microvasculature will be implemented by the demand for blood in the hardworking areas, which we will be stimulating in Jo's brain. His brain will be working with good EEG waves, the gamma waves. This is a pattern of neural electrical oscillation, with frequencies ranging from 25 to 140 Hertz (Hz), far beyond the well-known EEG routine exam waves. Delta waves (1 to 3 Hz) represent a brain in sluggish activity or perhaps sleepy. Theta (4 to 7 Hz) waves are related to drowsiness. Alpha waves (8-12 Hz) indicate focus and alertness related to creativity, and beta waves (frequencies > 12 Hz) denote great alertness, usually a brain performing calculations or extremely demanding tasks, like performing complex piano pieces[50]. Maestro, you will induce better circuitry throughout Jo's brain (Figure 10), but your work is cut for you! I apologize for the overflow of information; you have enough to deal with in your music alone."

---

[50] McDermott, B., Porter, E., Hughes, D., McGinley, B., Lang, M., O'Halloran, M., & Jones, M. (2018) 'Gamma Band Neural Stimulation in Humans and the Promise of a New Modality to Prevent and Treat Alzheimer's Disease,' *Journal of Alzheimer's Disease*, 65(2), 363-392. doi:10.3233/jad-180391.

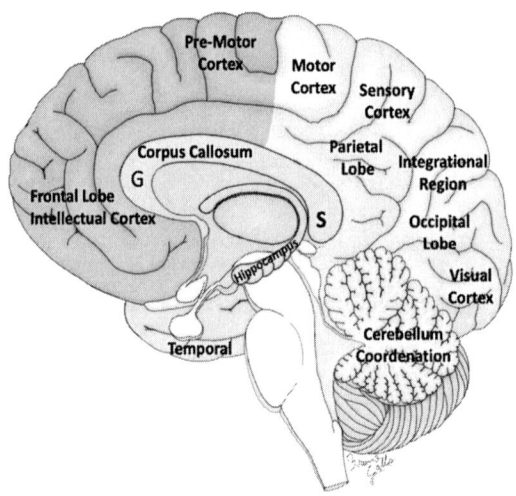

Figure 10: *Brain Regions related to Music*
This figure represents and names all brain areas related to musical performance. G is the Genus, and S is the Splenium of the Corpus Callosum (green). The Corpus Callosum is larger in musicians than non-musicians, showing that both hemispheres are highly in demand and integrated when music is played. A child's brain studying music exercises to increase these interhemispheric connections.

"Regarding Randy, Maestro, I am not worried about offering him any specific care. I have intensely tried to expose him to piano sounds since he was in my womb. Moreover, he has been playing piano since he was a toddler. I do want him to receive all the stimulation I just mentioned to you, which you will be doing for Jo anyway. But it will be a natural occurrence as he will be together with Jo. Randy is a curious and good-natured boy; he will naturally follow all your instructions to Jo.

"Regarding his motor skills, he has no difficulty playing, and he will improve through his own discipline and with your teaching. I already studied Randy's brain extensively with imaging because of his hamartoma. The size of the anterior portion of his corpus callosum is amazing; this structure connects the anterior portions of both brain hemispheres **(Figure 5-G)**. The size of this structure is highly related to the musician's intensity of training. Because of my fears about Randy's hamartoma, I developed his brain for music. I did it as an attempt to suppress the epileptic output from the hamartoma. I failed and had to use the Gamma Knife® to suppress the abnormal electrical firing coming from the hamartoma completely. The treatment was a success, so please take advantage of the brain he has and make him a great performer and an effective support for Jo.

"I want him to stay supportive of Jo, helpful to him, and take advantage of your teaching," said Jill.

"Jo's handicap touched Randy immensely. He felt guilty for winning the Julliard scholarship competition, taking it from Jo, which led to the tragedy that happened to Mr. Jin and Jo. It was a source of severe depression for Randy. Childhood depression is a complicated matter. It took me a lot of conversation and psychological support to help him accept that he had nothing to do with what happened to Jo's family. Randy is a very sensitive boy; his growing friendship with Jo helped him through his psychological woes. The thought that he was helping Jo's recovery was the strongest therapy for him. This sensitivity helps Randy with his musical performance, employing deep feelings and interpreting the great masters' compositions with nuanced sentiment. I believe he put all this sentimental reserve into his playing of the Beethoven Concert Number 3, helping him to distinguish himself from Jo's superb technical interpretation of Beethoven Concert Number 4 during the competition."

"I'll do my best; I am sure my many years of musical tribulations will help," said Maestro João.

"Maestro, your best is perfection," said Jill. "You showed it throughout your bright career. I am sure that under your tutorage, the boys will excel. I will try to be there to watch most of the concerts on the Brazilian tour you are organizing; I would love to see your country more extensively. Good luck with your work."

Chapter 38
Concerts

Music can name the unnamable and communicate the unknowable.
Leonard Bernstein

After a month of rehearsal, the first concert occurred at the Amazon Theater. This traditional theater in the north of the country was chosen by the Bachianas Orchestra director to launch the tour of the two prodigies. The concert was heavily advertised by Maestro João Carlos Martins. As director and founder of the orchestra, his name was sure to bring the event success. Linked to his name was his famous teaching program to find musical talent among needy children. The boys represented an example of such an initiative. Therefore, major support was obtained from government agencies and commercial entities. The traditional classical music house, constructed in 1896 in Manaus, was also an iconic tourist attraction in the Amazon region. Enrico Caruso once came to the theater to sing Giuseppe Verdi's 'Ernani Opera,' based on the 1830 play *Ernani*, written by Victor Hugo.

Maestro planned to popularize the boys throughout Brazil using traditional music halls through a secure tour. It was designed so that they would build their confidence and presentation throughout various Brazilian audiences, starting from the far north and culminating toward the larger audiences in the middle of the country. Manaus had a very sophisticated audience; it was the capital of the Amazon State. Moreover, it was a receptive city. The audience was easygoing, proud to have Maestro playing for them, and expected to give the boys unconditional support. After all, they represented a very exotic occurrence for the city, less so than in São Paulo and Rio de Janeiro, cities where the competition for recognition in music and arts at large was fiercer than in any other areas of the country. They were left for the end of their tour.

'Sala São Paulo' and 'Rio de Janeiro Municipal Theater' represented the most reputable venues for concerts in the country, where the critics would want to show off by giving the boys dubious reviews.

As expected, the boys did a great job, although Randy had to enter unexpectedly in several right-hand challenges for Jo. However, they were well rehearsed, so it happened in a seamless way. In his comments at the concert's end, the Maestro thanked the audience for their kindness. This was after a standing ovation of several minutes and after the boys had played the encore, 'Tico-Tico no Fubá' ('Sparrow in the Bran'), a Brazilian choro by Zequinha de Abreu. This popular piece, composed at the beginning of the last century, was an icon of Brazilian music, immortalized in over 15 movies produced in Hollywood, New York, and Brazil. Maestro had rehearsed the boys playing with the Bachianas Orchestra because he knew the young boys would touch the Brazilians' hearts with this piece, which is ingrained in the heart of every Brazilian classical music lover.

It was an immense success. It was featured on the major television channels and in the major country's magazines. Specifically, the 'Tico-Tico no Fubá' performance went viral on social media. Brazil was ready to receive the two boys in the major concert houses. 'Tico-Tico no Fubá' was also chosen because of the ease of the left hand. Jo caught the Brazilian rhythm amazingly fast, with Randy supporting the solo, the right hand **(Figure 11)**.

Figure 11: "Tico Tico no Fubá"
https://youtu.be/IZ-dB8lUU28

The boys left the stage, but the Orquestra Bachiana SESI-SP continued playing Beethoven's Fourth Symphony and some Brazilian classics. For the second part of the concert, Maestro João aimed to popularize Brazilian classical music in the world further, taking advantage of the audiences that the two young pianists would gather when they extended this into a worldwide tour. Like Samba and Bossa Nova, the trademark of Brazilian popular songs worldwide, representing Brazil's strong integration of races, its classical music also has strong shades of this integration. African rhythms mixed with European baroque music inspired the compositions, culminating in the 1700s when the country already had an elite who appreciated classical music. The dominant religion was Catholicism, which was brought by the Portuguese in the 1500s; therefore, music was heavily influenced by religion. The priest José Mauricio Nunes Garcia, known as Nunes Garcia, father of Brazilian classical music, lived from 1767 to 1830. He composed over 240 pieces of music. He was the Master of Music for the Royal Chapel when the Portuguese King John VI was in Brazil. He was in his South American colony, having fled from the political European woes caused by Napoleon's invasions.

Later, in the nineteenth and twentieth centuries (1887-1959), Heitor Villa-Lobos became one of the greatest Brazilian classic composers. Based on Brazilian 'folk' music, also a miscegenation of African, Indigenous, and European styles. He created the Bachianas Brasileiras, composing for instrument and voice. Villa-Lobos's massive work was over 2,000 compositions, including the Bachiana Number 5, which had brought Jo to tears when the dark-skinned young Brazilian singer was rehearsing when he first met Maestro João.

The successful concert was repeated in the main cities of the country, having outstanding reviews. It was a 'tour the force,' flying in a hired jet; in one month, they performed in 13 cities: Fortaleza, Belen, Recife, Salvador, Belo Horizonte, Porto Alegre, Florianopolis, Curitiba, Goiânia, Brasília, Cuiabá, Rio de Janeiro, and finally São Paulo.

Chapter 39
Beyond Music

Mastery is not perfection or even virtuosity. It is giving oneself love, forgiving one's mistakes, and not allowing earthly evidence to diminish one's view of oneself as a drop in the Ocean of Perfection.
Kenny Werner

After the successful 13-concert marathon, Maestro João called together the whole orchestra, Randy and Jo, for an analysis of their performance.

"I have often talked to my orchestra about the essence of being a musician. It goes beyond being a great technician; it is about making the audience feel the music. You are not focused on the applause. A true musician is completely taken by the playing, in such a way that, when they are playing, the audience is not even seen or present in his mind. There are no worries about making a mistake or what the audience thinks about the performance. Playing in a concert means giving yourself completely to music. Music emanates from inside the performer without effort or fear of making mistakes. Reaching this trance, despite the pressure of being in a concert hall, is difficult. It is when the musician's relationship with his instrument becomes entirely second nature. The practice has been so intense that playing comes naturally, without effort.

"The practice required to reach mastery is a given. For a musician to reach this level of performance, they must enjoy practicing. It only happens when love for the craft is ingrained in the music being played as if it emanates from the musician's soul. This was when playing became necessary for the musician's well-being; hours and hours flew without them noticing the time passing by. The pleasure of practice is craved. The musician is elated by it; he or she is in another space where the solitude of playing and the ecstasy of playing completely envelop the performer. The musician will be aware of the audience only when the piece is finished, with the applauses. The audience knows that the musician is not playing to impress them. They understand that they have the privilege of being inside the musician's space.

"Well," continued the Maestro. "Maybe this is difficult for you all to understand because you are still anxious about not making mistakes. On the other hand, if you believe in having dominated the technical side of music, ego takes over, and you lose the humility that the beauty of music transcends. You lose the view that you are small in front of it." He paused, giving time for the members of the orchestra and the boys to ask questions.

Jo was the first to ask a question. "Maestro, are you saying we didn't play as you expected?" Randy repeated the question, as both were anxious to please the Maestro and the audience.

"As you played perfectly, without any mistakes during the 13 concerts, I didn't want to call attention to details that would make any of you an effortless playing musician, as it would be an additional challenge that would complicate this initial training step. Our focus was taking the anxiety out of Jo. I am asking you to transcend to the next step of being a concert musician. I will ask you to watch videos of outstanding musicians, for example, Artur Rubinstein playing the Chopin—Piano Concert Number 2 in F Minor, opus 21 (https://youtu.be/B3r4EgwLqMM) and Vladimir Horowitz playing Schubert Impromptu Number 3 (https://youtu.be/FxhbAGwEYGQ). I want you to observe the ease with which these two consecrated pianists play. There was no anxiety, no faces, no extra body movements, only hands, and tranquil behavior, although they faced highly critical audiences. They were playing for pleasure, for themselves, and the audiences had the privilege of entering their world and their music space, not the other way around. You must create your own space in music," said the Maestro.

"They were not entering the audience's space. The listeners entered the same ecstasies in which they were enveloped, a trance in which the performer encompasses the audience. Andrés Segovia, the master of classical Spanish guitar, is also an example of this tranquility when performing. Listen to him playing Spanish Dance Number 10 in G (Danza Triste), a composition by Enrique Granados (https://youtu.be/X-vSnrPAems). The same can be observed in the Schubert Piano Quinteto D667 (The Trout) performed by Jaqueline Du Pré, Daniel Barenboim, Itzhak Perlman and Pinchas Zukerman (https://youtu.be/ZZdXoER96is). Their ensemble and their attitude show complete relaxation; they are smiling and obviously having a lot of fun together.

"There were no worries among them. In particular, Itzhak Perlman playing the violin is an example of this complete immersion in the world of music. Jaqueline Du Pré and her husband, Daniel Barenboim, were totally in tune with each other; his concentration on the flow of the ensemble is also impressive. They have played so many times, enjoying being imbibed in music together so much that it all came naturally to them; this is shown during their celebration backstage. Watch all these videos, which are easily available on YouTube. You are lucky to have this resource.

"I want you all to reach this level of ease when you play without pressure; it is for your pleasure. I saw it coming to you after the 10th concert. It was before we arrived in Rio de Janeiro and São Paulo. You got the deserved reviews when facing these two stringent and critical audiences.

"I want to see you pleasing yourselves, not me. Let me ask you an important question. Jo and Randy, did you have more fun playing for the audiences across Brazil, or when you arrived in Brazil and played in the hotel lobby alone, without your mothers knowing where you were?"

Randy answered. "I haven't thought about it, but without sounding ungrateful for all your teaching, it was easier and pleasanter at the hotel lobby. It was carefree!"

"This is exactly the point; you were playing for yourselves; you saw that piano there, idle in the lobby, you both set to do what you enjoyed doing when alone in your homes, as a game. The audience, passing by the lobby, had the privilege of seeing two geniuses playing. They entered into your world, your music space. Through you two, they lived a reality that might have populated their childhood dreams. How many people abandoned music due to the pressure of being a perfect musician? It is a very common occurrence for children to abandon their music classes when they reach their teens because of the pressure teachers and families put on them to be perfect musicians. You gave them an opportunity, an unexpected pleasure; they expressed gratitude by applauding your work. I want you to transfer that feeling into your concerts worldwide. You will see the world thanking you for the music you will be making. Don't worry, I will get you there!"

"It is difficult not to be anxious when I am afraid that my hands will not respond to my brain," said Jo.

Jill had come to Sao Paulo to watch their last concert; she was there, listening to the Maestro.

"May I talk?" She asked.

"Sure," answered the Maestro.

"Just to support what Maestro is saying, my husband asked his parents to stop his piano lessons because of the pressure he had from the teacher when he was a 10-year-old. He was under much pressure at school, as his father was a mathematician. He loved soccer and was a star in the school soccer team, so music was too much for him. Today, he regrets having stopped his piano lessons. There is a limit to how much pressure a child's brain can take. Let me explain why: It is important that Jo understands, but I believe it will also be valuable to the whole orchestra. Randy has heard this story so many times he might get bored, but let's do it."

"Jo, anxiety is a waste of brain power. Our brain needs an enormous amount of energy to function. It uses one-third of the energy that the whole body uses, although it represents less than 3% of the body weight. Anxiety occupies a large portion of the neural network without benefiting the task at hand, the motor task of playing piano, remembering all the notes, counting the rhythm, and harmonizing all this with the emotions that music brings. Although the musician does this automatically, the energy required is immense. The most extreme example of energy waste with anxiety occurs in patients with obsessive-compulsive disorder (OCD); they have so much anxiety about their obsession and their compulsive routines that they are not able to do anything else in life but work for their preoccupations[51].

"Anxiety chiefly occupies the brain area related to feelings and memory. Therefore, it has a major impact on your music playing. Jo, we have worked on your brain to maximize your neuronal network's ability to process music. Anxiety, because of its repetitive nature, impairs your practice and, most of all, disturbs your performance. The strategy of having Randy play with you was just to give you the comfortable feeling that you would not make mistakes notable to the audience. So, you can have fun with your friend, and most of all, progressively liberate you from the need for any help so you can continue your

---

[51] Santos BF, Gorgulho A, Saraiva CW, Lopes AC, Gomes JG, Pássaro De Salles A. (2019) 'Understanding gamma ventral capsulotomy: potential implications of diffusion tensor image tractography on target selectivity,' *Surg Neurol Int* 2019.

career independently, controlling your anxiety properly. We are sure you will achieve this ability. That is our plan, isn't it, Maestro?"

"Yes, it is, Jill. We have given Jo's brain a rest regarding his right hand. I see that he is using his right hand's fingers better. What do you think?" The Maestro asked looking at Randy.

"It is amazing, Maestro. After the 9th concert, the one given in Goiânia, I didn't need to intervene much to help Jo. He would go ahead playing the piece on his own. My mom asked me to let him go on when he was playing correctly and just to relax with him. Although I want to keep playing with him and dream of participating in the world tour with all of you, I don't think Jo needs me anymore."

"Yes, Randy," said Jill. "You have to concentrate in school as well. You love music; I have no doubt that you will continue with it for life. However, I want you to also have a strong academic background. You told me that, at some point, you would like to work with your dad in the laboratory. This is important, as a musical career is already possible for you. After your experience at Julliard, you will have a good vision of what a musician's life will be for you. Although it is a fun life, it also can be very hard financially. Not many musicians can live only from their music. Many have a main job, pursuing music on the side. Others really struggle to survive despite hours and hours of practice.

"A minority becomes famous and has an opulent life. You need to experiment with other opportunities; this is what your dad and I want to offer you. You will choose your life profession at the proper time, deciding where your love is: humanities, arts, science, economy, mathematics, or teaching. Sure, you will participate in the world concert tour, predominantly at the beginning, as we need to be sure that Jo will be able to on his own; then we can select the ones you will attend, depending on your school schedule."

"I agree," said the Maestro. "There was a time in my career when I had to stop to work as a businessman. If I hadn't had proper schooling, I would not have succeeded. It was such a desperate period, with my right hand failing, that I fell into severe depression. It was a lifesaver for me to be able to participate in an activity such as being a boxer's manager; it kept me close to audiences, a completely different audience, as you can imagine, but it did reinvigorate my desire to be a public person again. It is always important to have a plan B. Now, for example, I am living a plan B as a conductor, when in reality, I was trained throughout my entire life to be a concert pianist. I had to study again; returning to school after a certain age takes great determination. I was already 64 years old.

"Learning is no longer easy for an old guy, especially when I had already achieved a level in my career that meant changing direction was virtually impossible. Fortunately, music remained a healthy option. Leon Fleisher convinced me to try, but it took me learning how to be an orchestra conductor. Although my fulfillment in my youth differed from my current one, it was a good choice. I feel that I am very useful now, not as a dedicated teacher of an instrument, but of making music with the power of an orchestra. I also enjoy playing simple pieces with the orchestra during our performances."

"Maestro, what you are doing with a period of life in which most retired people waste on depression and sorrow is amazing. You are using the power of music, the wisdom of being a successful musician for your entire life, and your influence in the music world to help people and children with medical and social needs. I see it as a third life, after the first life as a pianist, a second life as a conductor, and a third life as a benefactor. It is very admirable. I am very grateful for your help with Jo's treatment.

"I also have to thank Randy for what he has done for his friend," Jill continued emotionally, "making us all successful and bringing Jo back to the career he always dreamed of for him and his parents, who fought so hard for him. What a great pleasure to have been in this country, learning its people's generosity and diversity. I never imagined that Jo and Randy would grow so much as musicians here. I also want to thank the whole orchestra for sharing your conductor. Let's keep on working together."

Randy told them that he had learned about a famous Brazilian musician in a book he read called *Effortless Master,* by Kenny Warner, a famous jazz pianist. He confessed in his writing that he came to Brazil in a moment of despair in his career to learn from the late pianist João Carlos Assis Brazil (1945-2021), a great interpreter of Villa-Lobos. He remembers João Carlos saying to him be kind to yourself while trying to help Kenny with his music breakdown. It was on this trip to Rio de Janeiro that Kenny learned to give himself to music without worrying about the audience. A five-minute exercise of hand tapping on the piano allowed him to rediscover the ease of playing and the understanding that we don't play for the audience but for our own enjoyment.

"This is the same advice Maestro João Carlos gave us," Randy said. "Kenny learned that perfection was not what the public looked for, as perfection is a given for a professional musician. Certainly, for the classical musician, this is not enough; the public needs to feel the performer on another level. It is when music emanates from the ethereal 'connection of humans with divinity,' a connection that has transcended generations through millennia. The most primitive homo sapiens already entered into trances with the rhythmic beat of the drum. His realization that music connects man to divinity inspired Kenny Warner to write his most recent book, *Becoming the Instrument*, which I am reading now, a complete embodiment of the musician with the instrument."

"Wow! You are really reading, Randy, congratulations," said Jill. "You should also read Joseph Ledoux; he dedicated his life to studying the pathways of emotion in the brain; he has an interesting theory on why music is so involved with human feelings. To him, it comes from fear and release of fear, explaining why we get the chills when we hear special tunes. It is like a wonderful groove when we listen to a composition that reaches our soul. A hardcore scientist, he does not talk about the soul but hypothesizes that having the chills does not translate to being afraid but relieved. In his animal studies, he showed that chills are important for furry animals, as they make them appear bigger when they are scared, intimidating the attacker. When the threat ceases, it corresponds to decreased neuronal activity in the amygdala, the structures located in the temporal lobes believed to be related to fear.

"Activity increases when the animal is in danger and decreases when the 'fight or flight response' has abated, a relief expressed in humans as the chills or shivers[52]. Studies are still necessary to support this theory completely, as we haven't yet imaged the brain in the moment of chills to be certain about the dynamics of the amygdala. However, we have proved in our animal experiments that when we block the amygdalae, we take away the animal's fear." [53]

---

[52] LeDoux, J (1996) *The emotional Brain. The Mysterious Underpinnings of Emotional Life*, Simon & Schuster.

[53] Langevin JP, De Salles AA, Kosoyan HP, Krahl SE (May 2010) 'Deep brain stimulation of the amygdala alleviates post-traumatic stress disorder symptoms in a rat model,' *J Psychiatr Res.*, **25**. (Epub ahead of print).

"Well," said the Maestro. "Too much science! It is time to rest and prepare for our next 13 concerts; we already have the tour set through Europe, Oceania, Asia, and North America. We are two months away; our last performance will be in the Carnegie Hall in New York. I always dreamed of returning there. I played there when I was a 26-year-old! It is incredible to be in that music house; I hope to be there with all of you."

Chapter 40
Meeting the Queen

Music once admitted to the soul,
becomes a sort of spirit and never dies.
Edward Bulwer Lytton

Randy, Jo, Jill, and Mrs. Jin left Brazil for a deserved vacation back home in Los Angeles. It was only a vacation from the concerts, as school was starting for Randy and Jo, and Jill was back to work at the university. Maestro oriented Randy and Jo to continue their practice together, with Jo progressively taking on the playing of all the Preludes with his right hand. Their task was for both to be able to play the 24 Preludes completely on their own, as the school would take precedence for Randy, and Jo might need help on the world tour. The Maestro had signed the contract with 13 music halls, seven in Europe and six in Asia, including performances in Beijing and Shanghai. Because Jo was adamant that he would be a concert pianist, Maestro wanted to give him great exposure in China, where he was well-known in the Chinese classical music circles.

Randy would not participate in the Asian portion of the tour; it would be the last leg, and school was his priority. Mrs. Jin and Jo never had in their minds that music would not be his career. He hadn't known another path in life since his years in China; music was his focus and an opportunity for the whole family. He had learned to enjoy music, love it, and live it despite his father's tough ways. The exhilarating feeling of having audiences admiring his playing was so ingrained in his early childhood that he didn't see life without it. There is a common problem with celebrity children; when they become adults and are no longer seen as gifted artists, they cannot tolerate an obscure life and become drug addicts to reach highs, becoming social pariahs. Mrs. Jin feared this outcome, so she was determined that Jo would excel in music throughout his life if it depended on her efforts.

The tour started in Amsterdam, where classical music was ubiquitous in schools, churches, and theaters. They were to give a concert in a church, invited by a government agency, offering free concerts for tourists. Brazilian music was exotic for tourists in northern Europe, where the Maestro was already well-known. Therefore, the second portion of the concert was very attractive for those interested in learning about global classical music. The audience would be eased into the concert with the boys playing the Preludes as a duo. The whole orchestra was excited about visiting the city, where they had been told that classical music was a natural love of the population. The city's charm, the old churches, the canals, and the possibility of them attending several concerts during their stay were very attractive to the Brazilian orchestra. Walking without any plan and entering one of the multitudes of churches could lead to the happy surprise of seeing chamber music groups playing heavenly tunes. They would be part of one of these carefree concerts as the audience would mainly be tourists with no desire to criticize.

Maestro João wanted to ease them into the European tour without putting too much pressure on his young players, allowing them to start playing for the pleasure of it, not to impress audiences. This environment was ideal for Jo, as Randy was instructed not to intervene. In the main theaters, the Maestro asked to have two pianos; they would sit separately, alternating the Preludes and completing them for each other when necessary. As he was already taking classes at school, Jill had organized for Randy to have classes online during the initial leg of the tour. They would spend three nights in Amsterdam, playing in two churches and the main music hall of the city, the Royal Concertgebouw. Their daily schedule was practicing for five hours in the morning, resting and tourism in the afternoon, and concerts from 7:00 pm to 9:00 pm. They were to be in bed no later than 11:00 pm as they practiced every day at 7:00 am. This schedule would continue in all the cities they were to play in.

The concerts in the two churches went well. The first was in the Church of Our Lady, a Catholic church built in 1854, now serving the Orthodox and Roman Catholic communities. The site was a beautiful neo-gothic church; some people were inside at 7:00 pm, a few tourists and Christian believers. The concert went without major problems. The Maestro was pleased with the boy's integration and orchestra performance. They were ready for the next concert in the English Reformed Church, one of the most traditional in Amsterdam, built in 1412. It was one of the first churches built in Holland.

Initially, it was a wooden building, but it was completely burned in a fire, which destroyed part of the city. It was rebuilt in the early 1600s, evolving to serve the English-speaking congregations in Amsterdam. In fact, it is one of the most beautiful buildings in the heart of Amsterdam. The concerts went well, except Jo felt his right-hand pinky curling. Maestro João noticed and signaled Randy to help. Nothing was noticed by the small audience in the church, but unfortunately, anxiety again invaded Jo's brain.

As the following day was their first European performance in a major theater, The Royal Concertgebouw, Maestro did not take chances; he asked Randy to take the leadership and play all Preludes as if he was the only one giving the concert. The audience stood up applauding when the concert ended, it was perfect with Jo also playing but without the pressure of being alone at the concert. In the second part after Beethoven's Fourth Symphony there was an encore with Ravel's Grande Cadenza and the second encore with the 'Tico-Tico no Fubá' was a great success. Great reviews appeared in the newspapers, helping to gather an audience for the concerts in Stockholm, the next city on their tour.

***

The home of the Royal Stockholm Philharmonic Orchestra, The Stockholm Concert Hall (Konserthuset Stockholm), was the next stop for the Maestro's orchestra and his boys. The amazing concert hall was designed by Ivar Tengbom, a famous neo-classical Swedish architect who lived from 1878 to 1968. He completed the traditional Roman facade in 1926. It also became the home for the annual Nobel Prize award ceremonies. So, it was a dream for any serious musician and scientist to have the honor of performing there. The venue is also famous for its popular music concerts. Maestro was worried about Jo's performance, as he had invited Queen Silvia Renate Sommerlath, the Germany-Brazilian who married Prince Carl Gustaf, sealing the romantic 1972 Munich Olympics love story. Prince Gustaf had met the exotic, beautiful Brazilian-looking woman as a participant in the Olympics, a personification of the 'Girl from Ipanema.'

The prince became King Carl XVI Gustaf of Sweden, succeeding his father to the throne, while the queen became loved by the Swedish people as a supporter of causes dedicated to children's protection and development worldwide.

The first preliminary concert in Sweden was in the Gamla Stan (Old Town), the oldest section of Stockholm, where the church 'Storkyrkan,' one of the oldest in the country, is located. Here, the concert went without difficulties; Randy and Jo played perfectly, assuring the Maestro that the performance the next day at the Nobel Prize home would go well. He was very interested in Queen Silvia's support for his work for children with dystonia and the poor children in Brazil. Jill came to Stockholm, too. She was also attracted by the opportunity to visit the Nobel Prize venue and Karolinska University, where the device that cured Randy, the Gamma Knife®, had been conceptualized.

Jill had the chance to meet Queen Silvia, an amazingly sweet woman who was mild and remarkably supportive of the boys' efforts. When Jill described the device implanted in Jo's brain, Queen Silvia was amazed. She wanted to learn more about the disease and how an electronic device inside a child's brain could help effectively, permitting him to play as a virtuoso. Jo was an amazing example of integrating an electrochemical machine like the brain and the electronic miniaturization of devices. The first question she asked after all the explanations was why such an invention had not yet been recognized by the Nobel Prize committees.

Jill promptly explained, "The understanding of Parkinson's disease, which has many features like dystonia, led to a Nobel Prize for the Swedish scientist Arvid Carlsson (1923-2018) for his work with the neurotransmitter dopamine. The integration of computers' electronics to chemical achievements like Carlsson's dopamine is the next step for human understanding of the brain, certainly worth a Nobel Prize. We are working on it. However, Swedish ingenuity has saved and improved millions of lives, for which the world is forever grateful, including our family. We used the Gamma Knife®, a Swedish neurosurgeon Lars Leksell invented and commercialized by a Swedish company, Elekta®, to treat a hamartoma in Randy's hypothalamus. It was giving him seizures and causing him to have uncontrolled aggressive behavior. He is now the intelligent and sensitive boy you watched playing with Jo."

"Dr. Morales, I know about the Gamma Knife®," said Queen Silvia. "It has helped millions of patients worldwide: people harboring the most difficult neurological diseases. We are very proud of our Elekta® company. You can count on our support to continue your studies on integrating electronics and pharmaceutics to cure neurological diseases. We are very proud of Arvid's and Leksell's work. We know Sweden has always been outstanding in the neurosciences. We want to see this continue. The work your team of scientists has done, with the influence of Maestro João and his orchestra, is impressive; I learned of Jo's and his father's tragedy through the news. It shocked Europe, where classical music is so prevalent, especially Sweden, where we have a strong tradition of protecting our children. I hope I can help you collaborate with our neuroscientists."

Knowing that the Swedish royal family was one of the wealthiest families in Europe, Jill gave the pitch for her research. "The integration of music and electrical stimulation of the brain is a very powerful influence on brain connectivity," remarked Jill. "This can be appreciated when you see musicians' MRIs. The neuronal network required for music performance is global; it runs throughout the brain. Feelings, motor function, sensory perception, and intellect are all required for a successful performance. The moment the musician is immersed in music, all these intricate functions are interconnected, although the feelings command all these senses, not the intellect alone. It is about playing without consciousness of playing but being one with the instrument. We still have much to understand about the mechanism of music invading and taking over the brain. It is amazing how we can flow from a sentiment of happiness to one of nostalgia and deep sadness to shed tears while a song progresses. I will be very grateful if you can help in any way our quest to understand the brain's electrochemical nuances and its reaction to music."

"I have a vested interest in helping you, Jill," Queen Silvia said. "It is part of my life's work to protect children. I chair the Royal Wedding Fund, which supports research in sports and athletics for disabled youth. I am proud of my Silvia Jubilee Fund for research on children with disabilities. Please contact our foundation; if we learn how to enhance youths' brains for the good, this world will be a better place."

Chapter 41
PTSD

Plasticity exists from the cradle to the grave.
Norman Doidge

After the successful performance in Sweden, they took a boat trip overnight from Stockholm to Helsinki, where the upcoming performances were scheduled, one in a church and the second in the main city's music hall. The Viking line is frequently a party boat for Swedes and Finns, taking advantage of the low prices for duty-free alcoholic drinks during the Baltic Sea crossing. They enjoy themselves on a pleasant overnight drinking trip. Music shows are common during these cruises. Therefore, the Maestro arranged for a short performance during the trip. He also scheduled a rehearsal with the whole orchestra in the morning before arriving in Helsinki, as they would play at the Helsinki Cathedral at 7:00 pm on the same day of their arrival. The boat left Stockholm harbor at 4:30 pm to arrive in Helsinki at 10:10 am, a 16- and 45-minute Baltic Sea crossing.

At 8:00 pm, the boys performed their Chopin Preludes successfully, finishing before 8:45 pm. After their performance, a Finnish musician returning home from an alcoholic round trip, tipsy, spontaneously sat at the piano and started playing the Beethoven Concert Number 3 and also recklessly moved to the Tchaikovsky Concert Number 1. Russian composers are very popular in Finland, as the Russian Tzars ruled the country until 1917. Even though it was partial and poor execution of the superb music pieces, they made Jo remember the day he lost the first piano competition of his life. He started to be agitated and sweating; his pupils became dilated when he started staring in a single direction. Mrs. Jin noticed immediately and called Jill's attention to the fact.

"Dr. Morales, Jo is not well. He is beginning a crisis. It looks like one of those he had in Los Angeles while in the hospital. I brought all the medications he used to take; I don't leave home without them. I always have been afraid of his reactions to Beethoven since that day in the ICU and of Tchaikovsky's pieces," said Mrs. Jin anxiously.

"Yes," answered Jill, "it is his Post-Traumatic Stress Disorder (PTSD) manifesting. Let's give him some time, and it will probably settle down. Please hug him and sing the lullabies you used to sing as a toddler; it will give him a soothing and secure feeling. It will send his bad memories away," smiled Jill, although worried.

She knew that this electrical and neurotransmitter manifestation could reverberate in his brain, waking up a dormant circuitry that took much of her and Charles' work to suppress. Mrs. Jin's hug did seem to release Jo from the spell. She hummed some of the pieces she and Jo enjoyed in his infancy. He remained serious, though, but the crisis did not evolve.

The next morning, after breakfast, still on the boat, they went to the rehearsal. When Jo started playing, something was wrong; he was playing without feeling, and his right hand was completely impaired, with all fingers curling. He was not performing as expected for an international tour. The Maestro had no doubt that his name and that of his orchestra were at stake, so he asked for Randy to play the whole concert. They were at the beginning of the tour, a bad performance before critics could harm their plans immensely. The problem was that the boys playing Bach's and Chopin's Preludes together were a great part of the concert's attraction. As it was advertised, the public expected to hear the phenomenon of the musical integration of the boys' brains.

Jill was observing the rehearsal and noticed the Maestro's and Mrs. Jin's anxiety. Although Jo's brain implant should not have failed, as the miniature computer held energy for a whole week without the need for recharging, something was clearly out of control. She had to figure it out, at least for the performance at the Helsinki Music Hall (*Helsingin Musiikkitalo*). The performance at Saint Nicholas' Church would probably have to be without Jo's right hand. She would have to check the device in his brain and probably recharge and reprogram it. She would have to contact her husband and Dr. Hillary in Los Angeles to exchange ideas with them. It looked like Jo's flashbacks were disturbing his motor circuitry. This emotional-motor interference had to be blocked. At the end of the rehearsal, the Maestro called Jill, Mrs. Jin, Randy, and Jo for a conversation.

They sat at the Maestro's cabin deck overlooking a beautiful view of the calm Baltic; it still had some ice blocks as the boat approached the harbor. They were almost in Helsinki and could see the city's skyline, in which Helsinki Cathedral, with its green domes, creates a unique view for those arriving at the city by the sea. The bucolic view of the church brought tears to Mrs. Jin's eyes, who was anxious about her son's promising career. Would he be incapable of performing in that famous city's landmark?

Helsinki Cathedral, one of the most visited buildings in the city, was built from 1830 to 1852 as a tribute to the Grand Duke of Finland, Tsar Nicholas I of Russia. It was also known as Saint Nicholas' Church until Finland's independence from Russia. Visited by more than 350,000 people per year, it promised to have a good audience for the already famous Brazilian Orchestra. Maestro João chose the site, hoping for a representative audience for the performance, introducing his musicians to musical circles in Eastern Europe.

It was a moment of anxiety for all of them. Randy was close to Jo when the Maestro started talking. In a friendly way, he was consoling his piano partner and reassuring him that he would be there for him no matter what the Maestro decided.

"Jo, what caused you so much trouble at the rehearsal?" The Maestro asked.

Jo timidly said, "I don't know. Bad memories came to me; my father and the music I played didn't sound right, and it all fogged my mind. I don't remember well; I had a frightened feeling, the one I used to have when I played poorly, and my dad got mad at me. I remember only when that man started playing Beethoven Concert Number 3, and then my mom hugged me. This morning, I didn't know why my right hand was stiff; it worried me, so I couldn't play well. I used my left hand as we had planned. Do you think it was not good enough, Maestro?"

"It was OK, but it came without true feeling for the music; the Preludes must be played with your soul. You were not into the music. It appeared you were mostly worried about your hand."

"Yes, I was. I played mechanically, worried about what was happening independently with my right hand; I couldn't stop it from curling. Do you think I will be able to play tonight?"

"I have a solution for the problem, but we will hear what Dr. Morales says."

"Well, I have been thinking about what to do. I will be working with Jo this afternoon. I want to check his brain device, recharge it, and try new programs. Together with the Maestro, we will set you up to play tonight. We are here to help you. Randy is also prepared to lend you a hand, so don't worry. I know it is difficult for you, but we have been through this before successfully, so we know how to handle it."

"OK," said Maestro. "I will have you wearing one of my gloves in your right hand; I expect you to play only single notes with the right hand and use only your index finger. Randy will fill in, as he can play the pieces by himself, and you can. This time, he will watch to ensure the Preludes' right-hand notes are completed. As I will be wearing gloves on both hands, it will appear that it is a strategy for our performance. I play with my gloves all the time, it works fine, as you have seen, so it will be easy for you."

"Maestro, I want to work with Jo this afternoon. I hope to have it all settled by 4 pm. Then you can have the boys and prepare them for the concert. What do you think about all of us going to the church then to review the boys' performance before the concert?"

"Sure, Jill; do you want to give your opinion, Mrs. Jin?" The Maestro asked.

"I must just thank you all for being so kind to Jo. He is calmer now; I am confident it will be fine. What do you think, Jo?"

"There was a time when I didn't use my right hand; Randy and I gave nice presenations then. Do you remember at the hotel lobby, Randy? There, we got no help from an orchestra or the Maestro's orientation. I am assured that Randy will be there for me, and I will do my best," said Jo, smiling.

"Jo, we will give a great concert. Play the left hand with gusto, and I will fill in strongly on the right. I will fill in when you need me; we know how to do this," said Randy.

They all left for lunch, preparing for an afternoon of intense work.

Chapter 42
Over Ethernet

*The brain is not an inanimate vessel that we fill;
rather, it is more like a living creature with an appetite,
one that can grow and change itself
with proper nourishment and exercise.*
Norman Doidge

After lunch, Mrs. Jin brought Jo to Jill's room to program his brain device. Jill connected the TV to the device programmer and linked Charles and Dr. Hillary in a Zoom call to discuss the steps for treating this new situation. Both appeared on the TV screen smiling.

"Hey, Jo, how is it going? A lot of success I heard," said Dr. Hillary

"Yes, but now I am scared; this hand curling was unexpected. I don't know what happened. Do you know?"

"No problem, Jo. Jill, Charles, and I had a meeting during lunch. We came up with a solution to program your brain. We will block the memories you described this morning to Maestro and Jill. We are positive that you will be able to play tonight and tomorrow. We will work over the Ethernet with you throughout your tour; don't worry, we will not leave you alone. How is your hand now?"

"It is still curling a bit. I don't think I can use it tonight," Jo said, looking sad.

"Well, we will work on it. The most important thing now is to block your bad memories so you can interpret and feel the music. You will make your mark with the left hand, no doubt. We want you to direct your brain to the musical interpretation; we don't want you to worry about performing with the right hand now; it will be too distracting. Let the right hand stay with Randy.

You both have these Preludes ingrained in your brains and your soul. And the concert's appeal is your seamless integration. It will be a success, I am sure."

Charles said, "Jo, put your little antenna over the device behind your ear. I will send the program I devised with Dr. Hillary and Jill through cyberspace. Jill will be examining you. Randy will be there observing so he can know when and where he will need to help you during the concert. You are an important and lucky guy to have this team of experts concentrating on your brain. So, rest assured, we will always be there for you."

"I am confident, thank you very much, Mr. Morales," said Jo.

"Now, Jill, as we decided over lunch in a video call, let's move the electrical fields anteriorly toward the cognitive portion of his pallidum so we can modulate the behavioral portion of the structure. Modulating its cognitive portion will block the interference from the lateral amygdala into this structure. Neuronal connections coming from the medial frontal lobe will be free to act. The more instinctive pallidum output will be blocked, while the more anterior and lateral portions of the frontal lobe, where Jo's intellectual, judgment, and music interpretation will flow freely. We will liberate a bit of the pallidum's motor function and check if his hands' dystonic movements get worse. If it happens, we can change the program to better moderate the motor control responsible for his hands."

The programming was set as planned. Jo sensed the change in his brain as if a shock were passing by. He felt well, but his right-hand continued curling. Jill suggested they go to the hotel lobby, where there was a piano, to test his playing. Randy went too, as he wanted to be prepared for the concert.

People gathered around the piano when they started playing in the hotel lobby. Jo's anxiety was obvious when he noticed the people around him and his right hand intensely curling; however, when Randy entered with the right-hand portions of the Preludes, he relaxed, and his left-hand playing became perfect and soulful. At this moment, Charles realizes that Jo will have one or another motor or cognitive help from the current device in his brain. The boys played the pieces flawlessly. Randy really dominated the portions that Jo tended to fail. They played the whole performance several times before Jill called Maestro João to judge their playing.

After hearing them, Maestro João looked at Jill and asked, "Is there nothing you can do about the right hand?"

"Apparently, we have to choose between perfect interpretation and right-hand motor skills today. What do you prefer? We have a backup strategy for the rest of the tour, but here in Helsinki, we must live with this limited solution."

"Fine, I want Jo to wear one of my gloves, though. It will signal to the audience that he has a problem in that hand. It will increase admiration for the quality of his playing, which is undoubtedly outstanding when Randy covers his right-hand deficits."

Jo put his head down, thinking the Maestro was unhappy.

"Hey, Jo, we came a long way," said the Maestro.

"We advertised that you and Randy played the Preludes together because of the dystonia in your right hand. The audiences expect that the performance will be joint, reflecting our assertion. They will not only give us complete support but will also see the phenomenon of brain integration through music you both achieved. We will ace our concerts! You can be sure." The Maestro smiled confidently.

"Thank you, Randy," said Jo, smiling. "Let's do it; I am always counting on you."

"I am ready; I am counting on you as well," said Randy.

That night, the boys delivered, as did the Bachianas Orchestra; the church's success was repeated in the *Helsingin Musiikkitalo*. The concert house was imposing. The incredible acoustics of the hall enhanced the audience's experience of the boys' technical and musical integration. Playing at the *Helsingin Musiikkitalo* was definitely an experience that Maestro João's musicians would never forget.

The boys admired the Finn musicians since they started classes at Colburn in Los Angeles because of the Los Angeles Philharmonic Conductor Esa-Pekka Salonen. Helsinki was the hometown of many famous composers and conductors who had been formed at the Sibelius Academy of Music in Helsinki. The modern *Helsingin Musiikkitalo* was the classical Finnish musicians' dream through the end of the last century. Its architectural design occurred from the twentieth to the twenty-first century. The building's groundbreaking started in 2008. It was inaugurated three years later by the Sibelius Academy students' presentations. Performances of the two main orchestras in Finland, the Helsinki Philharmonic and the Finnish Radio Symphony Orchestra, were also part of the inauguration program since the *Helsingin*

Musiikkitalo was home to both orchestras. There was also a complex presentation conducted by the violinist Jukka-Pekka with orchestra and coir, the highlight of the inauguration. Jukka-Pekka was a classmate of Esa-Pekka Salonen. The boys were very familiar with Maestro Esa-Pekka Salonen, as they attended many presentations and rehearsals of the famous conductor in Los Angeles.

Randy and Jo felt at home. Randy did a great job covering for Jo, so the performance was very smooth. Maestro João was delighted. He knew, however, that they had to solve Jo's problem; he could not spend his life depending on Randy. Jo had to support his own career, as he had decided to become a concert pianist. Like many other classical musicians who evolved from instrumentalists to maestros, a boy who loves classical music would probably follow in his footsteps.

After the successful concerts in Helsinki, Jill decided to go to Los Angeles to have a detailed conference with Dr. Hillary, Charles, and Dr. Wronsky, Jo's psychiatrist, to discuss how to control Jo's PTSD symptoms. She would have five days to work with them and organize her strategy. She knew she at least had to bring the LowFU device from there. She was convinced she needed to accompany the boys during the European tour.

She envisioned blocking the output from the lateral portion of Jo's amygdala, freeing him of his fear of failing with the right hand, allowing him to concentrate only on mastering the music. This was something she was not able to control by programming his current device, as it was specifically implanted to control motor symptoms. Indeed, she could direct a substantial part of the electrical output of the device to the anterior portion of the pallidum, leaving low energy in the posterior ventral pallidum (PVP). This was probably why the right hand was not being appropriately controlled. She planned to invert the stimulation in the following manner: low-frequency ultrasound to stimulate the lateral amygdala and the indwelling device to stimulate the PVP, controlling his cognitive and motor imbalance.

She had to improve her ability to selectively neuromodulate the instinctive and protective portion of Jo's brain. She had accomplished this before, with his motor function, when he was admitted to the ICU with a continuous dystonia crisis. She knew turning off the neuronal network responsible for Jo's bad memories would be possible. Using the LowFU, she had been able to take him out of the intensive care unit, evolving his therapy toward his recovery. It allowed Jo to make his mark as a musician and become admired worldwide. Now, the task promised to be easier than before.

What she could not allow was for Jo to develop a drug dependence that would indiscriminately affect all portions of his brain, everywhere medications blocked neurotransmitters or enhanced them. Specifically, modulating those cerebral areas leading to the symptoms was the best solution, keeping him at the peak of his performance. She would specifically try the lateral portion of the amygdala, as her experiments in the laboratory had shown this area was the culprit for his symptoms. Drugs would definitely be able to break the amygdala's influence but would also reduce his spark as a musician. They would completely sedate his feelings for music.

Chapter 43
All Together to Help

It was at once a magnificent and terrible sight to see they march on to the tune of their flutes, without any disorders in their ranks, any discomposure in their minds, or changes in their accountancies, calmly and cheerfully marching with music to the deadly fight.
Plutarch (46 A.D.-119 A.D.)

Arriving in Los Angeles, Jill called the meeting. Dr. Hillary was the first to arrive.

"Jill, we will have to be objective with this meeting. I have the operating room prepared for an emergency. We are missing you a lot here. I have been working double since you decided to embark on your European music tour. I realized the incredible volume of work you handle. I hope you are having a good time," said Dr. Hillary. He sounded almost jealous of Jill's opportunity to travel with the boys and the orchestra.

"Well, Professor, it has not been an easy vacation taking kids to fun rides and museums. I thought it would be nicer, but Jo is a demanding medical and technical challenge. I have been thinking, reading, and creating solutions 24-7. I go to bed thinking about how to solve his problems. I have been spending hours reading about the intricacies of brain pathways connecting myriads of neurons, synapses, and dendritic networks. Brain connectivity is an overwhelming topic; we know so little about it. Why do you think I came all the way from Europe to talk with the dream neuroscience team available here?"

"Don't feel that I am pressuring you to return to the demanding job of daily neurosurgery. I prefer you to keep pioneering the modulation of the musician's brain, as you are doing so well with Jo. Your opportunity with him is invaluable; he is an open music neuroscience book! Please take your time; I can do the job here; it is simply an assembly line for me after 40 years of brain surgery."

At this moment, Dr. Paul Wronsky, the psychiatrist, entered the room. "Hey, Jill, nice seeing you here. I guess Europe got boring for you; otherwise, you wouldn't be here. Thanks for inviting me to this discussion. I am anxious to hear more about Jo's PTSD symptoms. I cannot imagine how to help him without compromising his musical genius with sedation. Do you have one of your bright ideas?"

"Welcome, Paul. That is precisely what I want to ponder with you all. Do you have any easy fix with a pill to control Jo's memories of his father's harmful influence on his mind?" She hoped some new magic drug or behavior therapy had been developed recently. She didn't like to read pharmacology.

"Well, I understand from what you told me about Jo's reaction to Beethoven piano concert number 3 that he had a post-traumatic vegetative crisis, which you diagnosed as PTSD. Selected drugs aided by Cognitive Behavior Therapy (CBT) are usually the solution to it, but it is a very long process. I don't see it happening during the two-month music tour you are all engaged in. Completing a successful CBT program can take years. Do you want to take some medication with you just in case he needs it?" Wronsky asked.

"Unfortunately, he is very sensitive to drugs. He has a very low brain reserve. His brain's magnetic resonance (RM) shows that he lost a substantial volume of neurons in the hypoxic event due to the benzodiazepines. I feel wary of giving him medication while he is in Europe, away from our team supervision. He may become a zombie and not perform at concerts at all. We can have a two-week break here in Los Angeles before starting the Asian tour. Then we could try it if you are willing to manage his medication," answered Jill.

"Sure, I will try medications for him when he is here in Los Angeles, but what do you plan to do until then? How many concerts do you still have in Europe before you return?"

"We only finished the three concerts of the Scandinavian portion of the tour; we still have four cities to go through: Munich, Vienna, Madrid, and London. It will be challenging to keep Jo playing in all of them. Fortunately, the concerts will happen because Randy is doing very well. However, the audience expects to see them playing together. It was their integration that

Maestro João advertised. I plan to take our LowFU device to block his PTSD symptoms. I will have our magnetic transcranial stimulation (MTS) device as a backup. I will probably need several applications of both, one for his dystonia and the other for his depression. I imagine working with him daily. I don't have much time in Europe or here. The Maestro has them rehearsing through the mornings, so I only have part of the afternoon to work with Jo. They also need some rest. I need some light from you; I must return to Europe in two days. I need your steer on where I need to focus my stimulation efforts," said Jill.

"Did he have shivers during his neuro vegetative state?" Wronsky asked.

"As a matter of fact, he did," answered Jill.

"So, the Beethoven Number 3 concert is stimulating his lateral amygdala. There is a direct pathway coming from the auditory cortex, through the thalamus, to the amygdala. The pathway is believed to control chills and shivers as a response to music. This seemly primitive pathway has evolved in humans' neuronal network to provide a quasi-feeling of pleasure as an integration of a cognitive frontal cortex input coming from its interpretation of music as an unthreatening event. It resolves the feeling of being under threat recognized by the lateral amygdala before it surfaces as a dangerous message. Therefore, the person feels only the initial shivers caused by the sound.

"Jo is having the primitive chill reaction of a threatened animal, as the animal looks larger with its fur erection, scarring away the attacker. It is an immediate reaction of our primitive brain, which was progressively transformed into a pleasure sensation instead of an alarm for survival to humans. For example, a threatened furry animal has a generalized erection of its fur, while humans have only this primitive feeling of pleasurable chills displayed as goosebumps. This sensation is also felt during sexual foreplay."

"Yes, Paul, I read about this reaction to a threatening event," said Jill.

Dr. Wronsky continued, "I plan to give him a proven therapy that can control his PTSD symptoms relatively fast. I will organize it for the two weeks before you initiate the Asian tour. It is called the Eye Movement Desensitization and Reprocessing (EMDR) method. It has achieved remarkable results for some patients in a short period of time. Developed in the late 1980s by Francine Shapiro[54], it consists of a combination of making the patient occupy his brain with a repetitive task while he or she is going back

---

54 Shapiro, F. (2001) 'EMDR 12 years after its introduction: Past and future research,' Journal of Clinical Psychology, 58(1), 1-22. doi:10.1002/jclp.1126

through the traumatic memories that bring the PTSD symptoms. While the patient is experiencing his harmful memories, the therapist provokes repetitive eye movements by asking the subject to follow his finger with the eyes in a saccadic fashion. Apparently, this parallel task dissociates the traumatic memories from the patient's autonomic centers, causing the symptoms. I believe it will help him cope with unexpected tunes that bring him to his PTSD symptoms."

"The Beethoven Concert Number 3 is a threatening music for Jo," insisted Jill. "It is ingrained in his memory; it is possible that EMDR will help. The threat takes him all the way to a PTSD crisis and a severe neurovegetative response. If we can minimize those responses, it will be a great step in improving his performance. Additionally, if we manage to block his lateral amygdala, I believe we will stop his reaction to Beethoven's music bilaterally. We will be allaying his fear. The question I have is whether it will also remove his feelings for all music pieces, including the Preludes, which we so badly want Jo to feel. When we use all these techniques to invade his brain, we will possibly destroy his interpretation." Jill looked concerned.

"I don't believe so," intervened Dr. Hillary with his unending optimism. "He loves music; it is his passion. People who love music, as he does, have strong white matter connectivity between their auditory cortex and primitive brain structures related to pleasure, such as the accumbens, which are mainly controlled by the prefrontal cortex. The Foreway Bundle links these structures of the basal striatum. They come from primitive brainstem areas, are highly dopaminergic structures, and are intrinsic participants in pleasurable sensations. Therefore, they are prone to be involved in addiction and several impulsive activities, such as recreational drug intake, overeating, gambling, and sex. This means there is heavy connectivity going on from all brain areas with these basal primitive structures[55]. When an imbalance between these regions occurs, and the cognitive inhibition from cortical input fails, the person is vanquished by addiction.

---

[55] Ball T, Rahm B, Eickhoff SB, Schulze-Bonhage A, Speck O, et al (2007) 'Response Properties of Human Amygdala Subregions: Evidence Based on Functional MRI Combined with Probabilistic Anatomical Maps,' *PLoS ONE* 2(3): e307. doi:10.1371/journal.pone.0000307.

"The late neurologist and writer Oliver Sachs mentioned these pathways shortly before his death[56]. Only Beethoven brings back the tragic memories of the music competition and his father's reaction to his loss, which was painful and embarrassing for Jo. Obviously, we will only know for sure if we try to stop the input to his lateral amygdala with the LowFU; let's go ahead with your plan, Jill. I suggest that you take some clonazepam (Klonopin) with you just in case an emergency happens before a concert or a rehearsal. A few drops of clonazepam will calm Jo."

"Paul, I would like to explore your EDMR protocol; I will study it to take this option in my pocket. I will have five potential approaches: DBS, LowFU, TMS, EDMR, and drugs; I may need them all," said Jill. "Notice that I will keep drugs as a last resort, as once a dose is given, we lose control until it is metabolized, and worse, it will affect Jo's whole brain and body."

"Fine," said Dr. Hillary. "We have a plan. But now I have to run to the operating room. Thank you all. Have a good day."

---

[56] Sachs E Matthew, et al., (2016) 'Brain connectivity reflects human aesthetic responses to music,' *Social and Affective Neuroscience,* 1-8.

Chapter 44
Technology for Music and Brain

To achieve great things, two things are needed:
A plan and not quite enough time.
Leonard Bernstein

Jill organized all her devices and medication packages. She shipped them the day before her flight to Munich, where the orchestra had just arrived for the next concert. It would happen in three days' time at the Philharmonic Hall at the Gasteig in Munich. Still the largest music hall in the city, it was built in the 1980s, seating 2,387 folks in an interesting building resembling a seashell. The giant wooden shell was, unfortunately, built with poor acoustics. The famous American conductor Leonard Bernstein suggested that the Germans should burn it down. Despite this, Maestro João had selected it for its location, as the Gasteig also housed the Richard Strauss Conservatory, an 'Adult Education Center,' and a cozy shopping area with coffee shops and a library. He thought that the education center for arts would be an excellent site for the orchestra's musicians to wander around for food and entertainment.

The intense schedule called for morning rehearsal, freedom to rest in the afternoon, and one or two preparatory evening concerts in churches. However, as the concerts in Scandinavia had been successful, he decided to play only one concert there, skipping the church performances. The sold-out Philharmonic Hall seats demonstrated their remarkable fame, already spreading from Scandinavia throughout Europe.

After arriving at the hotel in Munich, Jill organized a complete non-invasive neuromodulation laboratory in a small conference room Maestro João had reserved for her work with Jo. She had a LowFU device, a TMS apparatus, a portable EEG recording machine with electrodes she could use to stimulate peripheral nerves across the skin, a brain robotic localizing device, and an infrared neuronavigational apparatus. She needed this stereotactic device based on reflective and non-invasive markers to precisely reach the proper sites for stimulation and/or inhibition of neurons, modulating deep nuclei and pathway structures responsible for the dystonia. Reaching Jo's brain at any location she deemed necessary. Additionally, she also had the EDMR protocols. The EDMR was to curb the anxiety and PTSD symptoms Jo could develop. She was trying all the psychiatric tricks she had learned in the crash course Dr. Wronsky had given her during the three days in Los Angeles. She would have two afternoons to work with Jo before the concert.

The fact that the concert was sold out created a lot of pressure on the orchestra and a fair reason for Jo's anxiety: in fact, for both boys, as they were the main attraction in Munich. The city media and press had extensively covered their unique success during the Scandinavian tour. To her dismay, Jo was beyond depressed. He had entered in a completely despondent mood. Mrs. Jin mentioned he was even having suicidal ideation. The Maestro had decided to only help Randy change the music score pages and play the piano during a few passages, all already planned with Randy. Randy had been instructed to play the pieces entirely.

Jill didn't waste time; she arrived in Munich in the afternoon, and that same night, she took Jo to her laboratory. She adjusted electrodes over his eyebrows and gave him a continuous three-hour brain stimulation. Electrical pulses entering through his ophthalmic branches of the trigeminal nerves invaded his brain. She worked on him from 7:00 pm to 10:00 pm. Additionally, she instructed Mrs. Jin to leave the electrodes in place and let him sleep with the stimulation on. Jo had a full night of sleep receiving high-frequency stimulation, spreading electricity throughout his brain. The trigeminal nerve is so-called because it has three converging branches that bring sensory input from the face and other regions of the head to the brain.

Jill targeted the stimulation through the ophthalmic branch, which is very accessible in the upper part of the eye socket. The electrical stimulation to the entire brain enters the skull through a small orifice over the orbit, marching through the skull base, where it meets its two accompanying branches, the maxillary and the mandibular. Together, they form the two trigeminal nerves, each entering the pons, part of the brainstem. There, they spread bilaterally, relaying the impulses in the sensory portion of the thalamus, reaching several brain regions after being reinforced in the sensory cortex. Impulses spread through the complex brain neuronal network, modifying the concentration of neurotransmitters throughout the synapses. As the synapses of this network become overworked by the prolonged high-frequency stimulation, the novel neurotransmitters' concentration changes to lift the patient's mood. Jill had studied this continuous and intense stimulation, as well as repetitive stimulation, knowing that continuously subcutaneous implanted electrodes improved depressed patients in a shorter time than sporadic treatment. She would have to maximize this technique, as she was not planning any surgery for Jo during the European tour.

The next morning, Jo woke up seeming a bit different. He accepted his breakfast without the need for Mrs. Jin's usual insistence. After breakfast, he spontaneously went to the hotel lobby piano and played. His right hand was completely curled, and he could not use it, but his left hand was useful. It was, however, still too rigid; he could not play well. He returned to the room without Mrs. Jin seeing him leaving. She was talking with Jill after their breakfast when they noticed that Jo was no longer playing in the lobby. They searched for him without avail. Mrs. Jin gave Jill a desperate look. Jill asked Mrs. Jin what worried her, as she did not understand what was happening. Mrs. Jin anxiously said that she was having a bad premonition. Immediately, she ran to the elevator, rushing to the room. When she entered, Jo had an open bottle of pills; his mouth was full of them, and he was holding a glass of water.

"What did you do, Jo?" Mrs. Jin screamed.

"I don't want to live anymore, Mom. If I can no longer play at the same level I always played at, life is not worth living. My life is a disaster; I want to die." He started crying.

Mrs. Jin immediately asked for Jill's help. They called an ambulance and rushed Jo to a hospital to pump his stomach. It all happened so fast that he didn't even lose consciousness. He only vomited and felt terrible that afternoon. Jill had a single day to help him recover from the concert. She had to be drastic in her approach. She planned to let Jo rest that night; the next day, she would try deep brain stimulation with the stereotactic neuronavigational device and the LowFU. She would also use the TMS if she felt that Jo's response to the LowFU stimulation was not sufficient to get him out of the deep depression before the concert that night.

She phoned Dr. Hillary, telling him what had happened with the trigeminal stimulation.

"Good, Jill, you took him out of depression, just enough for him to have the mental strength to try to kill himself. This is a possible reaction for very depressed patients. When severely depressed, they do not have even the drive to organize a suicide attempt. When they start to get out of the deep depression, they gather enough strength to go ahead and attempt suicide. It is my opinion that you have to continue with your approach. If you work diligently tomorrow using the LowFU, Jo may be able to participate fully in the concert. I'm optimistic he will get out of the depression. This indicated that broad stimulation of his neuronal network works."

Jill took Dr. Hillary's advice; the time for the concert in Munich was approaching. The Maestro explained how he had organized the boys' performance of the Preludes that night, enhancing Randy's role and decreasing Jo's as much as possible. However, he was hopeful the audience would still see a phenomenon of four hands. Randy was up to the task; he played the Preludes with extreme emotion. He transmits sadness in the proper passages, although the happiness is not quite there. Jo's resilience was felt by the audience; they saw a boy's extreme effort and his friend's desire to help him. The friendship between them was absolutely clear to the audience and throughout the world when it was broadcast by the media. The audience was taken by the collaboration between them. They clapped with gusto when they finished the Preludes.

The Maestro seamlessly completed the night with the Brazilian music program. At the conclusion, Jill hugged Mrs. Jin, both crying from happiness. Jill was exhausted; she could not celebrate with the orchestra that night. She took Randy to the hotel, and both slept for over 12 hours. They had to continue a four-hour speed train ride to Vienna the following afternoon. Mrs. Jin, who was still worried and dismayed by Jo's suicidal trial, did not take her eyes off him. However, Jo slept soundly that night and woke up in a stellar mood, as if nothing had happened.

Chapter 45
Vienna

Without music, life would be a mistake.
Friedrich Nietzsche

Playing in Vienna is a dream for every professional classical musician. The city exudes classical music everywhere. It was the capital of the Austro-Hungarian Empire during the period when Western classical music established itself. While music history goes back millennia, it was during the six centuries for which the Austro-Hungarian Empire dominated a large portion of Europe when investments in music halls became prevalent, allowing great classical compositions to be diffused through Europe. Vienna was the city with the most music halls in Europe. When Emperor Franz Joseph I married Elisabeth of Austria (Sisi), he commissioned the Vienna State Opera to house the performance of the most important composers and orchestras. Today, it is one of Europe's most traditional and sought-after classical music houses, competing favorably with La Scala in Milan, the Opera in Paris, the National Music Auditorium in Madrid, and the Albert Hall in London.

Surrounded by criticism of the proper Emperor and Vienna citizens, its construction claimed the life of the two men who conceptualized it. They died before the completion of the project in 1869. Working from 1861 to 1869 on the project, the architect Eduard van der Nüll was depressed by the critics of his design, leading him to suicide before seeing the birth of his brainchild. His partner in the construction, August Sicard von Sicardsburg, died weeks after Eduard's suicide, taken by tuberculosis. The tragedy did not halt the completion of the famous music hall where Maestro's musicians were being prepared to play; the biggest challenge was having Jo ready to play.

Jill worked on Jo's brain's functions the whole morning before the prestigious concert at the Vienna State Opera. She neuromodulated the lateral amygdala to curb the PTSD vegetative symptoms and the cortical subcallosal region to improve his depression using LowFU. Albeit with less specificity, she also stimulated the brain through the ophthalmic branch of the trigeminal nerve (TNS). This way, she was progressively improving his mental despondence. She fine-tuned his motor function with direct electrical stimulation of his posterior ventral pallidum (PVP) with the DBS. The cognitive frontal areas were managed with transcutaneous magnetic stimulation (TMS). That afternoon, Jo was another person. He interacted with his colleagues, who were always very close to Randy, and was playful with the orchestra's musicians. He displayed confidence and desire to play his portions of Bach's and Chopin's Preludes. Randy was most supportive of his desire, sharing with him the optimism of playing that night.

Jill and Randy went to the Maestro, asking him to change his mind about letting Jo change only the music score pages. Randy knew the virtuosity of his friend. The Maestro closely observed Jo's behavior during the afternoon, as Jill had assured him that she would change Jo's mindset. He became convinced that it was important to let Jo play; it would enhance his mood and redefine his desire to live, as music was indeed Jo's fuel for life; he had been playing for as long as he could remember. The Maestro had lived through similar dramas, so he was sympathetic to Jo's struggle. During the afternoon, Jill and the Maestro agreed that Jo was ready to try again, an amazing feat for only one morning of intense neuromodulation without using a single drug. The decision was made Jo would play. Randy spent three hours that afternoon playing the Preludes with Jo. He was totally convinced that Jo could perform well at the concert.

That night, the Vienna State Opera was packed; the orchestra entered to an ovation, followed by the two timid but confident boys. The audience stood up to greet them. The Maestro took the stage and talked about the amazing integration in the boys' brains, an achievement they had reached through music. He stressed how Chopin's Preludes had helped their healing, emphasizing the orchestra's pleasure and privilege in working with these exceptional boys, helping their growth as musicians, and enhancing their health. He confessed for the first time to an audience what an incredible opportunity it had been to teach such outstanding boys and to be in Vienna with such a warm, supportive audience. He explained the reason for their

European tour: bringing awareness about musician's dystonia, a disease capable of destroying a musician's career.

Additionally, he told a bit of his own story. Jill smiled, listening to the Maestro's confessions, knowing that she was saving Jo's career at that moment with the support of this outstanding and seasoned dystonic musician. Randy was also happy, although apprehensive; Jo's happiness was very important to him. He would do everything in his power and talent to ensure no doubts crossed Jo's mind.

What a wonderful friendship those boys had developed; one would not believe that one day, not so long ago, they had been in competition, leading to the dramatic event that overcame Jo and his family and the loss of life. The tragedy of Mr. Jin's suicide never left Randy's mind. He could not imagine losing his own father. Fortunately, he, his mother, and his father were able to help Jo, who had grown immensely in friendship and admiration for him. Jo was the incarnation of music. He had always loved music himself, but not with the intensity of Jo's love for it. Although they were very close, talking about everything, they never brought up the memories of the competition in Los Angeles, which had compromised Jo's health and piano-playing ability so severely. It would be too painful a memory to both.

The concert started with Randy playing alone, but soon Jo entered with his left hand in perfect execution. His confidence grew as the Preludes progressed, with such intensity that Randy felt confident, Jo played the parts perfectly with his right hand, always introducing feelings into his interpretation. The whole orchestra noticed Randy's generosity and consideration of his friend, always wanting the best for him without a trace of egotism. The audience also noticed Randy's continued efforts to enhance Jo's confidence, complementing any possible misstep seamlessly and generously.

Obviously, only a highly versed musician could appreciate the intensity of the friendship and the synchrony between the two young people, however the audience could feel the vibration between them.

Jill could not believe what she was hearing and seeing. Tears came to her eyes; she felt humbled by the power of science bound to music, her studies, and her son's art, maturity, and generosity. It was exhilarating to know that she had been able to help that child with such intensity. Emotion ran through her seeing Randy's efforts and the integration the boys achieved. Was her ability to sculpt Jo's brain, direct Randy's education, and the constant Charles' and hers Randy nurturing the reason for this incredible success? She realized that her kid embodied her and Charles' best traits: kindness, talents, generosity, and resilience. They had been able to educate Randy and treat his disease, making him an amazing musician.

When the audience continued clapping for several minutes, asking for encores, Maestro spoke explaining that the boys needed to rest. Not because Jo couldn't keep playing, but because Randy was crying with joy and excitement at what Jo had accomplished. Jo's complete recovery was an accomplishment that he wanted to see from the bottom of his heart. The Maestro entered with the Orquestra Bachiana SESI-SP playing Beethoven's Symphony number 4 and then on the piano with Ravel's great Cadenza, which was also a great success. The boys refreshed themselves and returned at the concert's end with the 'Tico-Tico no Fubá' encore, completing the night. Jill and Maestro knew they were ready to successfully conclude the European tour. They would continue to Madrid and London.

Chapter 46
One More Device

Success is not final; failure is not fatal:
It is the courage to continue that count.
Winston Churchill

Jill had learned a great deal while working on Jo's brain. What a feat she had achieved with her intense stimulation of Jo's diverse brain sites! It was the converse of what psychiatrists achieved with Electroconvulsive Therapy (ECT), in which a massive amount of electrical energy is delivered through the brain while the patient lies anesthetized. Instead, she could be specific, reaching targets to enhance the effect of neurotransmitter changes where it really matters. For example, it is well-known that ECT leads to memory loss in patients, especially after repeated treatments. Several sessions of ECT are necessary to take a patient out of a depression episode. Therefore, they receive a series of applications in anesthesia. Patients complain bitterly of their memory loss, although with time, this side effect improves.

Jill's specificity with LowFU and the more diffuse stimulation with TMS and TNS had provided a rapid improvement in Jo's depression. The response was almost immediately, as in a single day, she had been able to get him to play at a virtuoso level. Moreover, there was no trace of memory loss with the stimulation she had given him. The continuous overnight TNS was also a practical and effective way of approaching his depression. She was only worried because she could not follow Jo around the world to provide the treatment; he needed to continue performing at the level he had just reached in Vienna. Also, Randy would not always be available to support him. Randy must take care of his life and career, which might not be dedicated to music. She would have to offer Jo surgery again; it would be an implant of a similar device to the one in his PVP, although with a different shape, designed to completely cover the lateral portion of the amygdalae with an electrical field like the one she was achieving with the LowFU.

She had asked Charles to fashion the device, which would not be a 'Porcupine Fish' shape, but an oval. Another worry they would have to face would be the avoidance of seizures, as the amygdala is a highly epileptogenic structure. The feedback loop was also a challenge, as the input that turned on the device must be an impending threat, so they needed to work out how to record it. She sent all these thoughts to Charles; he would have to expedite his work, as after the concert in Madrid and London, they would be in Los Angeles for the tour break, and she wanted to do Jo's surgery then.

Charles received her requests and the news of the great success in Vienna. He reacted in his usual supportive way. "Jill, you are a nonstop worker. The worst is that I am obliged to keep up with your pace. Your ideas, which take split seconds for you to generate, represent a huge amount of work for me. It is not easy to be your husband."

"Come on, Honey, you are in heaven. You are at home, in your heavenly lab, without having to cook for us or drive Randy to school; you have all the time in the world to enjoy yourself. Please do the job!"

"OK, you think it is that easy. I will rack my brains to achieve what you are asking for. I do not know even where to start recording someone's fear signal. Do you?"

"No," answered Jill thoughtfully. "Have you heard of something called PUBMED? Dive into it, and you will find where someone feels afraid in the brain: the center of threat, if it exists."

"OK, great challenge. When you arrive in Los Angeles, I will have the device ready. You will study there as well to decide where the utopic site you are dreaming of is. I will talk with Dr. Hillary; he always has crazy ideas," said Charles, hopefully.

"Charles, we must provide Jo a long-term cure. He cannot depend on me and Randy forever. Randy's life has to continue beyond the world music tour. The reality is that it has not been even fun. It has been challenging. We had victories and setbacks, but it was an incredible opportunity for all of us. Randy has matured immensely. I have created and learned of solutions I would never have the opportunity to grasp if it were not for the urgency demanded by these high-level concerts Jo has endured. Randy and Jo are becoming buddies like those in the European trenches during the Second World War."

"Keep up the good work there. I will call a meeting with our team to discuss the signaling of the threat, Jill. I will let you know so you can concentrate on Jo's needs. Although he did wonderfully in Vienna, who knows what will come next? I hope not another suicide attempt. What a crazy move he did; I wish I could understand and do something about it. The device you are asking me to develop will be lifesaving. Thank you for this request; you always bring me remarkable medical puzzles to solve," said Charles.

"OK, we are a team, dear," answered Jill.

Chapter 47
More Concerts in Europe

It was according to ancient legend, the song of angels,
that induced unwilling soul to enter the body of Adam.
Kenny Werner

The Brazilian musicians arrived in London. Jill promptly requested the same setup she had organized in Munich and Vienna. Although Jo had played well at the show in Vienna, she needed to ensure she would have access to his brain with her stimulation devices. Jo was always a surprise! All of them were necessary for reaching the diverse sites related to Jo's perfect performance. He was very happy during the flight, but he was too active, in fact. He would not stay quiet in his seat. The flight attendant had to call his attention several times, asking him to fasten the seat belt, as he kept calling out to his friends. He continuously bothered Randy, who was trying to do his lessons, taking advantage of the two-hour and 20-minute flight from Vienna to London.

Something was different with Jo; Jill promptly made the diagnosis. He was in a manic state, a common reaction of a depressed patient who becomes exceedingly restless, bothersome, enthusiastic, and out of control. He was in the very opposite state of the depression that took him to the suicidal attempt. As this was a bipolar surge, she had to calm him down.

She alerted the Maestro. Although she believed that regaining control this time would be easier than dealing with depression and suicide, she needed to advise the orchestra's musicians and Randy that Jo was 'over-the-top.' He was too agitated; his colleagues had to understand that he could be inappropriate while in his manic state. This would prevent them from resenting him if he offended one of them or appeared to be too overbearing. Mainly, the Maestro needed to be understanding and patient with him. In fact, during the first rehearsal for the performance in the Albert Hall, he played too vehemently, not following Maestro João's cues very well. As Jill had advised, the Maestro was patient, letting Jo play alone for a while, then asked him to let Randy practice a little. However, his playing lacked the proper right-hand solo. Interestingly, Jo did not notice that his playing was defective. This was a real problem, as he had to let Randy enter when he noticed his right hand was failing.

Jill decided to give him a dose of valproic acid the night before the concert. Early in the morning, he was less overbearing than the day before, albeit a bit slow. Jill decided to watch the rehearsal before reaching any conclusion. Jo and Randy played well together; the Maestro made no comments regarding their playing. Jill quietly asked Randy if he had noticed any difference in Jo's behavior.

"Mom, I felt him a bit slow to react; maybe his rhythm was a bit off, but as I adapted to his play to avoid disturbing him, the Maestro did not comment. As we play the Preludes without the orchestra, a slight slowness is not noticeable; it does not disturb the other musicians or even the Maestro, who must notice but think it is fine."

"Do you think I need to adjust his brain?" Jill asked.

"No, Mom. Jo's slowness was so subtle that the Maestro didn't care or found it charming. I will make the whole thing right with my right hand. I just don't think you should give him any more medication," advised Randy, who had himself suffered the effects of overmedication.

"I am afraid he will be agitated by the immense Royal Albert Hall stage. The half-life of the valproic acid that he took yesterday is 7.2 hours. He probably will not have medication when you start the concert tonight. What will you do if he is too fast?" Jill asked.

"Nothing, I will just let him play. If he gets stuck, I will join in, as always. Don't worry, Mom, we have done this concert so many times that it has become second nature for us. We are mastering it. I don't get anxious with the Preludes anymore. I followed Jo's lead and completed his work. It is fun for me; I enjoy living through Chopin's Preludes. I will take care of making Jo shine."

Jill was impressed by Randy's confidence. She was not as confident as he seemed to be. Perhaps it was because he knew he could play all the Preludes on his own, living life in his own music space, a phenomenon well-described by Warner[57]. Whether Jo had problems or not, it would not make any difference to Randy's performance. On the other hand, she had no control whatsoever of Jo's behavior on stage.

***

That night, the Royal Albert Hall was packed. Prince Albert envisioned the Hall to provide art for the masses. His desire was reached, although he did not live to appreciate it. He died in 1861, before the completion of the building. The venue was built by a British military engineer commissioned to construct the theater to accommodate a massive crowd of 5,000 people. It had served the British people with the most eclectic collection of musicians for over 150 years, perpetuating Prince Albert's desire and his name. His wife insisted that the theater be called Albert. Special musicians such as the Beetles, Frank Sinatra, and various rock stars and bands have presented at Prince Albert's Hall; from pop to the most classic shows, the hall is constantly packed, exciting crowds with tears and mad behavior.

Maestro João had always dreamed of taking his orchestra there. The boys together were the 'icing on the cake.' They were already loved in Europe and recognized as phenomena of mental integration. It was amazing how silent and focused the over 5,000 people were that night. Randy and Jo looked at each other and started playing with such coordination and enchantment that the audience made no noise until the boys stood up to bow. Then the crowd exploded, clapping, recognizing the art of those children. It was admirable how they could capture the audience, of course, with the captivating explanations and help of Maestro João. The orchestra presented the remainder of the program easily, confident of success. The encore of the Brazilian piece was received with excitement by the standing audience, which kept clapping for several minutes after the musicians left. It was a magical night.

When they arrived at the hotel, Jill asked Randy how Jo was playing.

"Amazing," he answered.

"Was Jo too slow? I had the impression that he was being dragged by you."

"No, it was the other way around. He was a bit too fast, but obviously, the audience loved his pace. I just followed him, amazed with his dexterity, on the

---

[57] Kenny Warner (2022) *Becoming an Instrument. Lessons on Self-Mastery from Music to Life*, Sweet Lo Press, New York.

left and the right hand. I felt he only allowed me to play because he was so generous. He is a true friend, a partner. His massive suffering, the American way of teaching, and the Maestro's constant instructions have made Jo understand the banality of competitiveness. As Bela Bartok said, 'Competitions are for horses, not for artists.' Jo is an artist; he learned to feel the music within his soul, not worrying about his technique, the perfection of which is given at the level we are playing. Despite his age and woes, he is already a true master. Mom, you did a great job with his brain. I admire your work and dedication and the incredible mom you are." Randy's eyes were shining as he hugged his mom.

"No, I did not fix his brain! We all did: the Maestro, you, your dad, the orchestra, Mrs. Jin, the audience, and the music. Most of all, Jo's resilience and desire to improve. It has been teamwork completed with incredible scientific support from our team in Los Angeles under the leadership of Dr. Hillary, the psychiatrist, the neurologist, the neuroradiologist, and all the technical people who helped us. Yes, it took a crowd to seal this victory for Jo. We will finish our tour of this continent with the performance in Madrid and finally head home.

"We will have to perform another surgery to complete the cure of Jo's PTSD. Your dad is developing the device we will implant in his amygdala bilaterally. The basics of the device have been developed already, so it should not be difficult to adapt it to the amygdala. I hope that, after the surgery, Jo will not need us during the Asian tour, which will finally seal his career in China and complete his dream.

"It is time for us to concentrate on our own lives," said Jill, looking sternly into Randy's shining eyes.

"Mom, I want to do what you and Dad do. It is amazing to see you helping people the way you do; I know there is a lot of work ahead of me to achieve your level of mastery, but the rewards are indescribable and invaluable. Music is great, but what you do is incredible: helping people when they most need help is what I want to do. You are right, Mom; it is time for me to follow your and Dad's steps. From now on, Jo can fly on his own."

"He will, but if he needs us, we will be there for him," reassured Jill. "That is what we are all about, a team!"

Chapter 48
Perfect Teamwork

Virtuosos love their job with obsessive perfection,
sparking admiration on cultured and uncultured people.
Antonio De Salles

Jill wanted perfection, offering a complete cure to Jo. She only had to intervene one more time in his brain for a stellar performance at the National Music Auditorium in Madrid, hopefully, her last intervention in his brain in Europe. She applied a light LowFU stimulation to his amygdala, bilaterally, to ensure he would not have vegetative symptoms triggered by his natural stage fright. She was careful about not overdoing the stimulation, as a manic state was to be avoided at all costs. They had been lucky in London with the balance she achieved by giving him valproic acid 24 hours before the performance. She would not risk overdoing the stimulation again with the consequence of having to medicate him, jeopardizing Jo's last European performance. They had gone through rough moments, with moments of stress in almost every city. They needed a relaxing time in Madrid to close the tour smoothly, giving Jo the confidence to continue alone on his Asian tour.

More than 2,000 people were in the concert hall. Randy, mirroring his mother, strove for perfection during their performance, not only to play the Preludes perfectly but also to ensure Jo was ready to be on his own. He was adamant about letting him play as confidently as possible, so Jo would not think their success had only been achieved because of his help. Despite their concert being booked out, it was certainly not as intimidating and overwhelming as the audience in the Royal Albert Hall.

The facade of the Madrid National Music Auditorium was designed by the architect José María García de Paredes and completed in 1988. It was built following the simple and elegant Spanish architecture style. The constructors took advantage of the 1980s economic boom in the post-Franco era. The Spanish society invested in an austere, clean, and minimalistic design, although astonishingly beautiful inside. Jose Maria envisioned an inviting and efficient music hall, contrary to the opulent music houses in Europe already experienced by the Maestro's boys. The minimalistic aspect put Jo in a less anxious mode.

Jo felt confident everything would be fine, though he relied on Randy's help. They started playing perfectly well. As Randy let Jo play alone, he winked at him, signaling that he should keep playing as long as he felt comfortable. Jo needed it all to take the leadership, playing with his whole might. Randy added some of the notes in unison to show their cooperation to the eager audience wanting both playing. Their performance was again a total success. Randy and Jill had achieved their goal of giving complete confidence to Jo. The boy's happiness radiated to the audience and the orchestra as the musicians understood Randy's good deed. They were proud of both boys, one for the support he had given his friend and the other for being capable of humbly receiving help, taking the protagonist role at the proper moment as a real champion does.

After finishing the orchestra program and the encore, they felt the happiness of a team that had gone through a championship together. But it was a championship without competition, the feeling of friendship felt only by winners who fought together for a single goal: the victory of curing someone. The Maestro invited all of them to a paella restaurant for the last party in Europe, a tradition in Madrid.

Chapter 49
Another Surgery

Genius is one percent inspiration and ninety-nine percent perspiration.
Thomas A. Edison

Although the exhilarating feeling of victory after the Madrid performance was engraved into Jo's mind, giving him the strength to go forward in his music career, Jill knew he had a weakness she needed to circumvent for him. His slightly hypoxic brain, which had led to motor failures, and the added anxiety from the traumatic event with his father made Jo prone to weakening at the first sign of adversity. It happened on a Baltic Sea crossing ship. She recognized that the safety Randy had represented to Jo throughout the European tour was not a reality for the life of a high-performance musician. The plan had always been to completely recover Jo's artistic prowess, self-control, and ability to spearhead his own talent alone.

She had to offer him what had been missing in his personality when he migrated from China to the United States. It had been missing what Daniel Goleman called 'Emotional Intelligence' (EI) [58]. Added to the fact he came without the EI level that most endowed Western musicians have, he acquired the handicap of dystonia and PTSD. The dystonia was being controlled by the implant in his pallidum; now, she had to complete the implantation of another device to solve his PTSD. This had to be done in the amygdala, where Emotional Intelligence can be controlled in the human brain.

Charles had the device to control Jo's amygdala when the boys returned from Europe to Los Angeles. One of the issues was the amygdala volume,

---

[58] Goleman D. (1995) *Emotional Intelligence: Why it can matter more than IQ*, Bantam Books, Random House, Penguin Random House.

which needed to be influenced by his device. The amygdala is a complex structure divided into multiple sections. Its volume in humans varies immensely, not only in normal subjects but also in diseased brains. Additionally, there are also gender differences. The literature suggested a range in volume of 1.7 cm^3 on the left and right[59] to 3.4 cm^3 on the left and right[60] **(Figure 12)**. While this huge variation in size made it difficult for Charles to determine the potency of his implant to spread electricity to the whole amygdala, he calculated his electrical fields based on the size of Jo's amygdala, using the MRIs he had obtained in his first surgery. As he planned to implant the 4 mm diameter device in the center of the structure, it would allow the implant to stimulate the whole structure's volume, depending on Jo's reactions.

As for the amygdala, he created a device capable of producing an almond-shaped electrical field that approached the amygdala contours. It was possible to precisely target this inside the structure, not sending the electric impulses to regions beyond the target. He presented his plans to Jill, who was adamant that they needed to focus the impulses on the lateral amygdala. Charles discussed with her whether it would be interesting to have access to the medial side as well, especially knowing that the output of the amygdala toward the hypothalamus was via its medial extension. Medial access would allow them to balance the effects of the stimulation in case of agonistic and antagonistic activities inside the diverse subsections of the amygdala.

---

[59] Brierley, B., Shaw, P., & David, A. S. (2002) 'The human amygdala: a systematic review and meta-analysis of volumetric magnetic resonance imaging,' *Brain Research Reviews,* 39(1), 84-105. doi:10.1016/s0165-0173(02)00160-1.

[60] Watson, C., Andermann, F., Gloor, P., Jones-Gotman, M., Peters, T., Evans, A., ... Leroux, G. (1992) 'Anatomic basis of amygdaloid and hippocampal volume measurement by magnetic resonance imaging,' **Neurology**, 42(9), 1743-1743. doi:10.1212/wnl.42.9.1743.

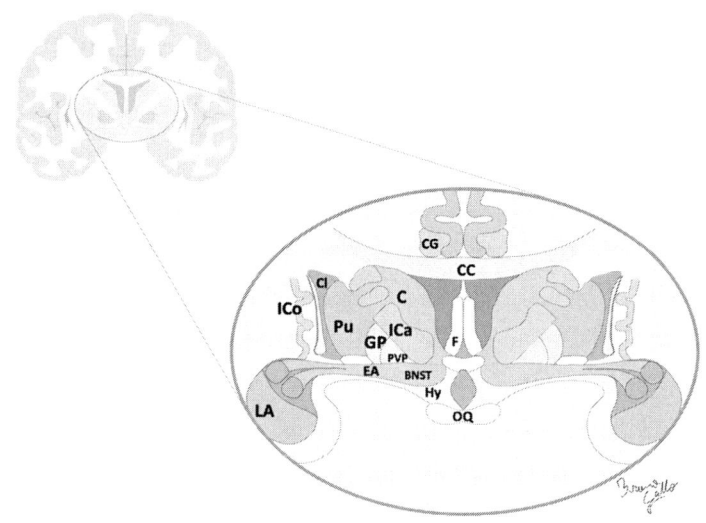

***Figure 12:** Integration of Memory and Feelings*
Notice the lateral amygdala in green (LA) and the direct output through the extended amygdala (EA) toward the hypothalamus (Hy), passing by the Bed Nucleus of the Stria Terminalis (BNST). Threatening memories arrive in the basal ganglia (globus pallidus (GP), putamen (Pu), and Caudate (C)) through this pathway. The close relationship of the amygdala with the hippocampus, back and forth, ensures that bad memories reach the amygdala. Information from diverse sensations enters the lateral amygdala, already reinforced by the frontal cortex judgment, and is distributed by the thalamus. Alternatively, the information goes directly into the amygdala when an emergency is signaled. There is a direct thalamus-amygdala highway, as the amygdala is the protective organ in the brain. Notice the strong connection of the amygdala with the basal ganglia, hypothalamus, and hippocampus. CC is the corpus callosum, which integrates the two cerebral hemispheres. CG is the cingulate gyrus, part of the limbic system completing the Papez circuit. The posterior ventral pallidum (PVP) is related to motor control. OQ is the optic chiasm, where the visual information from both eyes is integrated, passing information from both eyes to both cerebral hemispheres. (Simplified drawing from Pereira et al)[61].

"Charles," said Jill, "Let's discuss the best site to install the stimulator in the amygdala with our team. I know that to block Jo's PTSD symptoms, we will have to stimulate the lateral amygdala. I learned this by steering the field

---

[61] Pereira JB, Downes A, Gorgulho A, Patel V, Malkasian D, De Salles A. (2014) 'Alzheimer's disease: The role for neurosurgery,' *Surg Neurol Int.*, 5:S385-90.

of his current device toward the anterior portion of the pallidum and toward the lateral amygdala, blocking its medial output **(Figure 12)**. I could thus control his symptoms fairly well during the crisis he was having when we arrived in Helsinki. I was amazed at how fast he got better and gave the concert despite losing control of the dystonic right hand after I removed the stimulation of his posterior ventral pallidum (PVP). Fortunately, Randy was there to cover for his right hand, so it all went fine, and the concert was a success."

"Jill, I already conferred with Dr. Hillary to develop the shape of the device for the PTSD symptoms," insisted Charles. "He was of the opinion that we need to cover all the amygdala's volume to give us latitude programming. Do you think we need to call the whole team again? Imagine if the group decides that we must change the device's size and shape. It will set us back months. Moreover, Jo will lose the timing for going to Asia."

"So be it, Charles! What we cannot do is implant the wrong device and risk having to operate on Jo's amygdala twice. I certainly don't believe we will have to change much of what you have done, but putting the team's brains at work will only improve the quality of our final product. I will call the team to get everybody's opinion."

It was not necessary; Dr. Hillary was clearly on Charles' side. He started the meeting by saying he had thought the issue through and explained his reasons.

"I discussed the creation of the device and its location with Paul Wronsky and Robert Howard. Both agreed that we must cover the whole amygdala's extension, as this nut-shaped structure's input and output must be totally controlled. The amygdala is the guardian of the fear response. The information about a threat enters through the lateral amygdala; it is modulated with memories and information coming from the frontal lobes, thalamus, and the hippocampus and sent toward the hypothalamus for a fight-or-flight reaction, leading to the proper hormonal release necessary, as well as modulation of the commands for motor and cognitive decisions. It can be a well-thought-through decision or an emergency one. When this system is not modulated appropriately, we see the 'Emotional Hijack,' also described by Daniel Goleman[62].

---

[62] Goleman D. (1995) *Emotional Intelligence: Why it can matter more than IQ*, Bantam Books, Random House, Penguin Random House.

"It is a sudden reaction to the threat or aggression, which is no longer necessary in many modern relationships, especially in social relationships like those in the workplace. The person then shows a lack of 'Emotional Intelligence,' for instance, Jo's reaction against the judges when he lost the competition for the Julliard Music School. We need to help him control this weakness, as hearing Beethoven Concert Number 3 and the trauma from his father are the triggers for his PTSD attacks. We can block his reaction to the memory of these events with the electrical stimulation, as Jill did so many times using the LowFU device."

After Dr. Hillary's discourse, Jill accepted that the team was ready to act. "Well, Charles, clearly, you guys already had the discussion I was planning to have. I am convinced, Dr. Hillary, I will schedule the surgery. I hope we can offer him the ability to be *angry with the right person, to the right degree, at the right time, for the right purpose, in the right way.* It is the Aristotle Challenge, the definition of Emotional Intelligence."

***

The surgery procedures were straightforward, identical to the ones for implanting the device in the PVP since the target site was approximately 1 cm lateral to the PVP and slightly ventral (**Figure 12**). The responses to stimulation in such an interesting site were expected to be remarkable. Indeed, while awake in the surgery, the reactions to stimulation of the amygdala were very telling. Jo's PTSD symptoms were all reproduced on the operating table. Jill had invited a psychologist to participate in the studies of stimulating Jo's amygdala during the period he was awake, as someone dedicated to careful observations was necessary to ensure that unacceptable side effects would not be missed.

The placement of Charles' devices in the center of both amygdalae progressed smoothly. Once Jill and Dr. Hillary gave the green light for stimulation, they started the psychological studies. Dr. Wolf woke Jo up slowly to maintain his calm, without distress at waking up in the strange environment of the operating room. After an hour or so, Jo was free of drugs, still lying on the operating table, ready to collaborate with the studies. First, the declarative memory was tested. The psychologist asked him to recollect memories that usually triggered his PTSD symptoms. The cells in the lateral amygdala became very active, as detected by the spikes of the recording and stimulating device. These patterns were identified and defined with certainty that when they became active, the PTSD symptoms would promptly follow. These would be the biomarkers, the activity signature triggering the need to turn on the stimulation in the lateral amygdala to block its output. An overwhelming electrical discharge from the device would stop the initiation of the PTSD symptoms in its tracks[63].

"Charles, did you pick up the activity generated by Jo's traumatic memories?" Jill asked.

"Amazingly, they are very robust beta band waves, traveling medially through the BNST in the direction of the hypothalamus. It is just as you predicted. They will trigger the 'fight or flight' reaction if they arrive there. It will be quite simple to block them with an electrical discharge. They are neural oscillations in a frequency above 12.5 Hz. They range from 12.5 Hz to 30 Hz. Therefore, if we program a trend of stimulation above 30Hz, we can block them completely. I will program the device to kick in at the threshold of 12.5Hz with a trend of at least 30 seconds, just to block waves traveling through the BNST while still allowing the prompt return of the fast brain wave activity, which is indispensable for his good performance. Do you want to see?"

"Sure," said Dr. Hillary excitedly. "Isn't that the goal of this surgery? If you manage to block these lateral amygdala discharges, we will have controlled his PTSD symptoms and his 'Emotional Hijack,' as well."

"The question is whether we will block his nondeclarative memory," remarked the psychologist. "We don't want to block it. It should be detected when he recalls music, pleasant memories, and thoughts without threatening connotations. The nondeclarative memory should be accessed when he plays pieces of music randomly, in general, the ones that give him pleasure. He will play them almost unconsciously, mastering them, a simple natural performance rather than a recollection of music scores. Then it will be the true master playing."

Immediately, Jill asked Jo to imagine playing the Preludes with Randy. Tellingly, the cells in the lateral amygdala were very quiet while he was imagining this, while the PVP cells, recorded by the device in the pallidum, showed moderate firing, very well controlled, and modulated. This was the

---

[63] Spencer Q (2018) *Amygdala, Rewire the Limbic System in Your Brain*, Audiobook, narrated, Eric Boozer.

pattern necessary for motor delicacy in executing the Preludes as if he was, in fact, playing.

Dr. Hillary jumped to the conclusion. "This is amazing, so it matches the theory that if a person imagines playing a piece, bingo, the brain plays it, even without the muscles being commanded. It confirms that the exercise we suggested Jo did with his imagination, improving the dystonic manifestations in his hand, really was helping him."

"For sure, it was helping," said Jill. "He really improved his playing with the mental exercises."

"Well, here we have the evidence that the thinking exercises are effective. This is being shown scientifically for the first time, Charles. Your device is amazing; I believe we can even input algorithms into your device that will help a musician learn pieces and master them."

"Let's not go that far," said Jill. "The dexterity will have to be developed. A perfect coordination of these brainwaves with the actual activity of the muscles must be developed, don't you think?"

"Yes, but I believe a well-designed algorithm will help. This is for the future, though; now we needed to free Jo from his PTSD crisis. I have no doubt we have achieved it with this amazing surgery, Jill. Congratulations again for the coordinated work, you two. Today, at least here in the operating room, a superb neuroscientific feat was achieved. Will it work in a music hall?"

"Don't worry, Dr. Hillary. I have already developed the possibility of programming Jo's device through Ethernet. We can block his PTSD symptoms even if he is playing on the other side of the world, in Shanghai, for example. We can control these devices anywhere in the world if we need to. We can change the programs through the Ethernet, blocking the output of his lateral amygdala at our will. We have a very powerful tool to help Jo."

"What a marvelous device you developed, Charles. Have you already patented the algorithm?"

"Sure, the university has it. We turned the specifications in to the patent office. Our laboratory and our team will have 1.5% of the profits! If this becomes a worldwide spread technique, we will not have funding problems in our laboratory again."

Chapter 50
Maestro's Gratitude

*Music neuromodulates the brain in so many ways and sites,
which surgical interventions are far from reaching.*
Antonio De Salles

Jo stayed in Los Angeles for three weeks, recovering from his surgery, and then went to Shanghai to fulfill his life's dream of a concert there. It was to be in the city's most traditional theater. The Nanking Theater was designed to foster classical music in China. Inaugurated in 1930 with over 1000 seats, it evolved over the last century as a movie theater in the 1950s, the Beijing Theater. Finally, it became the first dedicated music house in China, the Cadillac Music Hall. Jo was starting his solo musician life by fulfilling his father's dream of playing in this most cherished site for a Chinese musician. In Shanghai, the little boy Jo had started his successful career. He wanted to show his peers how he had reached the acumen of the world's classical music circles. He was counting on the help of the Brazilian Maestro, who had fought his whole life against dystonia. He was also deeply grateful to the American doctors and scientists who had performed two successful surgeries to help him.

Jo was already quite a celebrity, as the story of the chips implanted in his brain to facilitate his playing spread around the world. The city felt honored to be receiving him and proud of being his original home. He wanted to impress all the musicians against whom he had once competed. He wanted to show how the opportunity he had created for himself had brought him to being a world-class concert pianist. The anxiety of performing for his whole country in such a prestigious theater, with roughly 1.5 billion people rooting for him while watching the TV, was immense.

Maestro João Carlos Martins was already on the stage with his orchestra when Jo Pan Jin, the night star, entered through the audience's ovation. The little boy bowed and walked toward the piano to start the concert. He immediately felt a wave of electricity crossing his brain and reaching his fingers; his anxiety had triggered his amygdalae's devices. He smiled at Maestro João, signaling that his device had kicked in; he was ready for the show. He played Bach's and Chopin's Preludes seamlessly; they had been consecrated for him by his and Randy's performance with the Bachianas Orchestra throughout Europe. Maestro had endured the woes the boys went through while presenting during the European tour; what a rehearsal for this moment that trip was! It's always easier to just depend on yourself. After Jo's successful solo, the Orchestra continued with Beethoven's Symphony Number 4. After the interval Jo and the Orchestra played the Piano Concerto Number 1 Op. 23 by Tchaikovsky with Jo on piano, which came out sensitively and technically perfect (Figure 13). They continued to the end of the concert with the Maestro at the piano performing the Grande Cadenza from Ravel's Left-Hand Concerto. The Tchaikovsky Concerto caused Jo's post-traumatic stress symptoms, therefore they showed that his illness was really under control.

A  B

Figure 13:
Query codes for Tchaikovsky's Concerto Number 1
(A) https://youtu.be/46P8hKr-BDA and Ravel's Concerto for left hand
(B) https://youtu.be/VR3ggyf9PDs.

After the long ovation they received, the Maestro took the stage to talk about Jo's fight for health, telling the saga of their rehearsals, non-invasive brain stimulations, the surgeries Jo had endured, and his admiration for Jo's adamant desire to become a global musician, for himself, for his family, and his country. The Maestro received applause for these remarks and continued thanking science and music for his life. A life of so much success that he identified with Jo's life and struggles. The Maestro brought up his teenage success and compared Jo's patriotism to how he felt when he was 12 years old about his own country, Brazil. They continued for the encore with Maestro demonstraint his own skills playing Bach's Partita Number 5 and the Orchestra with Buffalo Gap (Figure 14) and some Brazilian pieces, which always made the European public stand up clapping, the same happened in Shanghai.

Figure 14:
(A) Bach's Partita 5 https://youtu.be/IGU1qsvoGsc
(B) Buffalo Gap https://www.youtube.com/watch?v=tRYiRy_2lu8

What a parallel he could see with his own recovery, so many times and through so many years, after several hopeful surgeries, meeting well-intentioned doctors, offering him the best of their knowledge and the best of science available in the second half of the twentieth century. The combination of medical efforts and their resilience had provided, both to Jo and himself, salvation in their careers. The Maestro always stressed the respect doctors and humanity have for art. The art of music, combined with science, allows an amazing and beneficial modulation of the human brain. Finally, he thanked Jo, the little boy who was 70 years his junior, for the lesson he was giving to the world. By being an example of strength and commitment to art and to his own people. Jo showed the world that where there is a will, there is a way, even when an art as complex as music is the challenge. It is a challenge that requires the combination of all human functions for execution, intellect, motor finesse, physical acumen and sensitivity to all the senses.

Yes, music is a challenge of personal strength for anyone trying to use their brain to its full capacity. Those who challenge themselves and have difficulty with an illness, like Maestro and little Jo suffered, would like to have a magic pill to solve everything. However, Pharmacology is far from achieving this feat, due to the side effects that medications bring to the whole body and to the complex brain electrochemical network.

Jo, humbly standing beside his Maestro, received the well-deserved acclamation of his peers and compatriots. His career was on the rise, thanks to a pair of chips sitting in key sites of his brain, controlled from the other side of the world, fortunately by outstanding scientists. The side effects that drugs cause systemically were avoided with a focal, reversible and a programmable solution, sparing areas in our body that cannot be affected, as they would compromise intellect, art and especially the human quality of life.

Jo knew he would continue to fight dystonia, hopeful because he was counting on the dedication and wonderful work his neurosurgeons and neuroscientists had done in his brain. Achievements of science that would certainly continue to be implemented with improvements in technology, medicines, and understanding of brain plasticity. He would use music to obtain resources that would allow him to support scientists working on genetic research, which promises to finally achieve a cure for dystonia in its hereditary forms. Music would be his strength and guide, following the example of his mentor Martins, who despite the scars in his seventy years of battles against dystonia, remains faithful to his love of music as a war winner.

Epilogue

After a century of amazing scientific findings, we saw represented in this epic-tragic story the control of a devastating genetic disease, dystonia, which can be triggered by toxic drugs, ischemic episodes, and hypoxic events. These injuries to the nervous tissue led to plastic maladaptation of the neural circuitry, which persists but can be corrected using bioelectronics. This is a possibility Cajal did not even dreamed of at the beginning of the last century. Although this story is fictional, it reflects the daily reality in advanced medical centers worldwide, albeit with less advanced electronic devices than those depicted in this story. After the speed of science in the last century, at the turn of the twenty-first century, humans have partially conquered the genomics and the electronics of living species. Developments in physics and chemistry have provided the necessary tools. This is knowledge accumulated by homo sapiens due to the unique capacity to pass acquired wisdom on through generations.

Consequently, during the last few decades, homo sapiens started seeing the wiring (connectivity) described by Cajal and the functioning (molecular and metabolic) of the living brain through molecular and functional imaging. These can now be seen in such impressive detail that they allow us to treat the central nervous system as an electrochemical switchboard, with the potential to be modified by intelligent microchips. We showed in this story that the living brain is an electrochemical network that can correct itself, leading to real treatment of diseases and even ethically controversial enhancement of its intelligent functions.

Our deep knowledge of the brain started with the visualization of the microscopic connections by Cajal & Golgi, who earned the Nobel Prize in 1906 for their description of cellular network, underpinning our understanding of this living machine as being plastic, in other words, adaptable over its entire life to the demands of the environment. The evolution of radiology began with Roentgen, who received the first Nobel Prize in 1901. The series of imaging-related Nobel Prizes continued with the Curies in 1903 and the Prize for Egas

Muniz in 1949 (he controversially won it for the controversial manipulation of mental circuitry using the lobotomy when he should have won it for his development of cerebral angiography, instead), and finally the Prize for Cormack & Hounsfield in 1979, for the computer algorithm to obtain computerized x-ray imaging. The possibility of imaging by nuclear magnetic resonance relaxation was introduced by Bloemberger, who won the Nobel Prize in 1981 (NMR), and finally, the Mansfield & Lauterbur Nobel Prize was awarded for expediting the MRI acquisition in 2003.

Through all this, our understanding of brain functioning has skyrocketed. Molecular imaging using Positron Emission Tomography (PET) will probably also lead to a Nobel Prize for its undisputable importance in medicine, although it is controversial who deserves the prize honor. It has been a conundrum for the Nobel Prize committee to decide who deserves to be credited as the PET inventor. The 1975 paper describing the pioneer PET device has led to numerous controversies. The study of transduction in the nervous tissue by Karlsson, Greengard, and Kandel deserved the Nobel Prize in 2000, as it set the stage for our understanding of the brain's neurochemical underpinnings. This knowledge is now used to neuromodulate the brain with medication and electronics.

We are at a scientific moment of using ever more sophisticated information, with the possibility of correcting the human genome. Techniques of gene modification, such as CRISPR, are currently readily available. Engineering of the genetic code will possibly bring in the near future the correction of the genetic forms of dystonia, the subject of this story, and cure to a multitude of other genetic diseases. Molecular biology disclosed the DNA structure, a feat achieved jointly by Watson, Crick, and Wilkins, which deserved the Nobel Prize in Physiology or Medicine in 1962. With the CRISPR engineering of the genome, Doudna & Charpentier won the Chemistry Nobel Prize in 2020, which brought medicine to a new stage, the era of manipulating life, diseases, and species.

These inventive scientists led us to the point where future scientists have to debate the controversial work of changing the essence of life, enhancing plants, and modifying animals to improve the foods available to the ever-growing homo sapiens population. Equally important is the cure of genetic diseases. These include cancer, neurodegenerations, and a multitude of malfunctions of development and metabolism that rob humans of the possibility of enjoying normal life; these all now have the potential to be cured based on the most unexpected but robust findings.

However, the possibility of enhancing humans, pre- and post-birth, is ethically controversial. This story has raised some burning questions: where are art and science taking humans in the era of implants and CRISPR? Who will deal with the ethical issues of genetically boosted humans aided by implantable chips? Will the social disparity among humans increase? These technologies are extremely expensive now, meaning only the wealthy can benefit from their prowess. At least, that will be true until they reach the masses, like computers did!

Psychiatric Inspirations

The countries where I worked after spending time in Sweden, where the late Prof. Dr. Laurie Laitinen taught me the craft, had restrictive laws about helping psychiatric patients with neurosurgery. Professor Laitinen was one of the editors of an impressive book titled *Psychosurgery,* published in 1976, which discusses neurosurgeons' efforts to help psychiatric patients worldwide. My slow productivity in psychiatric surgery in the USA and Brazil from 1990 to 2024, for 33 years, is explained by being barred by the backward laws that prevented psychiatric patients from benefiting from modern neurosurgery, laws that still exist today. They are impeding neurosurgery based on precise anatomical computerized images of brain functions, neuronavigational techniques, and methods that allow surgeries without incisions.

Surgeries supported by evidence-based medicine in benchmarked and randomized clinical trials are ready to help patients and their families[64,65]. This

---

[64] Lopes, A. C., Greenberg, B. D., Canteras, M. M., Batistuzzo, M. C., Hoexter, M. Q., Gentil, A. F., … Miguel, E. C. (2014) 'Gamma Ventral Capsulotomy for Obsessive-Compulsive Disorder,' *JAMA Psychiatry*, 71(9), 1066. doi:10.1001/jamapsychiatry.2014

[65] Wu H, Hariz M, Visser-Vandewalle V, Zrinzo L, Coenen VA, Sheth SA, Bervoets C, Naesström M, Blomstedt P, Coyne T, Hamani C, Slavin K, Krauss JK, Kahl KG, Taira T, Zhang C, Sun B, Toda H, Schlaepfer T, Chang JW, Régis J, Schuurman R, Schulder M, Doshi P, Mosley P, Poologaindran A, Lázaro-Muñoz G, Pepper J, Schechtmann G, Fytagoridis A, Huys D, Gonçalves-Ferreira A, D'Haese PF, Neimat J, Broggi G, Vilela-Filho O, Voges J, Alkhani A, Nakajima T, Richieri R, Djurfeldt D, Fontaine P, Martinez-Alvarez R, Okamura Y, Chandler J, Watanabe K, Barcia JA,

absurd impediment led me to my first book, *Why Fly over the Cuckoos' Nest? Psychosurgery in My Brain, Please.* It was written to teach the lay reader about the harmful laws spearheaded by the similarly titled book and Oscar winner movie of 1978. Harmful laws have endured through the progress of our brain understanding. Our quest to bring accessibility of cures to psychiatric diseases has now been translated into four languages, with a more telling title in other languages: *The Brain of a Player, Love, and Soccer, which the second edition was just advanced by Austin Macauley Publishers.* This present scientific musical novel continues the quest to allow a full range of neurosurgeries to improve neurologic and neuropsychiatric patients' quality of life (Figure 15).

Figure 15: Giant black paella
(A) Giant black paella, squid ink rice, and seafood, representing disorganized music scores, and the 'porcupine fish device,' which inspired and allowed the music organization in Jo's brain. (B) Team of doctors after performing a successful Gamma Ventral Capsulotomy to organize a psychiatric patient's thoughts in Spain[66]. This is an example of commemorating the victory of helping someone over a traditional paella dinner in Madrid, mentioned in Chapter 48. From left to right: Drs. Antonio De Salles and Maria Alice Ferragut workers at NeuroSapiens® in Brazil, and Drs. Roberto Martinez-Alvarez[67] and Nuria Martinez Moreno workers at the Ruber International Hospital in Spain.

Reneses B, Lozano A, Gabriëls L, De Salles A, Halpern CH, Matthews K, Fins JJ, Nuttin B (Jan. 2021) 'Deep brain stimulation for refractory obsessive-compulsive disorder (OCD): emerging or established therapy?,' *Mol Psychiatry*, **26**(1):60-65. doi: 10.1038/s41380-020-

[66] Miguel, E. C. (2014) 'Gamma Ventral Capsulotomy for Obsessive-Compulsive Disorder,' *JAMA Psychiatry*, **71**(9), 1066. doi:10.1001/jamapsychiatry.

[67] Mikhail F. Chernov, Jamil A. Rzaev, Roberto Martínez-Álvarez (2022) 'Neurosurgical Management of Psychiatric Disorder,' *Parte 2 Elsevier*

Books Published by Antonio De Salles

1. De Salles AAF (1986) *Brain Acidosis Following Severe Head Injury* (Ph.D. thesis dissertation), Virginia Commonwealth University.
2. De Salles AAF, Goetsch SJ (eds.) (1993) *Stereotactic Surgery and Radiosurgery*, Medical Physics Publishing Corporation, Madison, Wisconsin.
3. De Salles AAF, Lufkin R (1997) *Minimally Invasive Therapy of the Brain,* Thieme Medical Publishers.
4. King W, Frazee J, De Salles AAF (1998) *Endoscopy of the Central and Peripheral Nervous System,* Thieme Medical Publishers.
5. De Salles AAF (July 2011) *Why Fly Over the Cuckoo's Nest? Psychosurgery in My Brain, Please,* Writers Guild of America. CreateSpace, Amazon.com.
6. De Salles AAF, Agazaryan A, Selch M, Gorgulho AA, Slotman B, Editors (April 2011) *Shaped Beam Radiosurgery*, Springer.
7. Kim W, De Salles A, Pouratian N (Editors) (2013) *Neuromodulation of the Peripheral and Central Nervous System.*
8. Bomin Sun, Antonio De Salles (2014) *Psychiatric Disorders Surgery*, Springer.
9. De Salles A (2018) O Cérebro do Jogador, Amor e Futebol. Bonecker, Rio de Janeiro, Brazil. Translated to Spanish, Hindi, English (another title, item 5-original writing).
10. Osama Abelaziz and Antonio De Salles (2023) *NeuroRadiosurgery: Case Review Atlas*, Springer.
11. De Salles A (2024) *The Brain of the Player, Love, and Soccer*, Austin Macauley, New York.
12. De Salles A (2025) *The Musician's Brain-Science and Sensibility*, English in press, Austin-Macauley, New York. (Translated to Spanish, and Portuguese)